PRAISE FOR

The Light of Luna Park

"Is there anything better than falling into a novel that asks an ethical question and then answers it with a big story that arrows straight into the question's heart? No, I would say: Nothing better. *What would you do to save a child?* Addison Armstrong asks in this assured debut that ushers us deep into a fascinating moment in history, where obstetrics and women's choices and the shadow line between circus and science combine. *The Light of Luna Park* got me, took me, taught me, and in the end, shook me."

—Sarah Blake, author of *The Guest Book*

"A dual timeline, a fascinating historical setting, a baby, a nurse, and above all, courage. This is my kind of story! Thank you, Addison Armstrong, for writing such an intriguing and heartfelt novel." —Diane Chamberlain, author of *Big Lies in a Small Town*

"At once a fascinating slice of history and a compelling story filled with relatable characters. Addison Armstrong has woven a beautiful tale around the sacrifices and hard choices made for love, and highlights the work of the extraordinary individuals who stood up against the widespread, harsh beliefs of the time. This is a wonderful debut. Congratulations to Ms. Armstrong!"

—Louise Fein, author of *Daughter of the Reich*

"Compassionate and evocative, filled with fascinating historical detail, *The Light of Luna Park* is the story of a woman finding the strength to face impossible decisions as she struggles to protect the life of a child."   —Fiona Valpy, author of *The Dressmaker's Gift*

"*The Light of Luna Park* is a gripping story of one woman's determination to save a premature baby and a daughter's quest to discover the truth about her mother, intertwined with the fascinating history of the incubator. It's an emotional and at times suspenseful novel about the strength of love and the importance of perseverance that will capture the reader's heart."
                    —Georgie Blalock, author of *The Other Windsor Girl*

"In *The Light of Luna Park*, author Addison Armstrong re-creates the surreal time when most preterm babies were cast aside to die, while a few dedicated nurses and a doctor on Coney Island saved them, then offered them as an amusement park sideshow. It's a story of a grieving daughter—a teacher of special-needs children—who must first unravel her own story by uncovering family secrets before she can understand and fully love herself, her husband, and her students. Taking place more than twenty years apart, these two stories collide in an unforgettable, heart-wrenching account of the power of a mother's love."
                    —Tracey Enerson Wood, author of *The Engineer's Wife*

THE
Light
of
Luna Park

ADDISON ARMSTRONG

G. P. PUTNAM'S SONS

NEW YORK

PUTNAM
— EST. 1838 —

G. P. PUTNAM'S SONS
Publishers Since 1838
An imprint of Penguin Random House LLC
penguinrandomhouse.com

Copyright © 2021 by Addison Armstrong
Penguin supports copyright. Copyright fuels creativity, encourages diverse
voices, promotes free speech, and creates a vibrant culture. Thank you for
buying an authorized edition of this book and for complying with copyright
laws by not reproducing, scanning, or distributing any part of it in any form
without permission. You are supporting writers and allowing Penguin to
continue to publish books for every reader.

Library of Congress Cataloging-in-Publication Data

Names: Armstrong, Addison, author.
Title: The light of Luna Park / Addison Armstrong.
Description: New York: G. P. Putnam's Sons, 2021. |
Identifiers: LCCN 2021015009 (print) | LCCN 2021015010 (ebook) |
ISBN 9780593328040 (trade paperback) | ISBN 9780593328057 (ebook)
Subjects: LCSH: Nurses—Fiction. | Premature infants—Fiction. |
Incubators (Pediatrics)—Fiction. | Luna Park (New York, N.Y.)—Fiction. |
Mothers and daughters—Fiction. | GSAFD: Historical fiction.
Classification: LCC PS3601.R5744 L54 2021 (print) |
LCC PS3601.R5744 (ebook) | DDC 813/.6—dc23
LC record available at https://lccn.loc.gov/2021015009
LC ebook record available at https://lccn.loc.gov/2021015010

Printed in the United States of America
1st Printing

BOOK DESIGN BY KRISTIN DEL ROSARIO

To my parents, Eric and Ellen Armstrong,
who would have joined the Coney Island sideshow themselves
if it meant making me happy—

Thanks for everything, Mom and Dad.
I couldn't be luckier to have you.

THE LIGHT OF LUNA PARK

CHAPTER ONE

Althea Anderson, June 1926

No baby is happy about being pushed into this world. But never have I seen one so entirely unprepared for its entrance. Three months premature, the infant before me contorts her shiny face to scream. Her tiny lungs convulse with the effort, and the skin on her chest stretches and snaps back to make room. Her matchstick legs kick; her coin-sized hands twitch. The girl's mother wails, and I fear her deep, gurgling gasps may snatch away the oxygen so craved by her infant. I fix my eyes on the newborn as if I can send her what she needs.

Keep breathing, I will the baby girl.

Her torso is the size of two fists, the size of two beating hearts.

Though we both know it, the doctor is the one to say the truth aloud. He puts down the forceps and sets his mouth in a firm line. "She won't live." He does nothing to sugarcoat the truth.

The father's neck tenses, tendons like claws. The poor mother's eyes widen, and she wipes her left as a drop of sweat drips into it from her brow line. Yes, the doctor's words are blunt, but he leaves out the perspectives that would render them downright cruel. He doesn't reveal that the medical term for a baby like this one is *weakling*. He doesn't suggest, as many doctors would, that such infants are better off dead. But still the reality stands stark. Already, the girl is struggling to breathe; she is unable to suckle. Her body temperature and weight are low.

Three months early, two pounds, two ounces. She has little chance of survival.

"Cybil," the girl's mother breathes. Her voice comes out half whisper, half sob, but it echoes in my mind like a scream. The baby has a name now.

"Nurse Anderson." Dr. Bricknell breaks through the litany of my thoughts. "The hallway."

I trail obediently after him, nervous. I've rarely had direct conversation with the doctor, but our head nurse is out today.

I look one more time at the family clustered together as I go. However much my medically trained hands itch to do something, *anything*, for baby Cybil, the parents deserve a moment alone with their infant.

In the corridor, Dr. Bricknell checks his wristwatch and grunts. "I can't stay."

I wait. The doctors never bother speaking to me unless orders are coming.

"But you'll need to make sure the parents see her suffer as little as possible."

I nod, mentally running through the list of small mercies I can provide: a heated water bottle, a blanket. I only wish there were something I could do to save the baby rather than merely ease her transition into death, and I ball my hands into fists at my side. They brush against the scratchy fabric of my uniform, and paper crinkles. I stiffen. The article! I'd cut it from the paper when I began my obstetrics cycle weeks ago, hoping to ask the doctors about it once they came to know me. As Dr. Bricknell has proved himself a rather stuffy, unapproachable sort, I'd completely forgotten. But with the head nurse back tomorrow, this may be my only chance.

"Doctor." I pull the crumpled newspaper clipping from my pinafore. "I do wonder if there is a way to save the baby."

Dr. Bricknell's brow creases. More in annoyance than interest, I'm afraid, but I press on. "It's about the incubator wards at Coney Island. There's a doctor there who takes premature babies free of charge—"

The doctor interrupts. "Free for the parents, but it costs ten cents a person to get in and see the babies."

"See them?"

"They're part of a freak show, Nurse Anderson. That 'doctor' is nothing but a quack."

A freak show. I picture Cybil lost in a woman's bristly beard or held in the grip of a man with three arms. I see her trampled under the feet of a giant or squeezed between the two heads of conjoined twins.

No. I'm a nurse, not a dime novelist. I deal in information, not imagination. "The article reports that Dr. Couney has saved thousands of premature infants," I say, "some of them as tiny as Cybil at birth."

"Cybil?"

"The baby." I gesture behind us, struggling to hide my disgust that he's already forgotten her name.

Dr. Bricknell sighs. "I'm sorry, Nurse Anderson, but that baby simply isn't fit to live. No freak show or circus man can change that."

"Should I ask the parents whether—"

"No, Nurse Anderson. It is not our place to question God's plan. Now"—he checks his wristwatch again—"I really must go. I trust you will do as I have asked of you—and not do anything to jeopardize your job?"

He leaves me standing in the hallway, crumpled article clenched in my fist.

I purse my lips and fight tears as I fold the paper to put back in my pocket. A nurse does not cry on the job. However much she may wish to.

My expression softens as I reenter the hospital room. Cybil is cradled in her mother's palm, her tiny arms the length of her mother's bloated pinky but half as wide.

It is not our place to question God's plan, Dr. Bricknell said. But surely God cannot want this baby to die. I swallow the urge to burst out into the hallway, chase the doctor down, and shake him. *God brought Dr. Couney to Coney Island*, I want to scream. *This is his modern miracle.*

But it is not my place. If I defy Dr. Bricknell, I will lose my job, lose everything I've worked for my whole life. Without nursing, I would have nothing; it's my lifeblood, my purpose. With each infant I safely help to deliver, the debt I owe my mother eases.

But I'm not the only one who might suffer. If Dr. Couney is

the con artist the doctor believes, Cybil would die despite it all. Her parents would lose their hope and their daughter a second time. Could they survive that?

I cannot give them hope and then destroy it, not when I know nothing about Couney beyond what's in the papers.

So I gather the blankets as Cybil's cries turn into desperate gulps for air. I tuck her bony legs under the fabric and swaddle the girl's shivering body. I think of Dr. Bricknell's words, circuses and freak shows, and I bite my tongue.

I nearly swallow it as I watch the girl die.

I have seen babies die before. I've helped deliver the stillborn and seen infants' hearts stop before the expulsion of the afterbirth. Is it wrenching every time? Of course it is. But when those babies have passed, they have done so because we were unable to save them.

Not because we decided not to try.

CHAPTER TWO

Stella Wright, December 1950

December 15: Mom's been gone three months to the day. It's not the date's reminder that stings, for it's not as if I have the luxury of forgetting her on the 11th or the 13th or the 27th. Every day, I grieve her.

What burns is the fact that it's been three months: that three months after Mom died, I still haven't "gotten over it." Foolish me; I thought a month would be enough to start waking up with a clear head. Instead, I'm lying here after ninety-one days with a skull that feels as if I've stuffed it with weights. I wonder sometimes if I cry in my sleep, the way my skin feels so tight and stretched in the morning, but I'm too afraid of the answer to ask my husband.

On cue, Jack enters the room with a tray. His silhouette in the light of the hallway glows, and his curly blond hair is ablaze. I never thought I'd marry straight out of college, if ever, but this right here is exactly why I did. Jack's barely cooked a day in his life, but here he is with his first pancakes: lumpy, misshapen, and made with care. Somehow they make me chuckle despite my pain. That's Jack's gift—he can always make me smile, make me laugh. Our second wedding anniversary will be in June of next year, just as I finish my second year of teaching, but his easy laugh and sense of humor never get old.

Jack sets the tray down beside me, almost spilling the glass of orange juice balanced precariously on its edge.

"Jack." I chuckle again to see the pancakes up close. "I'm almost afraid to eat these."

He shrugs. "They're good, I had one." He licks his lips and then turns briefly serious. "I thought it might be a tough day for you."

I squeeze his hand. He is thoughtful in a way that I'm not, my husband. If only I knew how to be as supportive of his episodes as he is of mine.

But it's different. He knows what I'm feeling and why, whereas I don't have that luxury. I've witnessed dozens of Jack's war flashbacks over this first year and a half of our marriage, but I can't see inside his head. I watch him thrash, tangled in the sheets of our bed; I watch him collapse under the weight of a thunderclap. But I cannot see past his reactions to what's inside, and I'm left to imagine the worst. Is he reliving near misses from his time in France? Maybe he just avoided crawling over a land mine at Normandy, a comrade blowing to pieces in his stead. Maybe a spray of bullets grazed his chest, so close he couldn't breathe.

Maybe, had he moved a fraction of a second earlier or later, I wouldn't even have him.

The alternative is almost more frightening. My husband—sweet, light, always armed with a joke—could be mired in guilt rather than fear. How many men did he kill? Could he see their faces as he pulled the trigger?

I shake my head to rid myself of the image. I sleep next to Jack every night, our bodies cleaved together. I don't want to imagine him a killer.

I look at him now. I'd be able to support him so much better if he would just tell me what he sees, but I don't have the energy to coax him out of his stubborn silence today, exhausted as I am by my own grief.

My mother died at forty-eight. We should have had decades left together. Her death robbed us of a future.

"Damn cancer," I whisper.

"Damn cancer." Jack squeezes my hand.

I take a sip of the orange juice. It's fresh and tangy enough to dispel the fuzz in my brain, and I exhale with relief. I gulp down the whole glass as Jack dresses, but I can't stomach more than a bite of the pancakes. Too heavy on a day I already feel like I'm dragging. Too sticky with syrup when I already feel stuck and immobile.

I force myself from bed and dress for school as Jack brushes his teeth in the bathroom. My kids' lives are hard enough without my looking like a zombie, so I make up my face and curl my hair. I eschew my typical dresses for a green blouse and cigarette pants; let the principal say what he will. Today is not a day I want to worry about whether I can cross my legs reading a story.

Jack pops up like he's reading my mind. "Am I allowed to say your legs look good in those?"

I swat Jack's hand away as he reaches for my waist and tugs at my tucked blouse. "Even breakfast in bed can't get you that far." I raise an eyebrow at him. "Not right before school."

"The kids would never know." Jack raises his eyebrows in return.

"*I* would."

He pretends to pout as I brush my teeth, the toothpaste sour after the juice. Jack's cute act is pretty persuasive, but he ruins it with what he says next.

"Too bad, since I heard that mornings are the best time to make mini Jacks or Stellas."

I spit my toothpaste violently into the sink and turn to Jack in exasperation. "Where on earth did you hear that? A television ad for breakfast cereal?"

"Sorry." Jack puts his hands up as he backs away.

I wince as I rinse my mouth. My tone was sharper than it needed to be. But Jack should have known better than to bring up babies on a day like today. I was reluctant to have kids before my mother died; now that she's gone, I don't know how I could possibly become a mother myself.

The kids at school are enough for me. They're practically *too* much for me. When I decided to be a teacher, it was because I appreciated the way kids were so honest and fresh. I thought I could help little girls like me keep their voices as they grew older, not try to quash them like most every teacher I'd ever had. I never planned on taking this job in special education—special education hardly existed when I was in school—but that was all that was available here for a newlywed. And Jack couldn't bear to move to the city after the war; he wanted to stay somewhere familiar: the place he'd always called home, the place we'd both gone to college. Slow, suburban Poughkeepsie. Maybe I'd understand better if I knew what he saw in France—but no. God forbid he confide in his wife.

I haven't returned to the city since my mom's funeral, either. Jack is afraid of its noises: the bomb threats from anarchists and terrorists, the roar of trains like the roar of artillery. I am afraid of its memories. We're selling the old apartment—where I grew up, and where my mom spent the last five years of her life alone—in February, and Jack helped me arrange for it to be cataloged and cleared by a company in the city. I can't bear to do it myself.

I sigh as I stare into the mirror. Blue smudges the space below my eyes, and I massage them gingerly. It's not that I don't love my students. I do. But I'm not trained to teach them, and it shows. They're run as ragged as I am. Some days, I have to grit my teeth and force myself to walk to the school building in the morning, because I know that nothing will be easy once I'm there. It's not the kids that make me drag my feet, though—it's the principal.

The principal. Today is the final day before Christmas break, and while I'd normally be relieved to have a vacation, the end of this semester is different.

My hands start to shake as I twist my hair into rolls, remembering the strange smirk on Principal Gardner's face after our confrontation over supplies two weeks ago. The fight had been long overdue; in our basement classroom, I have eight desks for eleven kids, three reading primers, four notebooks. God only knows what possessed me to suffer in silence for a year and a half; it shouldn't have taken my kids fighting over a pair of scissors and nearly stabbing their eyes out for me to demand a change.

Whether it was really the scissors, the exhaustion, or the grief over my mom, I don't know. But whatever it was, I locked the steel scissors in a drawer two weeks ago today and marched straight up to the principal's office. Channeling all my fury at Gardner and the universe, I gave the principal an ultimatum. If he didn't provide me with at least the basics by the end of the semester, he'd lose me.

I'd returned home exultant, sure I'd have a well-stocked classroom in two weeks' time, but Jack was more hesitant. He was afraid I'd been rash, acted out of grief rather than reason. But I know Gardner, and he won't do anything to make his life harder. Where on earth would he find another woman willing to teach the very same kids that the rest of the district sought to abandon? He'll never fire me.

At least, I hope not. My hope is tempered with nerves now that the day is finally here. The fact that it's the three-month anniversary of my mom's death only compounds my anxiety, and it was foolish of me not to realize earlier what the date would be. But then, I haven't been thinking clearly.

I hate myself for wondering if Jack could be right after all.

He inches back into the bathroom now, briefcase in hand. "I'm sorry for upsetting you, honey. Good luck with Gardner today."

"Thanks." I look back at the lumpy pancakes and smile gently. It's not Jack's fault that I'm not like the other women we graduated with, many of whom have already replaced work with children. It's just that I want to make the world a better place before I bring kids into it; I always have. "I think it will be good."

I'm trying to convince myself as much as I am him. I want my rashness to have helped my kids, not condemned them; I want to see their faces shining with delight when they return to a classroom in January stocked with colorful world maps, construction paper, books, and more.

Jack gives me a peck on the cheek as he goes, and I wave. As I finish getting ready, my thoughts remain on the things I love about my job: the hugs, the smiles, the constant busyness that keeps my mind from returning to the hole left by my mother's death.

Her dying left not just an emotional hole but a physical one, too. I no longer pick up the telephone to call my mom every weekend. That stiff pillow that only my mom found comfortable lies unused in our guest room. The kitchen cabinets are a mess, Mom being the only one who ever bothered to organize them. It took me five minutes to find paprika the other day.

Now, I root through the messy pantry for bread, check it to make sure it's still good, and smear it with peanut butter to take with me for lunch. It's time to go.

"Wish me luck, Mom." I look up at the ceiling and march out to meet the day.

CHAPTER THREE

Althea Anderson, July 1926

I cannot speak to Cybil's mother as I check her vitals. I chose not to speak when I could have pleaded, commanded, convinced. I cannot find it in me to make conversation after the fact.

But the woman is desperate to talk. "We named her after my mother," she offers, "Cybil."

"She was beautiful," I murmur. And she was. I only wish I could think about the little girl's splendor without also thinking of her death. Without hating Dr. Bricknell for letting it happen.

And without hating myself. The poor mother's grief pierces me as if it were my own. One moment she is sobbing, her speech so desperate and rushed that even my trained ears can only pick out the occasional word: *baby, hope, room, grandchild, love, why.* Again and again, *why*—a question I don't want to answer. The mother sobs and gasps and babbles and then, as if a switch has flipped, stops. Like Cybil's life, here and then suddenly snuffed out. And then the mother is back to tripping over her words, picking up speed before another inevitable stumble.

The father is the opposite. He doesn't string together meaningless words or stammer. He doesn't open his mouth at all. No stories, no questions, no tears. Instead, he shrinks into the corner and stands still as his daughter's lifeless body. Not even his face moves, and each time I shift my gaze from his wife to make a note, I see his eyes staring wide. I know that, even wide open, they don't see me. They don't see me or his wife in bed or the hospital room.

All they see is Cybil, and I can't help but wonder whether those eyes could have one day looked at Cybil as a child, a teenager, a young adult—if not for my silence.

If I, who have taken the nurse's pledge to devote myself to those committed to my care, had spoken.

But I didn't.

I let that sweet girl die.

dream of Cybil for weeks. Sometimes she is reproachful, tiny fists flying. Other times, she is broken, eye-droplet tears leaking from heavy-lidded eyes. And occasionally, she is kind. In these dreams, she shoots into girlhood, cheeks flaming with health. "I forgive you." She smiles to reveal straight, white teeth, and I wake up sobbing. The idea of what Cybil would have been, the thought of forgiveness undeserved—no more exquisite torment exists. And I fear that this particular torment will plague me for eternity.

July 5, I nearly miss my morning shift at the hospital. Not because I am sleeping off any Independence Day revelry; in fact, I am not sleeping at all. I woke at four a.m. unable to return to unconsciousness, and though I've escaped the dreams, wakefulness is not much better. Sitting alone at the table in the downstairs parlor, I watch Cybil in my mind's eye as she transforms into my own mother. I cannot judge the accuracy of the image; the whole of my recollection of my mother flows from one solemn portrait: dark hair, dark eyes, body encased in the high-necked ruffles of her era. She could be anyone. I know nothing of my mother, thanks to the cruelest of all life's ironies: that it was my introduction to the world that forced her out of it. My birth that caused her death. *At least she and my father are reunited again*, I tell myself. Since my father's death two years ago, I've been alone—but I try to comfort myself with the knowledge that my parents are together.

It never works. My worn, well-traveled thoughts trap me in amber. Cybil and my mother, dying as I stand silently by. Though my father never spoke of my mother's death, I remain horribly capable of imagining its various incarnations: slow, sudden, desperate, angry. Never do I picture her peaceful; always, her face is contorted as she gazes down at the daughter that has killed her. At me.

Those twisted lips and pained eyes are all I can see when Ida, a fellow nurse in residence here at 26th Street, rouses me from my stupor. "Thank you," I murmur as I run upstairs to grab my coat. Ida, with her flushed cheeks and unruly hair, is always the last nurse to sprint into Bellevue in the morning. Though I am typically the first, I barely make it today.

Once I do arrive at the hospital, I am restored to myself. Busy hands keep the guilt at bay as I fetch tools, check mothers' vitals, and study reports to summarize for the doctors.

At eleven a.m., Dr. Bricknell calls the head nurse and me in to assist with a premature labor. Working in obstetrics this term has been my greatest joy, however incongruent with my past it appears. Perhaps I feel that I can pay back my own debt to my parents by aiding others—or that's the motivation my father ascribed to my work before he died, anyway. Though I could have chosen it for a love of blood and corpses, and my father wouldn't have stopped me. For him, what mattered was the relief that I was out of his house. If I had a career, he reasoned, he didn't need to confront my face every morning: the face that both resembled his wife's and stole her from him.

Fitting that the inheritance he left me, however small, has funded my nursing education. It's why I'm able to be here doing what I've always wanted so desperately to do: assisting the doctors in delivering babies safely, saving them and their mothers.

I turn to the young woman in the hospital bed. Hattie, the head nurse has informed me. Due in September, her baby is ten weeks early. But now is not the time to point out the complications that may arise. Instead, I smile reassuringly at the woman as I squeeze her delicate fingers.

"But he has been kicking," the mother assures me, as if I'd told her he was not. "He kicked all night." Her voice verges on hysteria. "He's strong," she insists. "He's *healthy*." The poor woman's blond curls bounce with conviction. As if a firm enough belief can disrupt the course of nature.

But when the baby arrives, she—not he, as Hattie had predicted—is not breathing.

"Ice water," Dr. Bricknell commands, his calm steadying my hands as I obey. I pass him the tub, and he plunges a silent child, red marks on her head where the forceps grasped it, into the water and pulls out a wailing one.

"He's alive!" Hattie cries. "Alive!"

But Dr. Bricknell's words are grim as he peers over my shoulder. I am weighing her: 1,133 grams. Two pounds and a half, and drops of water still clinging to her, too. "Bring in the father," Dr. Bricknell commands. "This may be his only chance to meet his daughter."

"Daughter?" Hattie interrupts.

"Daughter," I confirm.

"Oh," Hattie falters. "Oh." But then a smile spreads across her face again. "Margaret, then."

Once both parents are in the room, Dr. Bricknell gives them the grim news. "She's too small to survive."

Hattie's face contorts, and for a moment I see Cybil's older, dark-haired mother in her place. No matter that Hattie's hair falls in golden ringlets around her unlined face and the other woman's brown hair was lank and straight; no matter that Hattie is shapely and youthful while Cybil's mother was thin and drawn. A mother's grief is universal.

But Hattie's grief isn't inevitable.

"Yes, she's too small to survive." I repeat Dr. Bricknell's statement but add a qualifier. "Too small to survive *here*."

The head nurse snaps her eyes in my direction as if to scare me into silence. For once, I ignore her.

"What do you mean?" His voice cold, Hattie's husband responds to my claim but keeps his eyes trained on Dr. Bricknell. I avoid looking the same way as I speak.

"We don't have incubators here, but there's a doctor at Coney

Island who does. There's no guarantee that your daughter will survive if we take her, but there's a chance. Here, she doesn't even have that."

Hattie inhales. "Incubators? How do we—"

Then the father's voice, overpowering. "You're suggesting that we put our daughter in a circus sideshow."

Dr. Bricknell turns toward me. "Yes, Nurse Anderson. I'd also like to know. Is that what you're suggesting?"

I straighten my spine. "I'm suggesting we save her life."

"Do they work? The incubators?" Hattie interjects.

"Sometimes," Dr. Bricknell admits, though he sounds anything but happy about it. "Likely through chance rather than skill. The man at Coney Island is by many accounts a liar and a fraud. Not trained as I am." He straightens.

The baby's father nods vigorously at the end of Dr. Bricknell's little speech. "Yes, yes. And you"—he turns to me—"you want my daughter displayed alongside burlesque dancers? Fire-eaters? Midgets?"

Cybil, Cybil, Cybil. Her name beats with a pulse stronger than that of this new baby's heart. "The facility is quite separate from all that," I promise the man, "just like a hospital." I'm practically parroting the news article, and I pray it's correct. I haven't yet had a free day to go and see for myself. Not with these hours. "Trained nurses and doctors, sanitary conditions, the newest technology. Several babies sent from other hospitals are doing beautifully there."

"But it is entirely your choice." Dr. Bricknell comforts the man before tossing a glare in my direction. *Not yours,* his pursed lips tell me. *Be. Quiet.* The cardinal rule for nursing students: Tread carefully. Be quiet. And obey.

My words are useless anyway. The father scoffs. "A hospital on Coney Island's midway. Ha!"

"Michael . . ." the wife speaks quietly.

"No, Hattie. Our daughter is not a freak."

Hattie's pale lashes cast spidery shadows as she peers down at her child. "No," the woman whispers. "She's not."

"It's decided, then." The man—Michael—turns to us. "We will follow *God's* plan." He emphasizes *God* as if we had suggested instead that he bargain with the devil himself for his daughter's life. His words are eerily similar to Dr. Bricknell's the day Cybil died as he continues. "Our daughter will not be exploited by a quack."

Silence. Michael is waiting for us to affirm his decision; I am waiting for Hattie to refute it. And—yes—she lifts her head from the damp pillow and opens her mouth. *Thank God.* Air whooshes from between my lips in relief. And then Hattie collapses back again, her mouth closing. I look to her husband and see why: his eyes are narrowed, and he is sending his wife the same message Dr. Bricknell telegraphed to me just moments before. *Not your decision. Be quiet. Obey.*

Like me, Hattie acquiesces. A tear leaks from her eye as she nods. The infant, poor sweet girl, is trembling. Even shriveled and pale, she possesses her mother's beauty: big eyes, full lips, a pinprick nose.

"Well." Dr. Bricknell nods once, curtly, as if the situation is simply unavoidable. "We'll give you a moment alone."

He whisks me into the hallway with the head nurse. "The nurse and I have another delivery to attend to."

I try not to let it sting, that he refers to her as "the" nurse like I'm not one, too.

"I assume it goes without saying that you don't open your mouth again as you do what you can to keep the girl comfortable. And then?" He waits to be sure my eyes are locked on his. "Up to the director to decide whether you still graduate, but you're off obstetrics." And away he goes, spinning on his heel and leaving his words swirling in my head. *Off obstetrics.*

No. I didn't do anything wrong. I'll talk to the director, argue my case, do an extra round in surgery or emergency . . .

Stop, Althea. Planning may be my way to cope, but I don't have time for it now. No time for list writing when a baby is dying in the next room. Losing my job means nothing if I don't use my job to save lives while I still have it.

I stride back into the delivery room, masking my panic as urgency. "I'm going to find the baby a hot water bottle to warm her skin." I let Hattie kiss her daughter's forehead before I take her and wrap her in a blanket and Hattie grips my wrist. The strength of her grasp surprises me, her body limp and coated in sweat. "Margaret." She whispers her daughter's name like the girl has stolen her voice.

"Margaret," I repeat as the girl and I slip from the room. Her round eyes stare fearfully into mine.

"Oh." The word drops from my mouth like a tear.

I cannot let this girl die.

Not again.

CHAPTER FOUR

Stella Wright, December 1950

As if I weren't struggling enough to get through this dreary December 15, Mary Ellen wets herself in class. Sweet thing that she is, she does her best afterward. She refuses to sit, not wanting to dirty the classroom seats, and she doesn't cry.

But I'm tempted to. I may have turned twenty-four in September, but my emotions can run as wild as my children's. I've nearly a dozen kids in the classroom and no way to clean Mary Ellen without leaving them alone. No extra clothing, no cleaning supplies, no bathroom, no assistant. I wouldn't have a classroom at all if there were two fewer students to fill it.

If today's minor catastrophe were a onetime occurrence, I would laugh about it later with Jack, poke fun at what my own expression must have been upon noting the streak in Mary Ellen's stockings.

But, dear Lord. This is not a unique situation. I find the

strength to push through only because I know that today is the day it will change—that at the end of the day, boxes of supplies will await me. No more of Gardner's cruelty; for nearly two years, he has scoffed every time I asked him for rulers or protractors.

"They wouldn't use them anyway," he always insisted. "What do you expect them to do, quantum mechanics?" His following laugh—a guilty attempt at conviviality—sounded like a bark.

God bless these kids, whose classroom doesn't even have a window. They need the lift these new supplies will give us as much as I do. I suspect that the room was built as a storage cellar, though the school itself denies it. About the only perk is that we'll be the most likely to survive if the Russians do finally drop a bomb on New York—but assuming that doesn't happen, there's nothing good to say about the place. My "special" kids were shoved back here when the law decided they had to be taught—when Principal Gardner could no longer dismiss students with disabilities as uneducable.

But even after all those reforms, I have just the eleven. I try not to think about the others that surely exist here in Dutchess County. Most are sent away to live in old, crumbling institutions. Remnants of the Victorian age, all red brick and creeping vine. Homes for idiots, for the deficient.

But whatever the principal says, my kids don't belong there. My kids aren't uneducable. I know that like I know the number of fingers on my hand. And any fool who spent a day with them would realize it, too. Just one glance into Judy's reproachful eyes shows she understands every damn word you say against her. A quick perusal of James's extensive notes on ants' social hierarchy demonstrates his keen eye for detail. A squishy hug from Mary

Ellen when you need it the most proves that she's perceptive enough to pick up on even the things we adults believe we've kept hidden.

Sometimes it felt like Mom was the only one who understood. She never acted like the kids were interchangeable; she knew every one of their names. Like me, she questioned how they are expected to progress—in speech, in literacy, in social skills or hygiene or independence—when they are isolated like this. How, God willing, am I supposed to teach them? Their ages range from five to eleven. Giovanna speaks only Italian—in fact, I suspect her language is why she's here, as she has no discernible handicap. Two others use wheelchairs, and I must carry each down the stairs in the morning on my own. Four do not speak. Only James writes, and just a handful read. So, what do I teach?

The district's answer is "something the whole lot can do." They keep it vague so that if we're ever investigated by the government, they can blame *me* for failing to provide rigor. But they are the ones to hand me stacks of coloring pages and bone-dry markers passed down from the classrooms with newer ones, patting my hand condescendingly as they pass the boxes over.

This, I can't help but think each time, *is how my children go through life. Neglected, patronized. Condescended to.*

I grit my teeth now in the approximation of a smile. "James, Judy," I instruct. "Run up to the bathroom and get me a stack of paper towels."

James refuses, shaking his head. He's entrenched in whatever he's working on today, and I know better than to push him. I'm lucky the sharp smell of Mary Ellen's urine hasn't set him off. The last thing we need right now is a tantrum.

Judy rolls her eyes at James and leaves on her own, the swing of her walk proving her grateful to be given the modicum of independence. Perhaps I should stop her, send Giovanna—but Judy's hopeful eyes convey how badly she craves the responsibility. The same desire has always coursed through my own body, constrained as it is by womanhood.

Guilt hits before the words form fully in my head. I have independence. I'm here, aren't I? Teaching at work rather than cooking and cleaning at home for Jack.

Not that they're always so different, I note ruefully as Judy reappears with paper towels from the upstairs bathroom.

"Thanks, Judy."

She nods, her face devoid of hostility. I take it as a victory and smile before remembering my reason for sending Judy off in the first place.

"Mary Ellen," I beckon. "Come." The girl complies, and I roll her stockings down to her ankles. "Here." I hand her the papers. "Wipe." She bats them against her legs until I take them and dry her off myself. "Now put the rest in your panties." Clumsy, but the best we can do. At the very least, they'll keep her from getting a prickly red rash where she's wet.

The principal appears in the doorway just as I'm easing myself back to my feet. He watches me rise with an aloofness he likes to describe as composure. "Something the matter?"

Damn. He hates it when I send the kids upstairs. And *I* hate it when he takes it as an excuse to come down and check in.

"No."

He gives Mary Ellen a pointed look. "Yet we're taking off our clothing?"

"She was hot." I swallow. Who knows what he'll say about the poor girl if he knows the truth? Human dignity is not exactly a concept he seems to have grasped.

The principal's eyebrows rise like he's enjoying my discomfort. This is the same man, after all, who relishes the power in reminding married teachers that he could release them from their position at any time. And he could. Other women in my graduating class have been subject to that very fate. Mom threatened to write a letter to the principal when my friend Sarah got fired after appearing at school with a ring on her finger; the issue was one of the few on which my mother and I were equally matched in passion.

I miss her. Jack wouldn't understand the injustice of Gardner's threat like she would have. In his eyes, it's only a matter of time before I quit to have kids, anyway. He works at the bank because it pays; he doesn't understand that I've spent my whole life wanting to teach.

And after today I'll start to teach the way I've always dreamed of. "Will the supplies be arriving today?" I clench my fists behind my back as I await Principal Gardner's answer, unwilling to let him see how nervous I am. I try to remind myself what I've told Jack for two weeks now. The principal would never let me quit; the job is far too hard to fill.

"The shipment should come in at one p.m. I'll leave the boxes by the door."

I feel the smile bloom across my face, two weeks' worth of stress diffusing into the air. I'd been right to speak up. Because of my insistence, we'll get supplies and maybe even turn over a new leaf with the principal. For him to be willing to bring the boxes down to me is unprecedented; my threat of leaving must have truly rattled him.

"Thank you," I tell the principal. *Thank you for finally showing me and my kids a modicum of respect.*

A t ten thirty a.m., I corral the class and march them upstairs for recess. Halfway through the school year, the process is no less chaotic than the day we began. I have to carry Carol and Robby up the steps one at a time, all the while yelling after Judy to wait for me before she runs outside unsupervised. Mary Ellen clutches my pant leg in her little fist, and I have to grit my teeth to keep from toppling over and sending Carol tumbling. What should be a simple task leaves me drenched in sweat, and I feel as hot and defeated after climbing the stairs as I would after climbing the Sisyphean mountain.

I push open the outside door and bite back a curse. Sleet falls in thick sheets from the sky, obscuring the metal swing set and slide that are just six feet away. The wind howls, and I'm surprised we couldn't hear its roar even from our windowless basement.

Beside me, Mary Ellen starts to cry. Judy crosses her arms over her chest, and Robby's face sags in disappointment.

"Can we go out anyway?" Judy looks up at me like her question is a challenge, but I shake my head. When the rain outside is a drizzle, I often ignore it; a quarter of an hour free of our four brick walls and grim gray ceiling can keep us sane. But this? Letting the kids outside in a storm like this one would be akin to murder.

I let the door fall shut, the linoleum floor slick. Mary Ellen continues to cry beside me, and I fight the urge to clap my hands over my ears.

Or, even more tempting, to join in her wailing. Like the kids, I look forward every day to this brief respite outside. We finally made it up those goddamn stairs, coats and all, and now we have to turn around and go straight back down.

Fighting to keep my own tears inside, I shepherd my class back to the basement. Carrying the wheelchairs downstairs is easier than carrying them up, but also more nerve-racking.

Once we arrive safely back in the classroom, faces sour, I take a deep breath. I try to look forward to the end of the day when my boxes will arrive, try to enjoy my time with the kids before our two-week separation for Christmas. We play games like Red Rover in an attempt to use up the kids' energy, but there's no pretending it's working.

I'm nursing Mary Ellen's stubbed toe, deflecting James's questions about germ theory, and trying to brainstorm another game to play when Principal Gardner's face appears at the doorway. "It's noon," he announces. "Time to send the kiddos home!"

For a brief moment, I breathe in with relief. This day has been an endless stream of fights and tears. The sort of morning I would normally follow with a call to my mother. I want nothing more than to be able to do the same now.

I look up at the principal. His hair is pristine, his collared shirt starched. Meanwhile, sweat pools in the armpits of my blouse, and snot remains crusted at my breastbone after a child's early-morning bout of tears. "Has the storm stopped, then?"

The principal quirks his head. "No. It sounds like a locomotive out there. Are you going deaf, too?" He glances from me to Carol and back.

I grit my teeth. "She's only deaf in one ear, Principal Gardner. She can hear you." *And understand you, too.*

"Hmm. Well, it's time for your students to go home."

I stare at him. *I do not feel comfortable walking in this weather. Yet he expects children to?*

I close my eyes. "Surely they can stay until two o'clock with the rest of the students. With all due respect, sir, they cannot walk home in this storm."

"*With all due respect*, Mrs. Wright, some of them cannot walk at all." His joke is met with steely silence. It's all I can do not to slap him. "Mrs. Wright," Principal Gardner says. "It is time for your students to go home. The choir class is headed down the stairs this very minute. Your children have no choice."

While our dank little basement is no bigger than the upstairs classrooms, the lack of desks gives Miss Edwards's chorus class space to stand and dance. There's also room to sit underneath the powder-encrusted chalkboard and watch.

"Well, I will make a choice *for* them, then." I lift my chin. "They are staying here. And so am I."

I turn before he can respond and shepherd my kids to a spot behind my cluttered desk. "We're going to stay here for a little while," I explain. "So we can stay safe and dry."

Once Miss Edwards's choir class has filed in, I run upstairs. I hate to leave the kids, but we don't have a telephone in the basement. I go down the list alphabetically by last name, calling Carol's home first.

"Mrs. Barr? This is Stella Wright."

Carol's mother interrupts me before I can continue. "I'm so sorry." Her voice quivers with tears. "I haven't been able to leave the house yet. I'm so sorry you're stuck there with her—thank you—"

Now, I interrupt her. "Don't worry, Mrs. Barr. I'm calling to let you know the kids will be staying late today. I'll be here until the weather calms down." She tries to thank me again, but I say a quick good-bye. I hate to hear her apologize as if her daughter is a burden. I've seen them together—Carol's legs kicking with glee, her mother's face splitting into a sparkling smile. Is it so hard for Mrs. Barr to believe that I love her daughter, too?

My mother was always so proud of me. She never bragged about herself or my dad or her home, but she wouldn't miss an opportunity to boast about me. Be it my first word, my kindness on the school playground, my acceptance to Vassar, or my wedding, my mother weaved my accomplishments into every conversation she had. I had to smother a laugh when she praised my fashion sense in front of her friends; she always told me privately that I spent far too much money on dresses and hairstyles.

Pushing my mother from my mind, I call the rest of my students' parents. Every one of them practically begs my forgiveness, and I feel guilt for my earlier frustration with the kids. How sad, that these parents feel as if I'm making some sort of sacrifice by spending time with their children. I know it doesn't come from a lack of love—if their love for their children weren't infinite, the kids wouldn't be here. They'd be in institutions. Doctors and people like Principal Gardner tell them to take them there every day. I don't want to imagine the horrible things these parents have heard to make them think the way they do.

When I've called all eleven mothers, I set the phone down with a dull click.

Oh, Mom. I allow myself a second. *I miss you.*

I return to the classroom to find that my children missed me, too. Four of them are wailing, and two are fighting. Miss Edwards, back turned to face her choir, is studiously ignoring them as her students gape.

I inhale. "It's all right, darlings. I'm back." I pull my kids in close to me. "Let's do something to pass the time, shall we?" I reach up and grope blindly along my desk until I find a book. *My Father's Dragon.*

"*My Father's Dragon,*" I begin to read. "By Ruth Stiles Gannett. 'Chapter One: My Father Meets the Cat.' Oh, children! Look at this. The first line of the book sounds just like what we have here. 'One cold rainy day . . .'"

The choir class returns upstairs at one o'clock, but the storm rages on outside. Our failed excursion for recess feels like it was years ago. We're nearly halfway through the book, but the kids have grown bored: Mary Ellen is picking her nose, Robby is staring at the ceiling, and James is calculating something on his fingers.

Then I remember the boxes of supplies. If the storm didn't delay their delivery, they should be outside the classroom by now.

I crack the door open and check, straightening with a thrill to see two large cardboard boxes stacked neatly against the wall.

"Children," I cry, "we've new supplies to open!"

The kids gather around me as I fall to my knees and tear into the boxes. I rip off the tape, imagining the number of books the packages might hold or the maps and posters I can use to brighten up our somber walls. I know the principal won't have bought everything on my list—from books to art supplies and more—but I'm eager to see what he has provided.

The first item I pull out is made of bulky canvas, folded and heavier than its size would suggest. With a thrill, I realize it must be canvas for painting. My children have never even picked up a paintbrush, but already I'm thinking about all they could create. Self-portraits, a rainbow to make the room their own, imaginary worlds where men like Gardner don't control their every move.

The thick cloth falls open, and it takes me a moment to figure out what I'm looking at. It isn't a rectangle or a square like I expected. Instead, it's the shape of the letter T, like a shirt. My brain is still focused on art, and my first thought is that the item is a smock.

Then it hits me. I drop the cloth and jump back like it's on fire.

Principal Gardner has sent me a straitjacket.

My entire body tenses as I peer inside the box.

It can't be. I dig through the piles. Straitjacket, straitjacket, straitjacket, each one child-sized.

"What are they?" Giovanna asks, pride in her voice for asking the question in English.

I look up and nearly choke on a sob as I gaze at my kids' expectant faces. Instead of seeing them as they are in front of me, I imagine how they would look in the jackets: Mary Ellen trying to sign to me, her sweet, baby-fat hands trapped in the folds of her jacket. Robby's body revolting, seizing; saliva running down his chin. Judy shivering with anger so intense she could almost break out. And Carol's eyes dimming with betrayal.

"Canvas," I force out. "Canvas for painting."

Giovanna shakes her head like she doesn't understand, and Judy squints. "Painting?"

"Yes." I stand up quickly, thrusting the jackets behind me.

Only the fact that the kids are watching me keeps me from tears. Because I don't have a choice now, do I? If I'm not going to pack my kids into straitjackets, I have to quit.

Which makes today my last day with them.

My mind sparks with an idea.

"Judy," I say. "Go to Miss Bell's classroom upstairs and fetch us some paint. As much as she'll give you."

The other teachers are rarely willing to share, so I jot a note on a sheet of paper and thrust it toward Judy. "Here. This tells her that it's for a project Principal Gardner has asked us to complete for the new year." I'm honest by nature, but these are special circumstances.

Judy runs off, and I shoo the other kids into the classroom and then drag the boxes after them.

I enlist their help laying the jackets in a patchwork quilt on the floor. I grin even through my fury. By the time Gardner sees these straitjackets again, they'll be unusable.

As the rain slows to a trickle, I survey the kids' work. The canvases are streaked with red and yellow, green and blue, and mostly, where the colors have mixed, brown. They have tire tracks across them from Judy and Giovanna wheeling Carol and Robby across the canvas, and they're fraying where James picked apart the edges. The metal buckles are cracked open from the weight of the wheelchairs, and I smile smugly. There'll be no fastening the jackets now.

Standing on the paint-splattered floor, my own clothing spotted with color, I am being cracked open, too. Half of me feels victorious, nearly giddy with joy as I look over the art my children have created.

The other half of me wants to fall to the ground and bury myself under the jackets, because I know this has to be it.

My kids will be better off with someone else. Someone trained for this. Someone level-headed and sensible.

Someone other than me.

I want more than anything to fight for these children, but I clearly don't know how. Not when my attempt to help makes things worse, when in my rashness and my grief I try to force the principal to give the kids a basic level of supplies and instead get them sewn up in straitjackets like madmen.

I close my eyes against the image. *I'm sorry. But I give up.*

I take a deep breath. "I'm glad we had such a fun day," I tell the kids, "because today was, sadly, my last day with you. After winter break, you are going to have a wonderful new teacher." I force my voice to stay bright and cheery. "I know you're going to love her!"

I focus in on James's quizzical expression and push away my tears.

"I love you all"—I sign the basic phrase as I speak it—"and I will miss you so, so much."

Eleven pairs of eyes stare back in various stages of under-standing. Mary Ellen is signing. Her wide, flat hands are clumsy, but her meaning is clear: "I love you."

Once I've given the children hugs that I hope will last us forever, I bang on Gardner's office door and burst in with-out waiting for a response. Ignoring the receptionist, whose head is bowed as she hands the principal a file, I stand over them. "Straitjackets?" My voice is loud; it carries all the fury I'd pushed down for the sake of my students.

"Oh, good." Gardner waves the receptionist out and turns to me. "You've had a chance to look at the new supplies."

"New supplies?" I can barely control the pitch and volume of my voice. "New *supplies?*"

"Now, Mrs. Wright. I know they might seem upsetting to you, but they're highly recommended for children like yours. Rome State was kind enough to send us some extras at a discounted rate. They say several schools have found them particularly useful during class."

Rome State? The name is almost as jarring as the jackets them-selves. Rome State is one of the institutions where my children could have ended up—might still end up. The place is rife with disease and abuse.

"Rome State is anything but 'kind,'" I say. "My kids will not be wearing those jackets."

"I assure you, Mrs. Wright. This is standard practice."

I hate the way his voice makes Jack's and my last name sound dirty. "But—"

"If you are unable to implement what is widely regarded as the best form of treatment for these children, Mrs. Wright, perhaps you are not fit for the job."

I have thick skin. I've gotten into more than my fair share of arguments over the years; I can take a raised voice or an insult. But the principal's words strike home. *Perhaps you are not fit for the job.*

The words hurt because I fear they are true. I try to help my kids, and I hurt them. I try to fight for them, and the world just fights back harder.

"That's exactly why I'm standing here in your office." I channel my anger to keep from dissolving into tears. "Because, as I promised, I am quitting."

I spin on my heel and throw my last comment over my shoulder. "The straitjackets are in my classroom. Good luck getting your money back for them."

CHAPTER FIVE

Althea Anderson, July 1926

In the obstetrics supply room, I wrap a hot water bottle in cloth and nestle it against the infant's skin. She blinks in response, and the sight of her wide eyes propels me surely as a shot. I grab a box I'd brought inside this morning, a lifetime ago, when it overflowed with pillowcases and sheets. It will have to do, though the baby takes up a mere fraction of the space. I create a nest of blankets around her, my hands shaking. Sweat soaks my nylon stockings until they are scratchy and irritating, and my pinched toes tingle in my standard-issue nursing shoes.

Each breath this girl takes could be her last.

Wincing, I roll the infant so that she resembles a Coney Island hot dog more than she does a Coney Island baby. Only when I make my excuses to the receptionist downstairs, body flushed full with lies, do I pull the cloth over the baby's dumpling face. "I must go. Sick. I'm sorry." I direct the message toward the receptionist, but my apology is for the infant. *I'm sorry we must lie.* And for Cybil: *I'm sorry we didn't.*

Plunging into the thick summer air with the baby, I flag a hansom cab and clamber up and inside. I sit stiff-backed and hold the baby close to my chest. Choking on the smell of the horse's sweat, I dip my head and press my nose into the baby's skin. It is clean, so clean. Unmarred by the heady scent of fear or bitter regret, free of perfume's saccharine seduction or debauchery's dirty detritus.

My skin is anything but clean. I quiver with fear so intense it masquerades as love.

I am kidnapping this girl.

To Coney Island," I cry, a protective arm draped around the place where the lid of the box bends open. "As fast as you can."

Though the Brooklyn Bridge is in sight of Bellevue, Coney Island is on the far side of Brooklyn. It may as well be California, Margaret and I swelter so long in the carriage. Transportation in the city is always a gamble. Today, we navigate an obstacle course of stubborn horses, smoky exhaust, and oblivious throngs of people. Traffic stops completely a block from Surf Avenue, and I stuff a wad of bills up through the trapdoor in the carriage. "Thank you," I cry as I leap from the carriage, "thank you!"

Margaret and I are off before the driver responds. My fingers twitch around the edges of the box, but I am too afraid to pull it open to check whether the girl is still breathing. I keep my eyes trained ahead as I push through throngs of people. Laughing and shouting, they are blissfully unaware that a life within their midst hangs in the balance.

And then we are there, the white stone entryway magnificent in scope: LUNA PARK: THE HEART OF CONEY ISLAND. Absurdly, as if taking again my anatomy exam, I murmur "heart" aloud and clutch at the organ in my own chest. Surely my nerves and mad dash through the city set it to racing, but I cannot feel its beat. The arrhythmic cacophony of the crowd mutes its pulse, and I pray this too is the reason I can no longer sense Margaret's tiny heart beating or hear the strangled choke of her gasps. *Please, God, let that be the only reason.*

My nurse's uniform propels me to the front of the line, and I press a dime into the ticketer's meaty hand. "Welcome"—he brandishes my ticket before me—"to the heart of Coney Island!" Patient listening is part of my job, but I don't stay to hear what else this man is trained to say. I grab the ticket and run.

The Coney Island article, which I've memorized like a rosary in my guilt over Cybil, reports that the exhibit sits along the throbbing midway of the fair. But *throbbing* is the wrong word to describe this main thoroughfare. It can claim no semblance of pattern or regularity. Lights dance between every tower and roof and wall, and electricity zings through the air as if the park believes itself immune to fire. The current carries with it the sharp scent of salt—from where? The sea, the sweat that coats the bodies pressed around me, the pretzels and popcorn sold at every corner? I cannot concentrate long enough to tell. Children shriek as they fly by on a coaster of shivering planks. A woman wearing naught but a feathery fan appears briefly at a doorway and then disappears again, a flood of men in pursuit. A man so short his head would just hit the place where my corselet laces in the back pushes his way through the crowd amid points and cries of horrified joy.

I pull the box with the baby closer to me. I hope she can breathe in this packed, airless crowd. I myself am struggling to as I'm swept along with the crush of bodies.

I must hurry. But where is the Toboggan, the landmark referenced in the article? My breath clogs my throat like smoke; fear and the crowd's sticky heat have paralyzed me. A better question: what *is* the Toboggan? It cannot be a sled, not in this suffocating summer. I scan the crowd. And, oh, there it is—the very roller coaster that so startled me moments before. A sign proclaims it the "world-class Toboggan"—a claim I highly doubt. I half expect the wheeled carts full of children to fly off.

Still, I fight my way toward it, working my body into strange contortions to hold Margaret in her box above the fray.

"Live babies!" I make out the barker's call as we approach. "All the world loves a baby!" It doesn't seem right, expecting a man on stilts to promise a miracle when a doctor cannot. But this is the place. Blinking lights advertise Couney's famous incubators and their equally famous babies: live, ten cents a viewing.

Two minutes ago, I feared being lost in the crowd; now, I prickle as if I am a spectacle for its enjoyment. I fight the urge to wipe the sweat winding its slow, meandering way between my breasts. Wearing a corselet for a twelve-hour shift is bad enough; now, in the heat and the crowd, I can hardly breathe. The lace cuffs of my knickers rub and itch, and I must use all my self-control not to hike up my skirt and scratch.

"You'll be okay, Margaret." I whisper the comfort to a girl who may not be breathing. A girl who, even if she is, can surely not hear me above the crowd's uneven roar. "We're here."

Adopting the brisk, competent walk I have perfected at the hospital, I approach the barker. "Is the doctor in?"

The man grins jovially down at me, his sweaty face an ice cream melting in the sun. "All day, every day! Just one shiny dime and you can see his babies!"

I shake my head. "I *have* a baby," I call up to the man. "One for him to take, that is."

The man's exuberance fizzles into uncertainty, and his face loses its grotesque proportions. "I suppose you'd best go on in, then . . . or perhaps you ought to pay regardless . . ." He trails off, and I miss his final decision as I skirt behind him through the door of the exhibit.

"Oh." The word slips involuntarily from my lips. The contrast between the chaotic midway and the still, silent hospital is jarring. And indeed it is a hospital, regardless of its billing. Nurses bustle about clasping spoons and thermometers; babies rest in windowed boxes like tiny eggs in refrigerators.

"I have a baby." My voice is loud in the silence, and I bring a hand to my throat in shame.

A nurse appears immediately at my side, pulling Margaret from the box and checking her pulse. My toes curl in my shoes as I wait for the verdict. I have seen death, yes, but I have never witnessed the death of someone with whom I have gone on a journey such as this. Nor the death of one for whom I may have sacrificed my job. *Please, God, no.*

It is with relief that my toes unclench when the nurse turns her steady eyes up to me. "We may save her yet."

I breathe—*slow in, slow out*—to calm myself as the nurse carefully swaddles and feeds the infant. Her administration of the milk and brandy awes me; she tips one drop at a time into the baby's nostril with a spoon folded at the end like a serviette. I avert my eyes from the spoon when I note that its bowl is the same size as Margaret's whole forehead. Oblivious to my discomfort, the nurse tilts the milk down Margaret's nose. I wait for a choke, a splutter, but it goes down smoothly. Once Margaret is fed, the nurse assigns the girl her own incubator: a metal box on stilts like the barker's outside. Aside from the glass-paneled double doors that swing open as if to a mansion, the incubator resembles a modern icebox. Odd that a baby rests inside.

Now that I am less frantic, I have time to really look about the place. Incubators identical to Margaret's line the walls of the room. A wide, glistening pane of glass separates this area's calm from a second room—one in which I imagine the fluttering quiet of this space transforms into something livelier. There, babies lie in bassinets and clutched to the chests of wet nurses. That second room is a nursery more than it is a hospital, and I step closer. The babies in that parallel universe are small, certainly. Smaller than some newborns I've seen. But they are a world away from the ones in here, who appear doll-like in their size and glassy sheen. If this man can turn Margaret into one of those children—smiling, laughing, crying, and fully *alive*—the rest of it is immaterial. It does not matter, the backdrop of clowns and dancers like ushers into hell. It does not matter that a man on stilts serves as receptionist or that a doctor makes himself rich with the clamor of his audience.

Once Margaret has been settled in her fleece blanket, oxygen tubes adjusted, the doctor himself emerges. "Dr. Couney." He shakes my hand with a smile, his grip inviting. The man is not what I expected him to be. He is understated, if ebullient, and there is nothing flashy in his appearance. "You've met Nurse Louise Recht." He gestures to the stocky, competent nurse attending to Margaret, and I nod.

"You are lucky"—he raises his eyebrows—"that we had an incubator open for the little one."

"I am lucky"—I shake my head with wonderment—"that we even made it here. Thank you. For all of this."

He bows his head. "The babies deserve a chance."

It is such a simple statement, but tears well in my eyes. Many doctors do not believe in such a chance. Too many doubt that weaklings with such little hope deserve the resources it takes to give them a try. Still others are convinced that they should not live even if they can, that they will do naught but generate a line of their own weak, inferior babies. Coney Island itself serves as the backdrop for fitter family competitions; ironic that no Luna Park incubator baby's family could ever win one. Especially as Couney allows infants of any color into his ward, and certainly no immigrant or Black family would be deemed the American ideal.

I shake my head at the injustice of it all. I've helped to deliver babies of all colors and creeds at Bellevue—one of the only hospitals in the city that allow such. Each little infant's eyes tell the same story: that of humanity and love.

I thank the doctor a final time as he turns to leave. Looking at the girl again and searching for color in her sunken cheeks, I nearly miss the doctor's final words.

"Nurse Anderson," the doctor calls to me across the room. "She *is* going to live."

The efficient Coney Island nurses take care of everything, making it far too easy to get away with my deception. Hospitals barely keep track of babies—I read a story recently about one that accidentally sent two unrelated babies home with each other's mothers—and the incubator ward is no different. The information they record is medical, not personal: weight, length, months to term. All I need to give as proof of identity is the girl's name: Margaret Perkins. I write down her parents' names, Michael and Hattie, but put down my own address at the Nurses' Residence in the field that asks for theirs. Michael and Hattie can't know about Margaret until I'm sure she'll survive.

My legs shudder as I write my address. I cannot tell if they are quaking in relief that I've not been questioned, or in fear as the reality of my actions becomes clear.

Maye Couney, head nurse and wife of the doctor himself, chats companionably as she takes down the information. "It always surprises me how many parents don't bring the babies themselves," she muses. I search desperately for a plausible explanation, but Maye provides me one. "Suppose it's out of sight, out of mind. They can pretend their little one is tucked away in a hospital room rather than the circus."

I smile weakly. "Surely, they could never call this place the circus once they've come by."

Maye shrugs her slight shoulders. "Some of them never do. They live too far away or are too ill after the birth. Others"—she smiles—"come daily. Visit their babies, nourish them with their own milk."

A spasm of guilt hits me. Margaret's mother is one of those who will never come.

But no. I have nothing to apologize for. I have saved the baby's life.

Only—what will I tell the parents?

She passed." I dip my head as I return to the Perkinses' curtained bedside that evening.

Hattie crosses herself, and Michael stumbles back. I suppose condemning your daughter to death does not prepare you for the reality of it. But my pity is reserved for the woman, suffering as I have for an inability to speak up.

I slide forward with the wastebasket as Hattie retches. Little comes up; she has not eaten since her contractions began. But still her husband steps away as if she has coughed up blood. I keep from shooting him the look of disgust he deserves. His daughter has died, and all that matters to him is avoiding the splatter of vomit on his sewn leather shoes?

I turn back to Hattie. "You're going to be just fine," I soothe. And she will. She'll be all right soon enough, when I bring her daughter back to her. Once Margaret is five pounds, six. Once Margaret can suckle and breathe unassisted. Poor Hattie and her husband need only endure their grief a month, maybe two, before I can tell them what I've done.

"When can we go?" Michael too is looking toward the future.

I affix a patient smile as I swivel to face him. "We'll need to keep your wife in for at least three days."

"Why?"

"Monitoring." I glance behind me and lower my voice so as not to frighten poor Hattie. She's been through enough. "There's always a risk of blood clots, hemorrhaging, or infection." A hemorrhage killed my own mother, but infection is more likely here in the hospital.

"You couldn't save the baby." Michael raises his eyebrows. "Why should I trust you with my wife?"

We could *save the baby*, I want to tell him. *In fact, I did. You're the one who refused.* Instead, I keep my smile plastered on my face. "I assure you, it's for the best that she remain here."

"Yes. I want to stay," Hattie confirms. Her voice is high and girlish like a child's. I wonder if it's how Margaret's voice will sound too—if the baby girl lives long enough to speak. The uncertainty as to whether she will, the doubt, is all that keeps me from pouring the truth out to Hattie right now. Sparkle in her eyes or not, Margaret is helpless. She could succumb to anything: apnea, bradycardia, sepsis, jaundice, hemorrhaging in the brain. I can't feed Hattie hope and then take it away again. She looks younger than me—twenty, twenty-one? I don't know how much pain she can take.

"You'll stay," I assure her. "It's standard procedure."

She nods, and I wonder if she's even younger than I've guessed. Her open face is so desperate; she needs taking care of. I'm happy to have a task. Something to distract me from the crime I've just committed, and the possible loss of my job on top of it.

"Am I going to die?" Hattie's voice wavers.

"Of course not." I can't really make this promise, but I've already broken so many rules that the kindness feels worth it.

"Then why can't we go home?" Michael snaps.

I purse my lips. "*You* are welcome to go home. It's your wife who needs to stay."

"I'm not leaving her here with you," he grumbles.

I'd like to think he wants to stay because he cares about his wife, but I'm afraid he's acting more from a territorial instinct than a protective one.

"You will have a new nurse after tonight," I tell the man. "Perhaps you'll find her more competent."

Michael merely grunts, but Hattie wraps her bloated fingers around my bony wrist. "Do you have to go?"

"Not yet," I promise her. "What do you need?"

"I just have questions." Her whole body shudders, pale skin against pale sheets like a ghost. "I . . . Did she suffer?"

I bite my lip. "No."

"What was it that . . ." Hattie flounders. ". . . did it?"

"Hattie!" Michael's voice slams into us like the shutting of a door. "It's over. Let it go."

I want to ignore Michael's command, but I don't have an answer for Hattie. Instead, I provide the only human comfort I can, keeping my hands on her so she feels less alone. I smooth her hair and plump her curls. I rub my thumb over her unblemished white shoulder.

She drifts to sleep before my shift ends at seven o'clock, and I don't wake her to say good-bye. I'll see her again, and I'll have her daughter with me when I do.

Though my whole body aches, I can't go back to the Nurses' Residence yet. Instead, I knock on the door of Miss Rottman's office. The plaque outside, *Director of Nursing Service*, usually thrills me. Today, it terrifies me.

"Come in." The principal's stern voice penetrates the door.

I enter.

"Nurse Anderson."

"Good evening."

"How can I help you?"

I inhale. "I've had a slight difference of opinion with Dr. Bricknell, and he's asked for a new nurse in obstetrics."

Miss Rottman's eyes narrow behind her thin, perfectly round glasses. "I've never known you to be oblique, Nurse Anderson. What was this 'difference in opinion'?"

"Dr. Bricknell informed the parents of a premature infant that their daughter would not survive here at the hospital. I agreed with him, but felt it was my duty to tell the parents about the incubator wards on Coney Island." Just mentioning the island sets my armpits sweating. I have the absurd fear that Miss Rottman can smell the salt on my skin. "Dr. Bricknell was . . . displeased. He felt that I was usurping his authority."

"You were." Miss Rottman's voice is curt, and my heart plummets. If I didn't smell like salty ocean air before, surely I do now: not from the beachy breezes but from the sweat that clings to my body like panic. "But"—Miss Rottman almost smiles—"occasionally, we must do that."

"We must . . ." I pause. "Excuse me?"

"We must occasionally usurp the man's authority. I wouldn't be here if we hadn't, would I?" This time, she does smile. Despite the stiff collar and the buttons that march from Miss Rottman's waist to her chin, I can imagine how she might have looked as a student here nearly two decades ago. She's stern now, but she would have been a spitfire.

"I suppose you're right." My own smile echoes hers.

"However." Miss Rottman raises her eyebrows. "There are no other positions available in obstetrics."

I bow my head.

"Where are you in your rotations?"

"I've done psychopathy, Pavilions A and B, the tuberculosis ward, and surgery."

The woman nods. "I avoid saying this as a matter of principle, but you have been one of our best nurses. In fact, though I've got decades left in me, I can almost imagine you taking over my position one day. I certainly don't want to keep you from graduating. How many mothers have you delivered?"

I can barely keep my voice level. My head swims from her compliment. "Over fifty, ma'am. I've done two of the three months in obstetrics."

Miss Rottman closes her eyes. "Don't make me regret this, Nurse Anderson. We don't take exceptions lightly."

I tip forward on my toes, desperate for good news.

"But I can move you to the emergency ward in Pavilion G. We've been over capacity every day for months, and we need a night nurse. Seven p.m. to seven a.m."

"I'll take anything, ma'am."

"You'll be on probation. Another complaint and you're out."

"Of course. I understand. Thank you." I would hug the woman

if I didn't suspect she is as standoffish as I am. "You don't know how much this means to me."

Miss Rottman fingers her pin. It is the same one I will receive at commencement next year: a crane on a round backdrop of gold. "I do know, Nurse Anderson. That is exactly why I've allowed it."

CHAPTER SIX

Stella Wright, December 1950

Jack arrives home from work at the bank just after five thirty p.m., and—miraculously, though I've just barely made it home myself—I've managed to get dinner on the table. I could have just picked something up on the way home, but I knew I'd fall apart without a task to do. I knew that as soon as I let myself stop and think, I'd break.

"How was your day?" I ask my husband at the door. Today, it's more reflex than genuine question.

"Better now that I'm here." He plants a kiss on my forehead and shrugs off his rain-splattered jacket. "How was yours? Did you get the supplies?"

Jack's coat slips off the coat rack and slumps to the floor, but I make no move to pick it up.

"I quit," I say. The words taste like poison in my mouth.

"Quit?" Jack's shock would look comical in any other situation, rain dripping from his hair onto the polished floor. "What happened?"

"Straitjackets. The supplies were straitjackets. He wants to make the kids wear them in class, and I just can't do it." My voice breaks, and I repeat myself in an effort to sound more sure. "I can't do it."

"Then don't," Jack says. "There has to be another option, something other than quitting. You love those kids."

"*I* do, but Principal Gardner doesn't. And I can't do anything for them when he's against me. I only make it worse."

Jack's eyebrows draw together like the kids have swiped a marker across his forehead. I recognize this look. He's about to give me a pep talk.

I hold up a finger. "Don't, Jack. Please."

But Jack surprises me, pulling me in to his chest so I smell his woodsy scent. "Stella, sweetheart. I know you're upset. What Principal Gardner did was wrong—God, he sounds like a monster. But . . ." Jack takes a breath. "I can't help but wonder whether your going through with quitting has more to do with your mom than with what happened. Because this—giving up—it isn't like you."

My mother's death was my final unraveling, I know. But the edges of my life have been fraying for longer than the past three months, the threads of overwork and undervalue splitting my days to the point of disintegration. How to make Jack understand the slow, steady crush of opposition? The slow, steady dissolution of the idealism that carried me through school despite the odds? I'd thought being a teacher would mean I could change things, teach girls to be fearless and confident the way boys were taught to be. When I'd accepted the job under Principal Gardner, I thought I could do the same—if not for young women, then for a group even more neglected.

But being a teacher is a woman's work, and that means it carries little power. I'm no agent of change; I'm part of the system. A system that wants to put kids in straitjackets just because they're different.

I shake my head. "Mom's dying might have pushed me over the precipice." After all, my mother always told me to speak up, and it was partly her voice ringing in my ears the day I gave Principal Gardner the ultimatum. "But does it matter?" I throw up my hands. "I'm hurting the kids, whatever the reason."

Jack squints at me as if trying to see me more clearly. "You're going to just walk out, then? Leave those kids worse off than they are now?"

I close my eyes, unable to bear the sight of Jack's disappointment. I've never been a quitter. Not as a first grader, when I campaigned for my classmates to bring in stuffed animals to donate to the Salvation Army during the Depression; not as a teenager, when I refused to drop out of physics and raised my grade from a D to a B.

But Jack is wrong. Another teacher might be able to get through to Principal Gardner, might know how to better reach the kids. I've never failed before; I never imagined that Principal Gardner would force my hand.

But I see no way around quitting now, not after what he's done. What I drove him to do.

I press my lips together. "Gardner hates me. If he uses my

attempts to help my kids to hurt them, the kids are better off without me." The words burn my tongue.

"Stella, I think you're being dramatic—"

"Stop," I snap. I'm tired of being called rash or dramatic. I'm no more dramatic than when he mistakes a thunderbolt for a gunshot, am I?

Jack pulls back, and I realize for the first time that today's storm must have been hard for him, too.

My level-headed mom would have thought of that. She never would have had this conversation with my dad in the first place. Mom probably would have smiled, told Dad she had to talk to him after supper, and let him enjoy his meal in peace. Meanwhile, our pork chops grow cold, and Jack's stomach rumbles.

But I'm not like my mom. I don't want to just lie down and swallow what I feel, or put the needs of the man of the house before my own. That's what women in my mom's generation did. And some part of Mom must have regretted it, because she always told me to speak up despite the fact that she seemed content to do the opposite.

Speak up. I tried that. I tried to speak up for my kids, and look what happened.

"I'm just bad for them," I finally say. I hardly recognize my own voice, it comes out so hoarse and quiet. "They're better off with someone else."

"No, Stella." Jack places a hand on my shoulder. "That's impossible. You love those kids more than anyone. You talk about them all the time, love them like they're your own."

Am I imagining the meaning behind his words? That if I had

loved these children less, maybe we would already have one of our own? I shrug away the unfair thoughts. "It doesn't matter. I told him already. I quit."

Jack hesitates. "Maybe you could learn to see this as a good thing."

"What?"

"I just hate seeing you like this. I want you to see the positive—like how you can focus on our future now. You can start thinking about your own children, kids no one will begrudge you for loving."

I narrow my eyes. "It's not the time to talk about our own children, Jack." Not so soon after Mom died. Not when I've just thrown my career away. Not when he still shuts me out of his own thoughts and fears.

"You're right." He holds up his hands. "Sorry."

When I don't answer right away, he bites his lip and then winces. "That's the second time today, isn't it?"

I nod, and he breathes in deeply. "I'm sorry. You have too much going on right now. I know that."

"Thanks," I whisper.

"Do you want to keep talking about it all?"

I shake my head. "Distract me."

We move to the table, and Jack lifts the pork chops and carries them back into the kitchen to reheat. He tells me to sit as he finishes, and then he joins me at the table.

"I have a good story," he says. "Very random. Very distracting."

"Okay." I smile. "Go ahead."

He launches into his telling of what might be the most ridiculous story I've heard. It's about Bill, a coworker of Jack's who has apparently decided he is allergic to facial hair. Jack explains how he and the others ended up having to do all of Bill's work today, because the ridiculous man couldn't bear to have a conversation or even sit in a meeting with a man who had a beard or a mustache. "And the worst part," Jack concludes finally, "is that, I swear to God, I sat down in front of this bearded guy that Bill forced me to meet with . . . and I sneezed! Six times in a row!"

Jack's story is so silly, so patently Jack, that I can't help but laugh. My husband is a goofball, and that's exactly why I fell in love with him.

I give his hand a squeeze as I get up from the table to clean the dishes. Only once I'm in the kitchen do my emotions hit me in full force again, and I breathe deeply over the sink.

Thank you. I look back at my husband in the other room. *Thank you for that half hour. Thank you for helping me forget.*

CHAPTER SEVEN

Althea Anderson, July 1926

Margaret has been at Coney Island but a day before I return to visit her. I am the only one who knows she is there, after all; she is my responsibility. I can't tell Hattie what I have done until I can assure her with certainty Margaret will pull through. The poor mother need not lose her daughter twice. I know grief leaves its scars. Absently, I reach into my purse for the one photograph I have of my mother. Dripping in ephemeral white lace, she grips my father's arm as if to root herself to the earth. Otherwise, I always thought as a child, she would float away like a cloud.

Now, the baby is asleep when I arrive. I gaze at her through the small glass doors of her incubator as her tiny, bony chest rises and falls. With her eyes closed, she is indistinguishable from the other babies; I recognize her only because her name is printed neatly on a card affixed to her unit. *Margaret.*

Funny, for she doesn't look like a Margaret to me. Margaret

is a name for an older generation of women, ones who didn't go into nursing or work in Coney Island or survive when they weren't supposed to. This little girl is a fighter. Her body is weak, but her eyes spark with power. She's as determined to live as Dr. Couney is to save her.

Behind me, a group of fairgoers enters the building. Their reflections move ghostlike and dim across the glass panes of Margaret's incubator until something catches the light. I turn quickly to see what is sparkling so and watch head nurse Louise Recht slip a ring off her finger and then slide it, glittering, up the leg of one of the infants. The crowd gasps, whether in horror or awe, and Louise deftly drops the ring back on her finger before tucking the baby safely away. "And even that small," she concludes with pride, "the baby will survive."

I turn again to Margaret. Her limbs, too, could be encircled by a ring meant for a woman's finger. Her veins, purple-red like a bruise, circumnavigate the entirety of her tiny torso like the lifeline of a palm.

I place my own palm on the glass that separates us. Those spidery veins, the thin lines of her ribs—they are begging to be filled with life. I want so desperately to pour it into them, to breathe into Margaret's knobby body and fill it with love.

I am a trained nurse, I remind myself. *Nearly registered.* When it comes to life, I must deal in numbers and facts. The love of a near stranger will never do what milk or oxygen does for an infant. I am a nurse, and I cannot afford the distracting comfort of superstition.

Beside my palm on the glass, Louise's reflection grows larger. I cringe, hoping she isn't going to make a spectacle of Margaret with the ring.

"Don't worry." She grins as I turn. "They're all gone, done with us and ready to move on to the burlesque dancers." I cannot tell if this bothers her or not, to be likened to such an act. "Anyway, this little one's too new yet. No ring tricks for her."

I nod, embarrassed that Louise so easily sensed my apprehension. I cannot afford to be so transparent, not when my career revolves around offering comfort to patients and their loved ones. Not when my presence here is a lie.

Louise smiles. "Do you want to hold her?"

Though shocked, I manage to control my expression. Surely, Louise cannot intend to take Margaret out of the incubator. But she does. The woman reaches past me to unlatch the doors. Gently, she pulls the sleeping Margaret from her cocoon of pumped heat and air.

"Is it time to feed her?" My voice is steady.

"Oh, no," Louise chuckles. "Not now. But we try to give them a human touch once in a while, bring some color to their cheeks."

The image of Margaret, alone and anonymous inside her incubator, makes a convincing case for Louise's point. But my years of schooling suggest the opposite. What if Louise passes a disease to little Margaret? The girl is already so weak that exposure to the air-conditioned room or separation from the otherworldly tubes of oxygen may be enough to kill her.

I open my mouth to respond, but a cry from the other room catches my attention. A curly-haired infant bawls with a vigor that penetrates the glass window, and I look over. The nurse changing the girl's diaper meets my eye briefly and shrugs. Her gaze returns with a patient smile to the infant.

I look back to Louise and sigh. "I suppose you know what

you're doing." Is it the image of the healthy baby that convinces me, or merely my desire to hold Margaret? I don't know. I am on the sidelines as so many babies enter into this world, but while I clean and weigh them, I don't ever hold them beyond those first precious moments. Like the umbilical cord, I am clipped away from them at birth. And so, getting the chance to hold baby Margaret now is something special.

I adjust her carefully, cradling her entire sleeping body. *Lifelines*, I think again, gazing down at Margaret's veins. I fight the senseless urge to unfurl her tiny fists, inquire where the pathways on her palms will lead her.

Afraid to transfer any germs that may endanger Margaret or her lungs, I lighten my own breath and exhale only softly through my nose. *Is this what it is to have a daughter?* I wonder. *To suppress your own breath of life for hers?*

My body quivers as I pass Margaret back over to Louise at the nurse's request, and my hands search for something else to occupy them in Margaret's absence. "She seems to be doing well," I tell the nurse, peeling back a hangnail on my left thumb. "I should be going, but"—the nail gives way, ripping off the skin beneath it—"I will certainly keep her mother apprised of her progress."

I clamp my thumb beneath the other fingers on my hand to stem the flow of blood. "Good-bye, Louise." I turn to go. "Good-bye, sweet Margaret."

Nights at Bellevue become my routine. Stitches and syringes and bandages, any number of minor emergencies that seem far less pressing than those faced by an infant. But when I enter the Nurses' Residence each morning, my thoughts turn again and again to Margaret. Sometimes, she is a comfort; I envision her eyes like a fighter's. Sometimes, she is fear, and I must focus on my work to avoid the image of Margaret's body turning as pale and lifeless as Cybil's had.

Then there is the other kind of fear. The fear of being discovered. What would happen to me, for stealing a child even temporarily from her parents and her doctor? I'd never work again. Never whisper comforts into an old woman's ear, never hold a baby kicking for the first time, never send a child back to carefree youth with a bandage and some tape. I wouldn't have a purpose, a reason for being.

I wouldn't have a way to make up for killing my mother, just by being born. My net balance in the world, my overall impact— it would be negative.

I shudder. Maybe sacrificing my work would be the end of my losses. Perhaps my timid femininity would save me, and I would be pardoned from any more serious consequence. Deemed insane or incompetent. The doctors consider us female nurses the latter already, do they not?

But that may not be enough. And I, Althea Anderson, exceptional student and well-mannered young lady, could end up on trial. I could stare into the hard eyes of a judge as he sentences me to waste away in dissolution the rest of my lonely life. Welfare Island's white stone penitentiary rears ugly and jagged in my mind. Other women have been sent there for less: Emma Goldman for distributing information on birth control, Becky Edelsohn for calling John D. Rockefeller a murderer. "Disturbing the peace," they called it for Edelsohn. What would they call my crime? Kidnapping?

I shudder. Boarding school had been bad enough, with its restrictions on my every movement and word and thought. But there, at least, I had hot meals to eat and a soft, warm bed to curl into at night. How would I survive in prison? With whom might I share a room? A thief? A murderer?

These thoughts terrorize me each time I turn a corner at Bellevue. Will someone question the circles under my eyes, the tremor in my hands, the blisters on my heels? Will someone recognize me from Coney's stifling crowds?

My fear comes to a head when Ida Berry, who has replaced me in obstetrics, stops me in the hallway at the end of her shift and the beginning of mine.

"Althea," she calls. "Are you in a hurry?"

I shake my head. I'm early as usual; I can't risk the doctors finding even the tiniest fault in my service.

"I wanted to let you know I filled out Margaret Perkins's death certificate."

My knees buckle beneath my apron, and I reach to the wall behind me to steady myself. "Margaret Perkins? Death certificate?" I'm too afraid to say anything more intelligent.

"Yes." Ida looks at me quizzically. "The newborn who died when you were still in obstetrics? You forgot to file the death certificate. I only realized because Dr. Bricknell was trying to get me out of his hair and made me organize all the records. As if anyone ever looks at them."

It's true. Bellevue is not known for its meticulous record keeping.

Ida looks around the hallway and lowers her voice. "Anyway, I found the birth certificate you'd signed, but no death certificate.

I didn't want you to get in trouble, so I went ahead and signed it for you." She shrugs, as if her words haven't altered the very foundation of my existence. "I can't blame you for forgetting. Everything gets chaotic when an infant dies." Her face sobers for the first time. "It's not something anyone should ever have to see."

I agree with her, stammer out a thank-you. But I retreat to the restroom to think as she whistles away. Now there is a death certificate for Margaret Perkins, who is not dead at all. What will happen when I bring her back to her parents? The danger is intensifying—not only for me, but for Ida, too. I never meant to implicate her in my wrongs.

But are they wrongs? Was I wrong to save a baby girl who could not save herself? We learned of Niccolò Machiavelli in school. Do my ends justify my means?

The thought is not a comforting one. Not when Machiavelli is a synonym for deceit and manipulation.

But, but, but. A line from *The Prince* bubbles to the surface of my murky mind, something we learned in school about nothing great being achieved without danger.

I am terrified. I am a liar and a crook. But I have done something great.

I have done the right thing, saving the girl for her parents.

And so it is that I return to Luna Park the next day, despite my twelve-hour shift overnight. It is Saturday, and revelers are out in full swing. Children scream with joy and exhaustion; mothers clutch wailing babies to their chests. Each step I take meets resistance, the sudden stop of a body before me or a syrupy puddle of beer around which I must step. My father used to ask me how I, so quiet and steady, could thrive in the chaos of the hospital, but what he never understood is that neither speed nor urgency translates into chaos. Medicine is an antidote to disorder, every procedure delineated with numbers and rules. Here at the carnival is the mayhem I have always sought to avoid. This wild world of Luna Park, Steeplechase's competing tower leering above, is an utter departure for me. Here, I've deviated not only from the steadfast rules of my profession but from its orderly realm.

But I will return to that other world once Margaret is healthy enough to go home to her mother. When she is part of a family like the ones jostling about: mothers, their own food abandoned as they feed their children bite by bite; fathers, oblivious as they shout across the masses to wives focused only on their children's erratic movements through the crowd.

I close my eyes. My own father was never one for such chatter, though perhaps he was different when my mother was alive. I'll never know.

I remind my feet to move, bump my way through the throng to reach the incubator facility. The barkers are familiar with me now and I slip in without paying the dime required for amusement's entry. With Hattie still in confinement, or so the nurses here believe, I am afforded the privileges of a mother.

The privilege and the pain. The sight of Margaret's pinprick body seizes me each time; always, I fixate on something different and excruciating. Today I am all too aware of the stubs of her tiny fingers, pale flesh where there should be brittle nail. I imagine that her toes are the same way, though they are wrapped securely in a fleece blanket and pink satin bow. This girl is still forming, still—for all intents and purposes—in the womb.

Even I, who never knew my mother, was granted the connection of being formed in her body. Poor Margaret is alone, half-formed. The tragedy of it makes me bold, and I search for Maye or Louise. Instead, I catch the good doctor himself as he emerges from the office area, and he greets me with a grin. "Nurse Anderson," he cries out, "how lovely of you to stop by."

I duck my head. "I must keep the mother apprised of Margaret's health."

"Of course, of course." Dr. Couney waves his hand as if we are discussing a game of checkers rather than a baby's life. Perhaps I should find his nonchalance off-putting, but his confidence in Margaret's survival sets me at ease. He and I see the same fighting spirit in the girl.

"I was wondering"—I breathe in—"whether I could hold her?" I am prepared with my defense—that Louise had let me just days ago—but it does not prove necessary.

"Absolutely." Dr. Couney grins. "You sanitized?"

"Of course." As is required, I had washed my hands with the provided soap and water upon entering the building. I smile slightly. "Twice."

"Good, good." Dr. Couney pats my back. The gesture is condescending, but I appreciate the words that accompany them. "I've fired a nurse or two for not washing her hands."

I watch Dr. Couney as he lifts Margaret gently into his arms. He's a strange man, this doctor. He's so against the fold in running this practice that doctors deem exploitative and dehumanizing, but he's also so rigid with the rules he does follow. All visitors must wash hands. No gawkers can touch the babies. Blankets must be wrapped just so. He cares about the babies in his facilities, that much is obvious. Does that make up for his methods?

Dr. Couney smiles as he surveys Margaret. "She's strong, this one," he whistles. "Two and a half pounds when she came in, was she not?"

I nod slightly, afraid to make any movement that might disrupt the girl.

Dr. Couney whistles again. "Our minimum," he tells me, "is two pounds."

I cringe. Cybil had been two pounds and two ounces. We could have brought her here. But we didn't.

I push the guilt away and focus on the doctor's words. "Any less than that and we won't be able to save them. Even two pounds"—he shakes his head—"even that is tempting fate."

But Margaret's a fighter, I remind myself. He said it himself: *strong, this one.* I carry the words with me as the doors release me back into the sticky July heat. The crowd moves en masse, thicker than usual and more unified. Where are they going? The flood of people pushes me in the direction of a banner stretched from one building to another: *Better Babies Contest July 10, 1926.*

Curiosity piqued, I let the crowd carry me closer. Is this something Dr. Couney has manufactured? How glorious, were he to show the world how babies like Margaret could survive.

But the babies I make out as I approach are not premature. They drip with rolls, their pudgy thighs visible in their nudity. But why are the babies naked before a crowd? And in this sun? Already, their pale skin—for they are all creamy white—is reddening like salmon. Behind each infant stands its mother, trying her hardest not to sweat: curls set, cloches jaunty, dresses sticking to thighs. Ring-studded fingers keep their babies balanced on the long bench serving as a stage. Many of the babies struggle to escape their mothers' clutches as a row of women in aprons and men in hats and ties poke and prod them, clipboards in hand. A baby on the far left wails as a woman wraps a measuring tape around his forehead, neck, torso, wrists, and ankles. Closer to where I stand in the opposite back corner of the crowd, a little girl stares unblinking at a man who pries open her lips and taps her teeth with his knuckles. Beside her, judges fan a collection of toys before a boy and take notes as he reaches and grasps. I recognize the gross motor skills evaluation, but why is it taking place here?

I squirm between the other spectators to get closer. A poster leaning against the wooden stand carries a catchphrase: *You are raising better cattle, better horses, and better hogs, why don't you raise better babies?*

The glint of a silver trophy turns my head. *Best baby, 1926.*

Tears pool in the corners of my eyes. I'd like to blame the painful reflection of the trophy in the sunlight, but I am picturing Margaret. Her purple gums. Her shrunken arms and legs. She would never win a better baby contest, no matter how much of a fighter she is. Nor would have Cybil, and perhaps that is part of the reason the world let her die. At a place like this, she'd be viewed as defective. Her parents would be suspected of illness or sin. The fitter family contests across the countries would eschew their participation as well as hers.

I turn to survey the crowd. German speakers, Italian speakers, snatches of English with that familiar Irish lilt. Even a few Black families dot the midway, and I clench my toes to keep from crying openly. So many children excluded from this inane, dehumanizing contest. So many men and women told they are less than. So many babies unvalued and abandoned.

And the contest itself. I am a nurse. I know the value of dental health, infant size, and physical coordination. But proclaiming the need for more babies like "this" means reducing the number of babies like "that." I've seen the flashing-light exhibits in the Hall of Science. "We need more normal people to be born," they say, "and fewer criminals." Fewer illiterate parents, they mean, fewer immigrant parents, fewer Black parents.

Yes, this is a movement for the babies' health. But only for certain babies.

It is a movement that would tear Margaret from her family and this world.

Disgusted, I turn away. Angling my narrow body so my right shoulder leads me through the crowd, I push away and toward the exit. Dr. Couney and his incubators are the only spot of light at this godforsaken fairground.

Today, only a small trickle files into the popular World Circus Sideshow as I pass. I suppose I ought not be surprised. After all, the freak show performers are no prizewinners like the chubby, healthy babies on display outside.

I pause. I typically stay far from the circus sideshow and its "freaks." My toes twitch at the very thought of going inside and taking advantage of these men, women, and even children who make a living off defections and deformities.

Like Margaret does? Tourists pay a dime to see my baby girl, too. Those hawk-eyed, gaping gawkers keep Margaret alive. They pay for her air and her warmth and her clothes and her food and her care.

I look again at the sign: *World Circus Sideshow.* Inhaling, I pay the fee and step inside. Dampness permeates, and darkness surrounds me. The place is a far cry from Dr. Couney's bright, clean incubator ward. I pause for a moment as my pupils dilate, and then I continue. The first exhibit consists of a pair of twins. *Pinheads Flip and Pip*, a banner reads above them. Both women are about my age, and their small, microcephalic heads are shaved smooth aside from a tuft of hair like a sprout at the top. Both girls wear large, childish bows and matching checkered dresses.

"Not half as good as Zip," a man mutters beside me. "Even though there are two of them! Should be twice as good." He laughs at his own weak joke.

"Excuse me?"

"Zip, the African Pinhead? Died earlier this year. Looked like a monkey. They billed him as the missing link. He did shows and all—much funnier than these girls."

The two girls giggle uncertainly, but my shoulders tense in horror. "I regret to inform you he was not the 'missing link.'" I lift my chin. "I am a nurse. That man and these girls are microcephalic. It's a neurodevelopmental disorder. It could very well have been *you* born like that." I am only momentarily mortified by my words, for the man's response assures me he deserved it.

"Yeah, right. My parents were good ol' Americans. Thank God these girls are locked up in here, huh?"

I close my eyes and take a deep breath. *That's not how it works*, I want to tell him. *Microcephaly is not always a genetic disease. It can be caused by anoxia at birth, infections during pregnancy . . . countless other curses of circumstance alone.* But the man is rolling his eyes, whites eerie in the darkness, and he moves away from me. I should call out and stop him, but the words clot like blood in my throat. The man wouldn't believe me, anyway. Wouldn't care if he did. Instead of pursuing the man, I pick up one of the pamphlets Flip offers me. *Twins from the Yucatan*, it proclaims. Twins? I look back to the girls. Impossible. And the claim that the girls are from the Yucatan is equally impossible. Chances are they come from Alabama or Georgia, states with economies still sagging decades after the War between the States. Wagner, Coney's circus director, has been known to make a pretty penny off children from down South. He buys them from their desperate mothers for pocket change, then turns around and makes a fortune off them. I doubt their families see a penny. Yes, Dr. Couney also makes money for what he does—but he saves people's babies in the process. Wagner takes the money and then the babies, too.

Slightly nauseous, I continue through the hallway. I throw the four-legged Myrtle Corbin a nervous smile as I pass her, anxious to get on. Perched beside Myrtle is Violetta, a woman with no legs and no arms. I try not to stare and continue toward the exit. I pass the bearded lady, the tattooed lady, the fat lady, and Scalo the seal boy. One room sits barricaded and guarded by a barker, the sign on the door declaring the spectacle inside suitable for "men only."

Just before the exit, a barker stands and advertises a show. "Five minutes," he calls. "Come see our world-famous contortionists!"

I shiver ever so slightly as I pass him with a polite denial, and a woman standing nearby grins sympathetically. "You find it eerie, too? My husband and kids are in there, but I can't bear to watch."

I purse my lips. "It's not that," I admit. To spill my thoughts to a stranger is unlike me, but I am filled to the brim with secrets. My feelings now are the only piece of me safe to share. "The whole thing feels exploitative. Those poor girls—Pip and Flip? And Myrtle? Hardly older than your kids, maybe?"

The lady shrugs. "Perhaps. But what other fifteen-year-old girl could make her own living? God knows Myrtle couldn't without the circus."

I hesitate. The lady is right. Girls are hard-pressed to find real work as it is. I cannot imagine the difficulty of doing so with a set of extra legs.

The lady shrugs. "Way I see things, the circus is a haven for people like that. Yeah, maybe it's dark and dirty and who knows how they're treated, but they'd be left to die anywhere else."

She's not wrong. They would be left to die the same way sweet Margaret would have been. "But still." I shake my head. "They shouldn't *have* to come here. This shouldn't be their only option." Again, I'm thinking of Margaret. Of Cybil, and how she should have been granted a chance at Bellevue just as Margaret is here at Luna Park. And maybe I'm thinking of myself, all too aware of how hard it is for a woman to support herself in this world. "They should be allowed to work in the real world."

The woman shifts uncomfortably. She speaks with less confidence now. "It's not the circus's fault they aren't able to do anything else."

"No." I shake my head. "I only wish we could force the rest of the world to see these people, too."

CHAPTER EIGHT

Stella Wright, December 1950

Christmas break is a somber affair without my mom. Jack's mother is a vibrant character, a cross between a movie star and a suffragist—she left Jack's dad, a drunk, two decades ago and has made a way for herself and Jack ever since. I love her for having raised Jack to love a woman who is as uninhibited as a man. But I miss the steadying presence of my own mother. While Jack and his mom laugh beside the fireplace on Christmas Eve, I steal away to the guest room and pull out my mom's worn copy of "The Gift of the Magi." She always left it here so we could read it over Christmas, a tradition born when I was a child. Mom would sit in the armchair by the fire, and I would sit cross-legged and eager at her feet. Father, a number of years older, was never comfortable on the floor, but he sat beside me those nights. After Dad died five years ago and I met Jack at Vassar, Jack took that place beside me. Together, we listened to the story of Della and Jim: Della who sells her hair for Jim's watch chain, and Jim who sells his watch for Della's hair combs. I loved the story before I was old enough to understand it, when all that mattered to me was the soothing cadence of my mother's voice as she read the prose like poetry. In primary school, I started getting suspicious. "Why does the writer say they were wise?" I asked my mom. "They can't even use their gifts." To me, that sounded like stupidity. But Mom smiled and stroked my hair.

"Stella, baby girl, it's not about the gifts. It's about the sacrifice."

"What's sacrifice mean?"

Mother hesitated, then slipped from her chair to sit on the floor in front of me. "Love," she said. "Sacrifice means love."

Now, I curl up on the guest bed and read the story through. Tears drip from my eyes onto the pages, and I can't tell whether they're tears of joy or of sadness.

Jack finds me wrapping my hair around my fingers twenty minutes later. He sees the book in my lap and smiles. "Thinking of selling your hair for me?"

"I would," I tell him, forcing a smile. "But I was thinking I'd sell it—and anything else, everything else—to get my mom back. Even just for one night."

Ever patient, Jack holds me as I sob. When I start to quiet, he strokes my hair the way my mom did so many years ago. "What do you say we start our own tradition?"

"Like?"

"Cookies for Santa?"

"That's not very creative, Jack."

"So?" He shrugs. "It's fun."

"Okay." I untangle myself from his arms and stand. "You're right. Let's do it."

Two hours later, we've baked and devoured two dozen cookies. Jack's mother is asleep in the guest bed, and Jack and I lie with full stomachs in our own.

"That was even better than making cookies for Santa," I say. "He gets enough cookies, anyway."

"You deem it a worthy tradition, then?"

I laugh. "Yes."

"Our kids will love it."

I stiffen. "We don't have kids."

"We will, though." Jack inches closer to me. "My mom asked about it again this afternoon. 'When are you giving me some grandchildren?'" He imitates his mom's voice exactly, but I don't laugh.

"I'm tired, Jack." I turn away. Having children would force me to accept that I don't have a job anymore to keep me out of the house. And Jack and I . . . we aren't ready. Not with his fears and episodes. I suspect that it's only the presence of his mother that keeps them from happening with as much regularity over the holidays, and I'm both grateful and perversely jealous that she can soothe my husband in a way that I can't.

But she will return to her winter home in Florida soon, and Jack will fall again into his patterns. We're not ready for kids, and I'm not ready without a mother to teach me how to be a mother myself.

I lie awake as Jack's breath flattens in sleep. It's an odd reversal; usually, he's the one whose anxiety troubles him in the nighttime.

I cringe to remember the first night I brushed up against it.

"Jack . . ." I had been uncharacteristically unsure of myself the morning after our one-week wedding anniversary. "Do you regret marrying me?"

I was scrambling eggs over the stove, and Jack's horrified shock made me grateful that he was not the one beside the hot stovetop.

"How could you ask me that?"

He sounded wounded, and I rushed to clarify. "You didn't sleep. Not a wink."

"Maybe I was too deliriously happy."

My husband is not an evasive man by nature, but I knew there was something he wasn't telling me. His words did not carry their usual direct certainty. "Jack, your eyes were scrunched so tight you wouldn't have seen the flames if I burned down the house. You were not 'happy.' In fact"—I give the eggs an aggressive whisk—"you looked like you were being tortured." At least I knew better than to mention the tears that seeped from beneath his closed lids in the early morning, or the ones I silently cried in response.

"Oh, Stella." He rubbed his forehead. "I'm sorry. It didn't have anything to do with you. I swear."

"What was it, then?" I asked because I didn't believe him. I was afraid he regretted marrying me, wished he'd settled with a sweet-natured girl who listened more than she talked and didn't insist on working after marriage. Looking back, I should have expected his answer. My father had been affected by the First World War. I knew from his years of silence that combat and its effects plague men in ways we don't yet understand. Back then, they called the men shell-shocked. Now, the term is *combat fatigue*. But those weren't things I'd ever associated with ebullient Jack, and I was surprised when the word fell hard from Jack's lips like a stone.

"War."

"Oh, Jack." I abandoned the still-runny eggs and slid into the chair next to him. "Jack, darling, tell me."

Tell me. A year and a half later, I recognize the naivety in such a demand.

He had stiffened. "No."

"No?"

"No."

"Jack. I'm your *wife*."

"There are some things that should never be told."

Even to me? His words stung.

I remember the frustration mounting in me like panic. *He's my husband. He's supposed to know me, and I'm supposed to know him. I'm supposed to comfort him when he needs me, but how can I do that without knowing the demons he battles?*

I couldn't put any of it into words back then, so I merely stared at my husband. "I don't agree."

"Stella." His voice became eerily calm. "It's not something you'll ever understand."

"Well, I won't, if you don't tell me!"

At that, Jack had left the room. He'd gone to work without a bite of the eggs or the bacon I'd made, and I kicked over the chair he'd vacated. Later, he confessed that he had left not to spite me but to keep from doing something he regretted. "I saw a lot of violence," he'd said evenly. "And I don't want you to."

I love Jack. I love his laugh and his face and his skin and his jokes and his thoughtfulness, so different from mine. But sometimes I hate him, too, for not letting me see these parts of him that mean so much. Maybe if it only happened in the nighttime, I could learn to live with it. But he falls apart in public, too, and he pushes me away. I want him to turn to me when he is frightened by a car starting or John Wayne whipping out a gun in an old western. But he closes in on himself instead, and I'm left alone on the outside. What am I supposed to do besides ask him what is wrong, what he's seeing, how I can help? What am I supposed to do when he doesn't answer?

Now I pull the sheets over my eyes, Jack soundly sleeping beside me. Can I love a man I don't really know?

Of course I can. I *do*. But can I have a baby with him?

That's the question, Stella.

I just wish my mother were still around to help me answer it.

Christmas Day passes without note, but I grow restless as the days blend together before New Year's. I miss my kids. I imagine going to visit each, bringing homemade play dough as a peace offering, but I know it will just confuse them further. It would be selfish; I've already hurt them enough.

Jack does his best to lift my spirits, and going to the movies and puzzling are welcome moments of escape from my otherwise dark and dizzying thoughts. But those escapes only go so far. When Jack goes back to work after the New Year, I imagine my students back at school with their new, better teacher while I'm left listless and alone. The housework is time-consuming enough to fill my days: cleaning, dusting, cooking, shopping—but my mind is left to wander. I cycle through guilt and grief and fear in equal measure. I've left my students alone, I've lost my mother, I don't know how to reconcile my husband's and my ideas on marriage and children.

I'm restless; worse, my mind is a cage. I need something to do. Something that matters.

'm going into the city," I tell Jack, the half-formed idea flying from my mouth as he walks in the door one evening the second week of January.

"What?"

To his credit, he doesn't panic. He knows me well enough to wait for an explanation.

"Not tonight," I clarify unnecessarily as I take his coat. "But I've decided I want to be the one to clean out my mother's place before it's sold next month."

Now, Jack glances up with dismay. "We've already hired people for that."

"I know," I say, "and I appreciate your help."

Help is an understatement; Jack had arranged everything for me. I'd been too grief-stricken to do it myself. "But things have changed. And it feels wrong to let strangers go through my mother's personal things." I think of her copy of "The Gift of the Magi," her favorite blanket, her well-thumbed books of poetry.

Jack shakes his head, uncomprehending. "What are you hoping to find?"

"I don't know, but I know I need to do it." I need my mother, and this is as close as I can get. I'm hopeful that the rummaging, sorting, cleaning, and selling—work with a finish line, unlike housework—will alleviate my restlessness. And that it will distract me from my grief and guilt, too. Dare I hope Mary Ellen's "I love you" and Robby's fat tears will forget me there in the city?

I don't know how to tell Jack that here, I begin each morning with a spray of forget-me-not guilt. A morning bouquet of free time to remind me that, after suffering the loss of my own mother, I've left my students the same way: alone. Bereft.

I cannot go to my mother for comfort or advice. I can't call her like I did in college to help me sort through these feelings that hit me all at once. I can't call her to vent about Jack and roll my eyes at her conciliatory suggestions before taking them anyway. But I can go back to the world we shared. I can drape myself in the clothes hanging in her closet and run my hands along the walls she painted. I can imagine myself closer to her. Imagine myself a tiny bit less alone.

Supper is quiet and stilted. Jack and I retire to bed early, but I can't sleep. Not because I'm having second thoughts about my decision to go to the city, but because Jack is. He lies awake next to me and twitches the whole night long. For the second time in a month, I'm kept awake with memories of that first night I witnessed his episodes after our marriage, and I am as sleepless and agitated as my husband when we rise the next morning.

We stand across from each other in the kitchen, the setting eerily similar to that long-ago day I asked him if he regretted our marriage.

"I'm still going." Though I don't mean for them to, the words reverberate like a slap. Exhausted, I can't think clearly enough to be gentle.

"And I'm still against it," Jack says. "Stella, I'm just worried about you. A woman alone—"

A woman alone. I nearly scoff. "My sweet, timid mom who didn't work a day in her life lived in that apartment building on her own for five years after Dad died. I think I'll be just fine as 'a woman alone.'"

"Okay." Jack lets a smile slip through. "You're right. You're too strong to be an easy target."

I give him a begrudging smile in return, appreciating his effort.

"But I'm just worried about you. I don't think it will do you any good to be rummaging through the past when you could focus on the future here. On what still matters."

Of course. The "future," also known as "having kids."

"My mom isn't 'the past,'" I say. "And you know we aren't ready for children."

I regret the words as soon as I say them. Jack didn't mention children explicitly; I shouldn't have brought them up. Things are complicated enough as it is.

"Your mom was twenty-four when you were born," Jack points out.

"Jack. It's not about our age. If we have a baby, that baby deserves to understand *both* his or her parents." I'm near tears now. My mother was my rock for so many years, my constant supporter and quiet strength. Who else would have understood the way I felt when I first found out about Jack's night terrors? Who else would have intuitively grasped the love I have for my students? I don't know how to survive without her. And I don't want to have a child who cannot rely on Jack and on me the same way. And yes, I admit it—I don't want to have a child when *I* cannot rely on Jack the same way. When I am forced to question how well I really know him.

"Okay." Jack shakes his head. "I'm sorry. It's not the time."

He uses that apology an awful lot, but I bite my tongue before I say something snappy in return. "Thank you," I say instead. "And you're right. We're talking about the city, about me cleaning out the old place."

But that's the problem, isn't it? Jack and I aren't good at talking about one thing at a time. I love him, but I can't help bringing all my fears and worries into every discussion we have: Do I know Jack as well as he knows me? How will we ever find ourselves ready for children? What if I never think he's ready; then what?

I take a deep breath, trying to focus. "I know it's hard for you when I go back."

He nods once, quickly. "You know I dislike the city."

I know he's afraid of it. The cacophony of car horns, the boring and drilling in the streets. But Manhattan is my hometown, and Jack's fear cuts deep. *I* am the city, with all its hustle and noise.

I force myself to stay calm. "It's where I grew up, Jack. I need to go back."

"Stella, please reconsider. There's no use reliving the past, Stell, not when you have a life here—"

All my efforts to be gentle dissolve, and I snap. "*Do* I have a life here? Without a job and with a husband who can't—or won't—confide in me?"

It's not fair and I know it, but I have lost so much of my life in these past months. Emptiness has been growing in me for weeks, and anger unfurls so neatly in its place.

Sorry, I'm about to say, but Jack is too quick for me.

"Without a job? Stella, you quit! It's not my fault that you couldn't handle some pushback from Principal Gardner—"

"Some pushback? Jack, he wanted me to put the kids in strait-jackets!"

"Look." Jack throws up his hands. "All I mean is that I went through a goddamn war. You're so desperate to hear me *talk* about it, tell you stories like they're fairy tales, but you don't understand. I held men in my arms as they died. I *killed* men. Meanwhile, you can't even stand up to an idiot boss without running. You think you could handle war?"

He's giving me a piece of what I want, sharing a fraction of the memories that haunt him. But all I hear is the last part. *You can't even stand up to an idiot boss without running.*

"I am a teacher," I hiss. "Not a soldier."

"You *were* a teacher. But you left."

I step back, nearly tripping over my chair.

"You're good at leaving," Jack continues. His voice barely sounds like his own. "You left your students. You left your mother in the hospital the night she died. And now it looks like you're trying to leave me."

I see my mother crumpled in her hospital gown. I hear the nurses telling me I can't go in. And even though I'd never obeyed an order my whole life, I listened. They were giving me a gift, letting me keep the image I had of my mother instead of forcing me to replace it with that of the weak creature she'd become.

So I obeyed. I let my mother die alone, and I regret it every day.

"You think I'm leaving you, Jack?" I look at him, a large tear shivering its way down my nose. "Fine. I'll go."

"No, Stella—I didn't mean—"

I grit my teeth, inhale, force my anger back down from boiling. "I'm sorry. But I am going. It's something I need to do."

"Stell . . ."

I wait, hoping against hope that Jack will offer to come along. My childhood home would seem so much less empty with his laughter, and I smile as I imagine him bringing me pancakes in the bed I slept in till I was eighteen. I've spent years taking care of other people's children, and now I've lost the one person who was always around to take care of me. Maybe Jack will put aside his own fears just this once?

"Fine," Jack finally says.

"Fine, what?"

"Fine, you can go."

My irritation returns in full force, fueled by hurt. "I wasn't asking for your permission," I huff as I turn from the room to pack.

CHAPTER NINE

Althea Anderson, August 1926

I should have known better than to skip the residence's weekly tea. I creep up the stairs and find the social directress, Miss Caswell, planted staunchly before my door.

"Hello." I smile politely, pressing my hairpins more firmly into the folds of my hair.

"Do you have time to sit down with me?" Miss Caswell inquires. "In the library, perhaps?"

I cannot say no. She knows as well as I that I need not be at the hospital until seven tonight. I have three hours.

"Of course." I smile weakly. "That would be lovely."

She leads me to the second story, and I am grateful the rest of the women are sipping tea downstairs so I don't have to field their looks of concern. One would think that years of living at a boarding school would have trained me well in socializing with other girls, but I have always been slightly inept in that regard. Too serious, too focused.

Miss Caswell and I settle into the library armchairs, facing each other with practiced decorum. "Remind me. What shift are you on?"

"Emergency. I just finished obstetrics."

She smiles. "What is your preference?"

I hesitate briefly but cannot lie. "Obstetrics."

She nods. "Many of our girls are partial to that ward."

I smile slightly and wait. Surely we don't sit here alone while the rest of the girls celebrate downstairs just to make small talk.

"And you are finding your accommodations here satisfactory?"

"I—yes, of course." I've been here two years already. "Always."

"The social events are to your liking?"

"Certainly." I search for an example to give her. Yesterday, I skipped visiting Margaret to play a game of tennis with the other girls. Not because I wanted to, of course, but because I thought it best to show my face. I don't want anyone questioning where I've been. Now, I'm grateful for my decision. "The tennis, the plays we've seen. I'm very appreciative."

"Hm. I simply wonder whether you find something lacking, Althea. Or perhaps whether our company is not enough for you?"

My thoughts snap back to Margaret. Could Miss Caswell be alluding to her, to my frequent visits to Coney Island? "I don't know what you mean."

"This may remind you." Miss Caswell pulls an envelope from the pocket of her coat and hands it over. "I am not familiar with any 'Michael Perkins' living in our ladies-only boardinghouse . . ." She looks up pointedly. "Are you?"

I suddenly understand why the women at the hospital scream when contractions begin. My stomach roils, and my vision clouds. I take the envelope blindly and force myself to look down at it until my sight returns.

Michael Perkins
Room 4B
440 East 26th St.
New York City, New York 10010

The return address is Margaret Perkins, 1208 Surf Ave. Thank God they didn't put Luna Park. But Michael Perkins's address is mine.

I roll my shoulders back, sit up straight. "Certainly you aren't suggesting that this letter arrived here intentionally."

Miss Caswell has the good grace to suck in her cheeks with embarrassment. "You know it is my responsibility to ensure that all my charges are safe, Althea. No matter how untoward it may seem."

Safe. She and I both know what that means: respectable, reputable. *Single, Christian, and of good breeding,* as the nursing application stressed.

I wonder briefly whether Miss Caswell would be more horrified by a man living in my room or by the truth. Whether a baby born out of wedlock or a kidnapping would be a greater sin in her eyes.

"Of course, Miss Caswell. I understand. And I am grateful. But for over two years I have lived here without a problem." I speak with a confidence I do not possess. "Frankly, I'm mortified that you could so much as suspect me of something such as . . . this."

Miss Caswell's cheeks color slightly. "I still must do my due diligence."

I am steady and reliable. I make decisions after weeks of deliberation. But now, for the second time in a month, I lie with the rashness of a man. As if I am as confident as I pretend to be.

"It must be a mistake," I repeat. "You can open the letter and see."

Miss Caswell arches an eyebrow as she slips her slender finger under the tongue of the envelope. I clench my toes as I remember Louise's silver ring, its dizzying never-ending sheen. I close my eyes briefly, regain my balance. I've no idea what is in that envelope. I had not expected the Couneys to send anything when I'd written my own address in place of the Perkinses'. Why on earth would they?

The answer to my own question rises like the wail of an infant. *Something has happened to Margaret.* I lurch forward. There are so many possibilities: breathing complications, malnutrition, choking, illness. Anything could have happened to the girl in the two days since I've seen her. She lies barely alive in a glass box at the fairground, and no one knows she is there. Tears begin to prick my eyes, and I squeeze my lids tightly. Why, why is Miss Caswell so painfully slow? With precision, she pulls the contents of the envelope from its mouth, perfectly slit. What comes out is not a letter but a card. Stiff white paper and printed words.

She lifts it to her eyes.

"What does it say?" I modulate my tone to mask my fear. But

Miss Caswell smiles, flips her fragile wrist so I can read the words on the sheet.

One month and still kicking! I love you, Mom and Dad.

Love from your daughter,
Margaret Perkins

Below the words sits a thumbprint, tiny as a comma. "Oh," I gasp. Margaret's little print presses into my throat so I can hardly breathe. Those whorls are so vulnerable, half-smudged where Margaret must have slipped or squirmed. Michael Perkins, who would have kept this fingerprint from existing in the world at all, does not deserve this note. But my anger is tempered by relief. Margaret is safe. Margaret is safe, and so am I. Nothing in this letter connects me to the child or the father.

Miss Caswell's bony frame has lost some of its rigidity; she is as grateful as I.

"Poor Mr. Perkins—and Mrs. Perkins, too," she laughs gaily. "Won't ever get their card. I do wonder about the competency of the postal workers, once in a while." Miss Caswell stands, tossing the sheet into the wastebasket. "Thank you, Miss Anderson. I hope you have not taken this personally. I have"—she nods—"been impressed by your conscientiousness these last years."

"Thank you." I bow my head. "I believe," I add, noting that she is waiting for me, "I will stay here in the library. I have some studying to do before my shift tonight."

"Quite right."

She steps from the library with a nod of approval, leaving me beside the wastebasket.

I pull the card out and fold it gently against my breast. Such a precious gift should not be wasted. I'll keep it, however undeserving Michael Perkins may be, and return it to him and his wife alongside their daughter.

I press my hand to my bosom, my thumb to Margaret's. For now, the note will be mine.

By the end of August, I'm living a double life. I'm in the emergency room every night and at Coney Island most days. The nurses at Luna Park have come to expect me, and more importantly, they expect Margaret not only to live but to lead an entirely normal life. At eight weeks, she is four pounds—still much lighter than the average newborn, but finally outside the most dangerous range. "Soon"—Louise pokes Margaret's tiny upturned nose fondly—"you'll be moving to the big kids' room!"

I laugh, looking past Louise and through the glass. Not a single one of those "big kids" can be more than five or six pounds.

"And it's a good thing, too." Louise looks up at me with lips creased in sobriety. "You know we close down at the end of the summer. When the park shuts down for the season."

Of course, I know this. I've been anxiously charting Margaret's growth, projecting what her weight will be at the end of her time here. Whether she'll be viable for life back home with Hattie and Michael.

"Yes." I resist the urge to take Margaret from Louise's arms.

"What do you do with the babies who are not ready to be released?"

The nurse shrugs. "We typically deliver them to various hospitals in the area, incubators included. It is far from the ideal solution, what with the transport and the lack of individualized care or training at the facilities, but we have no other options. You're lucky Margaret should be ready to go."

"I'm sorry," I say stupidly.

"Sorry?"

"I work at one of those hospitals. I'm sorry we don't have the incubators or the training."

"Well." Louise waves her hand. "I know how it is. It isn't as if you have a say. One day"—she smiles down at Margaret—"when all these babies are grown up and healthy, they'll see. Doctors, hospitals—they'll finally start saving them all."

One day is not good enough, I want to tell Louise. But she knows that. Why else is she here, after all, except to—slowly, steadily, against all odds—prove that these babies deserve a chance?

"Until then," she confirms, "we pray. 'Let the little children come to me.' Surely if the world cannot see these babies' value, their Creator can."

I murmur agreement. How could He not?

Then I think of Michael Perkins, Margaret's creator in the most literal way. My eyelids twitch. He could not see this girl's value. He does not deserve her.

I speak before my thoughts cross a dangerous line. "I cannot wait to take the girl back to her parents." I calibrate my expression to my words as I beam at Louise. "They will be overjoyed to see her again."

Louise's forehead creases in pity. "Isn't it a shame that they haven't been able to visit," she clucks, shaking her head. "Sadly, it isn't uncommon."

I bow my head. "Very much a shame. But . . . there is simply no way it would have been possible."

Louise's smile cuts with understanding. "Then you've been a blessing to them, haven't you?"

Blessing. From Old English *bledsian*.

To consecrate.

With blood.

But it is not blood Margaret begins coughing up the next week. Instead, green-yellow sputum seeps suddenly from between her round pink lips as I hold her late Sunday morning. "Louise!" I screech. "Maye!" I place my hand to Margaret's forehead—hot. Her breathing is labored. "Louise!"

The nurse appears instantly at my side. She pulls a stethoscope from the folds of her gown and presses it to my baby's lungs.

"Do you hear rales?"

Louise just nods, crossing herself. "*Que Dieu nous aide.*"

The terrible word unfurls from both our mouths in eerie lockstep: "Pneumonia."

I am not the calm, composed Nurse Anderson of Bellevue Hospital. I am frantic, desperate, rabid.

I take a deep breath but forget to exhale. I will not let Margaret succumb to this illness, not after she's reached the two-month milestone. We must act. "She's likely dehydrated." I pat the baby's diaper—dry.

Louise nods shortly, and I pass her the infant as I run for the eyedroppers. "Here, baby girl." I return, fighting Margaret's cough to get the milk down her throat. "You can do it, sweet Margaret. Swallow, Margaret, just swallow. You'll be all right."

She'll be all right if we get her to the hospital.

Welfare Island rears again in my mind. Would I survive a transformed life of labor and shackles if I were arrested? If we register Margaret at the hospital and they find out who we both are?

Althea. I am asking the wrong questions. What matters is this: Will Margaret survive this if we don't take her to the hospital? Or will she join Cybil in the ranks of those I have let die?

My voice changes as I look up at Louise. I don't want to prompt Margaret's registration and my own potential downfall. But I have to. I'd turn myself in to save her. "We need to take her to Coney Island Hospital, Louise. She needs medicine. The anti-serum."

"She needs the medicine." Louise nods. "But I don't think she needs the hospital."

"What?" Hope tears the word from my throat. "Why not?"

"If she catches another infection from the other patients, it will kill her—if getting her there doesn't do it first. She needs her incubator now more than ever."

Blessed relief envelops me, my legs wobbling like peach preserves. "I'll go, then. But they'll need to type her pneumonia." Treatment for one strain will cause complications for another. "Is there a capsule I can use to transport her sputum?" From there, if her pneumonia is pneumococcal, the doctors can type it and determine which serum will save her.

"Here." Louise shoves Margaret abruptly into my arms and sprints off. Her urgency both comforts and frightens me. Margaret is in good hands, but the situation, if capable Louise is ruffled, is dire. The infant's face contorts as her lips open and close in a desperate plea for air. The silence accompanying the movement sets me shaking more than the sickly green-yellow of her mucus.

"Margaret, baby? Say something," I beg her. "Make some sort of noise." *She's never been quiet before.* I rub my thumb gently across her flushed forehead where it fades into nose. "Please, baby girl. I'm here. You'll be all right."

I'm here. You'll be all right. Can I say such a thing? Do I have the power to save this baby? Or have I merely hurt her? What if my greedy visits and insistence on holding Margaret gave her this illness?

Overwhelmed, I doubt my ability to stay here and hold this baby while she shakes and wheezes and dies. But my body is stronger than my mind. "None of us can know what we are capable of until we are tested," Elizabeth Blackwell once said. The first woman to get a medical degree in the United States, Blackwell was capable of anything. I am capable of this. I was capable of risking my entire life to save Margaret from certain death, wasn't I?

Now, I force myself to calm so I can hold Margaret gently and whisper to her, talk to her, soothe her with words like a lullaby until Louise comes bustling back. "Take this." She thrusts a paper into my hands. "It's signed by the doctor. They'll understand the baby can't come in." She wields a bottle in her other hand and positions it beneath Margaret's lips.

"Give us a little cough, Marg." I thump her back. "Bring

something up for us." I am more confident now that I have a goal, a clear medical procedure to follow. Margaret chokes up more unnaturally yellow mucus, and Louise tips the neck of the bottle to catch it. Though each cough is painful to watch, we have enough sputum in the capsule for the doctors at the hospital to get a reading. Mouth grimly set, Louise seals the container. I am grateful she is beside me. Many would not be able to stomach such a task.

"Here." Louise passes me the sample. "*Dieu soit avec toi.* God be with you."

I run. The nearest hospital is just a mile away, and I can get there faster on foot than I could in a cab forced to sift through Coney Island traffic. I tear my hat from atop my head as I run and stuff it into the bosom of my dress. Even without the boning of decades past, my corselet makes it difficult to run without growing short of breath, and I count my steps to center me. At step 897, I feel the fabric at the heel of my right foot give way; at 905, the left. Both heels are bleeding by 1,000, and I doubt I am even halfway to the hospital. I bend quickly and remove my calfskin shoes. They dangle from their straps on my left fingers as I resume running. The sample is clutched in my right hand, and Louise's note is folded into my brassiere.

I make it to Ocean Parkway. Businessmen and young couples shoot me bewildered looks as I pass; surely, I am a sight to behold. Barefoot, bleeding, and with my hair slipping from its coiffure, I could be an escapee from an asylum. With this image in mind, I stop just before the hospital doors and slip my feet back into my shoes. I uncoil the mess of my hair, braid the length of it, and fold it back up. It will do.

After presenting my own credentials and Louise's note, and proving my expertise through an arduous description of Margaret's symptoms and sputum sample, the nurses at Coney Island Hospital take the container from me. "It will take at least six hours to get the results," they warn.

I cannot stay away from Margaret that long. Not when today—God forbid—may be the last time I see her. "I will be back in four, then," I promise. "I must go be with the girl."

Margaret's welfare no longer depends on my speed, but I run back to Luna Park regardless. I could not bear to arrive back too late to see her. I burst through the doors with uncharacteristic conspicuousness and dash straight to Margaret's station. Am I imagining the blue pallor snaking beneath her pale skin? I dig my nails into my palms to keep from reaching for her. I cannot risk transmitting anything more to her weak little system. "I'm here, Margaret. I'm here."

Arms wrapped around my torso, I sway before Margaret's incubator for hours. Though her eyes are closed, her tired body cannot find sleep. Coughing and fever make it impossible. I sing her quietly every lullaby I can muster, and my voice is sore and out of tune by the time five and a half hours have crept slowly by.

I place my palm on the glass door of Margaret's incubator. "I will be back, Marg. I will be back with something to save you."

I have half an hour to get to the hospital, and I walk briskly this time rather than run. I pray the whole journey, my lips moving silently. *Please, please, please, please, please.*

God hears my prayers. The nurse who greets me is not the same one I met just hours ago, but she too is brisk and confident. "The good news is that the infant's pneumonia is pneumococcal," she says, "so it can be treated with serum therapy. Since today is the first day with recognizable symptoms, the treatment will decrease her mortality risk from about half to just five percent." I sag in relief, but she continues. "The bad news is that the antiserum is typically administered intravenously. I assume Luna Park does not have the necessary technology for such a treatment?"

"No."

"I thought as much." She turns to walk down the corridor, indicating that I should follow. "Fortunately, your baby may respond to subcutaneous injection. She is young enough and small enough that the antibody buildup should still be enough. It may be better, actually." She turns to face me. "Injection this way will stave off chills and anaphylaxis."

Unaccustomed to being on the receiving end of this sort of conversation, I am grateful I have the training to understand everything the nurse is saying.

"I can provide you the serum, but you will have to administer it yourself," she finishes.

I nod.

"I also must tell you it is exceedingly expensive."

I shrug helplessly. "It's our only hope." I'll find a second job if I have to, work as a secretary somewhere or clean houses. I don't sleep as it is.

The nurse's smile is tinged with sadness. "I thought you'd say that." She stops walking and tells me to wait. She disappears through a door and returns a moment later with a capsule of liquid. "She'll need two thousand units a day." About 0.05 milligrams. "Start today, immediately, and continue as long as seems necessary."

"Thank you." I clasp my hands in prayer, the capsule between them. "Thank you."

"Of course. Nurse Recht's note said to send the bill to Dr. Couney."

My eyes widen, but only momentarily. Even such shocking kindness cannot captivate my interest for long with Margaret so ill. "Yes, please. And thank you. Thank you, so much."

I usually sleep part of the day, but I cannot succumb to my exhaustion with Margaret fighting to breathe. I remain in Luna Park with my gaze fixated on Margaret in her incubator. Already, her skin is losing its blue sheen. Her fever is lowering. Miraculously, the antiserum is working. And fast.

I leave at five p.m. for my shift at Bellevue, which I spend in dizzy distraction, adrenaline keeping me on my feet. I return to Luna Park the next morning, going on thirty hours without sleep. Margaret is better still, her cough no longer drowning in fluid. Louise has already given her today's dose of serum, and I wrap my arms around the woman in an uncharacteristic show of affection. "Thank you, Louise. You've saved her." *You've saved me, too*, I don't say aloud.

"I couldn't have done it on my own." Louise smiles at me. "I don't know if the mother herself could have been more devoted than you've been."

"Well." My real smile is replaced by a fake one. "Just part of being a nurse. You know."

Soon, I *will* go back to just being a nurse. Margaret is approaching her release, and I will take her back to Michael and Hattie and forget all about the whole affair.

Well. I could never forget. I'll always remember Margaret's bright green eyes and mussed hair and demanding wail. I'll never forget the sweat and the fear of that day in the carriage, the desperation of this bout of pneumonia, the exquisite pain of gazing upon her perfect little face. But I will be able to put my time with her aside. I will be able to live my life again, rather than hers. I will work at the hospital without fear of discovery, spend my few daily hours of freedom reading books and taking walks rather than shuttling to and from Coney Island.

But the thought does not fill me with joy. Instead, as I gaze upon Margaret's fitfully sleeping form, I cry all the tears I had held inside as we desperately battled her pneumonia. I wasn't ready for her to leave us. Will I be ready to leave her?

CHAPTER TEN

Stella Wright, January 1951

I stand before our old apartment building in Central Park West with my suitcase in my hand, feeling as if I could be back from college for Christmas break. I count the windows and find our place: third floor, fourth from the left. The windows to either side are brightly lit, but ours are dim. A grim reminder that I'm not in college anymore, that Mom isn't upstairs whipping together my favorite soup or standing ready to greet me at the door.

I've only been in the apartment once since she passed, and it was for the reception after the funeral. I was so busy feeding everyone and forcing myself to laugh at all their favorite stories about my mom that I didn't have time to notice how wrong the space felt without her. I've avoided my old home since then. Now, I'm almost afraid to go in.

Shifting my suitcase to my left hand, I pull open the door and climb the stairs slowly to the third floor. I fish the keys from the pocket of my coat, sweating in the stairway, and push open our door.

I don't know what I expected, but the nothingness hits me like a foghorn. The quiet in the apartment is unnatural; my mom should be here to take my coat and pull me in for a hug, to cluck over my appearance and offer me a glass of water.

Instead, I keep my coat on in the freezing apartment, frustrated with myself for not anticipating that the heat would be off. I don't even bother trying to turn on the lights. No one's paid electricity since the funeral.

I drop my purse and suitcase off in my old room and decide to start in the kitchen, where the natural light is strongest. I begin by sorting through the china and the silverware, the metal's cold seeping through the fingers of my deerskin gloves as if into my bones. I separate things into piles to give away and piles for Jack and me to keep. My coat starts to itch as I think about Jack. Our good-bye had been rushed, Jack leaving for work at the same time I was running out to catch the train. Not that either of us had anything we wanted to say. Not without starting another fight.

The damage had been done, anyway. I know that my leaving hurt him, but his inability to even consider coming along is hurting me. Pancakes and jokes are fine, but they aren't enough to keep me afloat here.

I push away my thoughts and try to focus on my task. I'd pictured hard, physical work wringing the sadness and shame from my body like sweat. Instead, I'm sorting through dusty flatware that was more ostentatious than my mother ever wanted in the first place. Were they wedding gifts, I wondered, or hand-me-downs? I let out a sob as I realize that now I'll never know.

Though I've not even been here an hour, the cold and the silence are more than I can bear. I refuse to think about whether that means Jack was right—that I shouldn't have come.

I lock up the apartment and stride quickly to the end of the street, head bowed to keep my eyes from the sting of the cold. I don't need to look up; the path from home to café is one my parents and I walked with comforting regularity my whole childhood. I smile to think of it now, my father's determined gait like we would topple off the sidewalk without him there to guide us. From girlhood, I was aware of the thin bubble of his pride that I knew never to pop; it hung shimmering and translucent till the day he died. Hard to believe it's been over five years since he did.

But that death was so much easier to take. My father died at sixty-three, and his passing coincided with the close of the Second World War. All around us were grieving widows, mothers without sons, infants without fathers. My dad's death was a tragedy, but it was a natural one. And Mom and I had each other to lean on. After his funeral, she was free to visit me at school as often as she liked; it was how she and Jack got to know each other so well despite his aversion to the city.

But now that Mom's gone, I don't know who to turn to.

I try to transport myself to an easier time as I step into the café. The warmth of the heated room seeps beneath my skin like the comfort of Mom's hand on my forehead, and the familiar hostess stands to greet me like nothing has changed since I came here last.

"Chicken soup," I order, solid and simple.

When the soup bowl arrives, I sit with it cupped in my hands and watch as customers stumble into the café and drift back out.

One young girl with wild red hair bursts into tears as her mother drags her out the door. Her high emotions, shared with abandon, remind me so much of my students in Poughkeepsie. I press the heels of my palms into my eyes to stem my tears. I wish Jack were here to put his warm arm around me—but no.

Stella, I admonish, reminding myself that I was the one to leave. That I didn't ask him to come—just expected him to know I wanted it.

I scald my throat as I gulp down my soup, but the pain is a welcome distraction. Maybe I'll burn my throat too badly to keep hurling out words I'll regret next time I see my husband. *Fine*, I'd told him. *I'll go.*

The café is warm, and I don't want to go. But I do want the scene replaying in my head—Jack's expression as I left, our stand-offish good-bye—to stop. I stand abruptly.

The wind howls around my ankles as I step outside, my swing coat flapping. I practically run to the corner store, where I stop to pick up snacks, a couple of flashlights, and candles.

I exhale in relief as I step into the apartment building and linger in the stairwell. I don't want to reenter the freezing unit, but I don't really have a choice. I try to convince myself that now is the best time, with the soup in my belly warming me from the inside.

You can't complain, I remind myself. *You wanted to be here.* And I did. I *do*. Yes, Jack had worried it would make me think of my mother and bring my spirits down—but what he doesn't understand is I don't think of her any less in Poughkeepsie. Especially now that I'm not working. Here, at least, I can think of her and feel just a little bit less far away.

Mom, I pray. *Was coming here the right thing to do?*

It's hard to know what her answer would have been. She never would've raised her voice to my dad; she obeyed him in all things. But she raised me to speak out despite her own complacency. "Use your voice," she would remind me as I went off to school each morning, a faint note of urgency in her voice. "Silence is dangerous, Stella."

The first time she said it had been after I told her about a girl at school who'd been mocked for her accent. The girl was German, and I didn't realize until years later that the hatred the other students felt for her was copied from the attitudes their parents had adopted after the First World War.

"What did *you* say?" Mom had asked me after I complained about the kids' jeers.

"I didn't say anything!" I'd been shocked, even wounded, that she'd asked. Surely she knew better than to think I would have joined in with such cruelty.

But she hadn't touched my cheek the way she did when she was proud of me. She'd shaken her head sadly. "Oh, Stella. Don't you know that staying silent means saying it's okay?"

The next day, I got in trouble for stomping one of the bullies on the toes when he called the girl a cabbage eater. My father was outraged, but I think Mom was secretly proud.

I wish I had her advice now, her wisdom. If she promised that my marriage would survive, I'd believe her.

Mom? I lift my eyes to the ceiling. *What would you have me do?*

Mom wouldn't have approved of the way I walked out. She adored Jack. "A comedian," she'd claimed after first meeting him.

"More like a goof," I'd laughed. But she wasn't wrong. Jack's silliness has always made me laugh. I'm lucky to have him, and I wonder sometimes—doubled over the kitchen table in hysterics—why my mom didn't marry someone who could make her laugh the same way, even if my dad was a good man. But who knows how my parents ended up together? It was a different time.

I sigh. Jack's humor is what I miss most of all when he retreats into anxiety and fear. Damn war. A wife shouldn't miss her own husband, not when she's sleeping right beside him every night.

I turn back to the task at hand. I've moved into my mother's closet, wanting to feel surrounded by her. The candles and flashlight are necessary in here, tucked away from the windows. They light upon mementos I remember and ones I don't, but even those I don't recognize carry the touch of my mother's hand. I warm my own hands in the folds of the clothes I wore as an infant, surprised my mother saved them.

I laugh to find an old checkered headband. I used to tuck my blond hair beneath it and pose in front of the mirror, proclaiming myself Nancy Drew. "Do you see the resemblance?" I'd ask, and Dad would always scrunch up his face like he was trying to decide. One bad winter when we hardly left the house, my mother left clues around the apartment so I could solve the "mystery of the missing cookbook." When I found it, triumphant and bouncing with glee, she let me pick a recipe to make alongside her for supper.

Only now with the benefit of hindsight can I see how different she was from other mothers. She was quiet and conservative, not one to wear trousers or sport a youthful bob. But she did let me explore in a way that other mothers didn't. She urged me from the time I started kindergarten to go to university. And my father, however traditional, was magnanimous to a fault. So to Vassar I went.

Now, I wish I'd coaxed my mother to answer the questions she used to brush off: *Why didn't you go to school? Didn't you ever want a job?*

I'll never know, I suppose. But I know she fought for me to have those things. To her, that was what mattered.

Thanks, Mom, I send up to the sky. *With love, from Stella Star.*

I 've saved my mother's charm box for last. I shouldn't be afraid; I know exactly what's in the treasure box. But I don't know how I'll react. Will I feel closer to my mother as I hold her life in my hands, or will the loss seem all the more real?

I force myself to think of the good, and I smile as I remember how my mother rechristened the box the "treasure box" at my insistence. I had just read *Treasure Island*, and Mom's keepsakes felt as valuable as gold: the pressed flower, the silky ribbon.

But around age sixteen I decided my mother's life was irrelevant. She was barely even born in this century, I scoffed. She grew up in the midst of Prohibition and most definitely followed every law. She adhered to every expectation: no college, marriage before twenty-five, daughter soon after.

My mother was predictable and rule-following: the teenager's definition of boring. Now I wonder if "mature" would be more accurate. Mom didn't have my sharp tongue or impulsiveness; she wouldn't have threatened to quit without weighing pros and cons. She didn't just plan in broad strokes—she wrote lists. Grocery lists, to-do lists, idea lists. Lists of colleges I could apply to, lists of test scores I'd gotten, lists of tuition and columns of calculations. Lists of books she wanted to read, quotes she liked, and restaurants she wanted to try.

She never tried most of them. My dad liked our corner café, which he said was convenient after a long day of work. Mom never argued.

And there, again, is what I always questioned. Why did she never go after what she wanted? *Did* she even want anything, other than my happiness, and then my father's?

I shake my head. I'm getting too philosophical. I'm here in New York to escape the voices in my head, not indulge them.

I lift the lid of my mother's charm box. I haven't looked at it since my father died and Mom and I put his ring in here for safekeeping.

I don't see the pink, satiny ribbon that I expect upon opening. Instead, a letter is folded just under the lid. I smooth out the sheet, the bottom third of the paper swinging as if it may rip off at the crease. Underneath is the pink bow I remember; this letter was added after the last time I opened the box.

I'm surprised to see the date on the top of the paper: July 5, 1946. The letter has been opened and closed so many times I would have guessed it was older.

Stranger is the salutation. *Dear Nurse Anderson*, it reads.

Anderson was my mother's maiden name, but she wasn't an Anderson in 1946. She hadn't been an Anderson since . . . what, 1925? Before I was born, anyway. And she'd certainly never been a nurse.

My mother was a homemaker my whole life. The closest she

got to a career was cooking for the PTA bake sale at Christmastime every year. Every letter she'd ever received had been addressed *Mrs.* or even *wife of.*

But there is no denying the carefully printed letters here. Nurse. Could Nurse Anderson be an aunt or a cousin of my mother's I've never known? It seems impossible, but less so than the alternative: that my mother had been a nurse. *That,* I would have known.

Curiosity makes me forget the cold, and I read the rest of the letter.

July 5, 1946

Dear Nurse Anderson,

My name is Hattie Perkins, and twenty years ago today you assisted in the delivery of my baby girl. Surely you have had a great many patients at Bellevue. But the tiny flicker of hope that you will recall my name or my daughter's, God bless her, compels me to write you this evening.

I don't know if you remember her: Margaret Perkins. But I do. Oh, how I remember. At twenty-one years old, I thought I could forget. I thought I could run away from heartbreak, forget it like the sting of a boy's rejection or last year's fashion. But I could not forget, have never forgotten. I have spent decades remembering Margaret's birth and the decisions we made then. I believe my childlessness in the decades since has been my punishment from God.

I wonder what could have been different. But I cannot

change the decision I made then. The best I can do is try to celebrate my baby girl. Stop running from my sins and from her memory.

You were the last one of us to see my precious daughter. Any recollections you have of her—from her expressions to her cry—would be appreciated. I don't even know my own daughter's eye color, God forgive me.

I hope that the decades since we have seen each other have blessed you in ways they never have me.

With great sorrow and fragile hope,

Hattie Perkins

The emotion in the letter strikes at my heart. I don't know these people, but I know grief. And to think this poor woman, Hattie, was plagued by it for decades. My grief has lasted months, and already I am worn down and wearied by it.

The address must be a mistake. A letter to the wrong Anderson. It's a common enough last name.

But if it was meant for a stranger, why did my mother keep it?

My heart aches to think that just a few months ago, I could have simply picked up the phone and asked my mom. For nearly four months, I've been unable to make new memories with my mom—but now, I have a chance to bring her back to life however thinly. I can find out why my mother kept this letter, find out who Nurse Anderson and Hattie Perkins were to her.

For the first time in weeks I feel a sense of purpose. Perhaps my mother's life can act as a signpost for my own.

I check the year on the letter again: 1946, when I was

finishing my freshman year at Vassar and Mom was still alive. Strange to think my world was so different not even five years ago. I had Mom, had just met Jack, hadn't yet been broken down by the realities of teaching.

I shake my head and reach for Mom's charm box again. Enough self-pity. I need to remind myself of the mother I knew, hold the familiar objects that will make her mine again. With the letter gone, the box looks just like I remember it. On top is the frayed pink bow I wore as an infant; I pull it out to put on, first rubbing the bow between my fingers and wondering at its worn softness. The ribbon is three fingers wide, and I tie it around my wrist now like a chunky bracelet.

Next is my father's golden wedding band. A wave of sadness washes over me as I turn it slowly between my thumb and forefinger, though my dad's death did not shake the earth I stand on like my mother's has. Years have softened the pain. Will they soften this pain, so much more intense?

Kissing the ring lightly, I slide it onto my thumb and reach for the flower and the photograph resting at the bottom of my mother's box. I look at the familiar creased photograph first. In it are my maternal grandparents, neither of whom I ever met. Both dark-haired like my mother, their faces radiate joy. I never knew any of my grandparents, but maybe that's part of why my mother and I were so close. It was just us and my dad for so many years, and then just us. I gaze again at the photograph. I don't know how my grandmother can breathe in her ruffled outfit, much less smile.

I look at the yellow witch hazel pressed between two sheets of paper. How foolish it seems now that I never asked my mom why the plant was so precious to her. Where did it come from? Did she press it, or did someone else?

The flower is still bright after so many years, its story forgotten.

I press the sheet to my nose, but whatever scent the flower once carried is long gone.

I hate the time I wasted too focused on myself to ask my mom about her own story.

As I move to place the flower back into the box, I see an unfamiliar envelope at the bottom.

I pull it out and gasp. It's addressed to Michael Perkins.

Perkins, again. Hattie's husband, Hattie's son? No, not Hattie's son. Her letter said she was childless apart from Margaret.

Margaret. I look at the return address, the girl's name unmistakable: *Margaret Perkins, 1208 Surf Ave., Brooklyn.*

But Margaret had died, hadn't she?

I open the envelope and slide out the stiff, expensive paper.

One month and still kicking! I love you, Mom and Dad.

> *Love from your daughter,*
> *Margaret Perkins*

Below the girl's name is an inked print, tiny and blurred. A thumbprint.

I shiver. So Margaret Perkins lived for at least a month, but she spent that time somewhere in Brooklyn without her parents. By 1946, Hattie was looking back on a life without her. She didn't even know the girl's eye color.

I put the thumbprint aside and pull out the letter addressed to

Nurse Anderson again. The mystery of Hattie and Margaret is a perplexing one, but it's not the one that matters. What I do need to know is why my mother has Hattie's letter in the first place—and what relation Nurse Anderson has to my mother.

Surrounded by the clothes in her closet, I breathe in my mother's scent. I know exactly which outfits were her favorite, which one she had the longest, which one she wore to my high school graduation. I know which dress she chose for my father's funeral, and I also know she never put it on again. I thought I knew everything about my mother. She never talked about herself much; I cringe as I realize that I assumed she didn't have much to say.

But maybe I was wrong. Is there a side to my mother I never knew?

And can I now, four months after losing her, find her again?

CHAPTER ELEVEN

Althea Anderson, September 1926

Three days later, Margaret is pink and white again like a pig. Her cheeks get rounder each day, and the hair on her head is thick enough now to identify it as blond. *Just like Hattie's.* Though I always picture Hattie as she was after Margaret's death, her curls weighed down with sweat, I force myself to remember her beauty. The woman is young and pretty, and Margaret will be, too. Hattie will know how to drape Margaret's clothes and style her hair.

I finger my own dark hair twisted under my cap. Well, a nurse has no time to worry about vanity. No matter that my face is pale and my nose sharp. A patient desperate for a shot of morphine or a woman on the brink of motherhood does not care what I look like. No, they care what I can do. And at Bellevue, the first Florence Nightingale–based nurses' training school in the entire country, I can do a lot.

So long as I stay quiet and keep my head down, that is.

I'm good at that.

Louise appears beside me as I reflect. "She's come a long way."

I nod.

"Her parents will be thrilled."

I nod again. I certainly hope so. But who knows what they will say? I've thought through a thousand speeches, but still I don't know how I'm going to tell Margaret's parents what I've done. Much less how they'll respond.

"Speaking of." Louise turns away from her own reflection in Margaret's glass incubator and faces me. "Will they be making the trip to pick her up, or will you deliver her to them?"

"They've asked me to take her," I lie. "So they can have everything prepared at the house ahead of time."

"She'll be in good hands," Louise says. "The best."

I flinch, not because I think she's wrong but because I'm afraid she's right. My hands are the ones that saved her. Are Hattie and Michael prepared to care for Margaret the way I know to?

I whisper my good-byes to the girl as I leave Coney Island for Manhattan. I hate leaving her each night, but I don't mind the work in the emergency department. It isn't as magical as delivering babies, but it's better than surgery. I crave the sense of being needed, of being valuable. The urgency occupies my mind.

Unfortunately, Bellevue's lead emergency doctor, despite twenty years of success with the nurse training program, makes clear his distaste for female medical workers. I spend half of my twelve-hour shift washing sheets and making beds. One patient whose water I have been sent to fetch is alone when I return. "Nurse," the man croaks, his voice frayed with nerves. "Please."

I turn from the door, sheets draped over my arm. "Sir?"

He points to his left eye, enshrouded in mist. A cataract. "What are they going to do to me, ma'am?"

First, retrobulbar anesthesia. Then, a six-millimeter incision. Saline and syringes for extraction of the cataract, and then iodine-treated catgut to suture the wound. You'll need a pair of aphakic lenses to take home, but your vision will return in the next month and a half.

I swallow my knowledge like soup that scalds the throat going down. What else can I do, with the surgeon's heavy footfalls approaching? "I'm but a nurse," I tell the man gently. "You'd best ask the doctor."

The man is disappointed. "You don't know."

I clench my toes as if to pin down and trample the words that yearn to fly free. "No," I reply softly, "I do not."

Forget the anatomy, alimentation, toxicology, dietetics, massage, biology, and hygiene. Forget the years of coursework and hours of practice. To qualify as a nurse, I must master it all. But to serve as one, I must pretend I know none of it. Too threatening is a woman who knows her medicine; one day, the doctors fear, we will rise up and take their coveted spots at the top of the medical world.

For now, I am quiet. But I hope the men's fear is founded.

I hope one day, we are the doctors.

I return to reality when the next patient enters the ER, a little boy with a sprained wrist and an overprotective grandmother. It's not exactly an emergency, which I explain as gently as possible before directing the indignant woman and her grandson to the children's pavilion. Next is an elderly man with chest pain, whom I send immediately to Resuscitation.

I nearly have to be resuscitated myself when I recognize the next patient. "M-Mrs. Perkins," I stammer, her startling green eyes and blond ringlets unmistakable despite the horrifying condition of the rest of her face. Her once-perfect little nose is bulging and twisted out of place, bruising spreading along both sides and pooling beneath her eyes. A faint smudge of blood remains on the woman's skin, the rest of it wiped hurriedly onto the loose sleeve of her pale yellow dress.

Hardly able to breathe, I turn away from the sight of Margaret's real mother and dig into the icebox. I pull out more ice cubes than I can hold, and the excess pieces spill from my hands and skitter across the floor. I watch helplessly as they slide every which way, leaving pale glimmering trails of water pointing back at me like accusatory arrows. I grit my teeth and wrap the remaining ice in cloth, angry at myself for being so careless. It's not like me to get rattled. I can smile calmly and offer words of comfort to children with shards of bone jutting from their skin, victims of fires with flesh hanging in charred folds from their faces, elderly patients on the cusp of death. But here I am, flustered and incompetent in the face of a broken nose?

Of course, it isn't the broken nose that's thrown me. It's the sight of Hattie Perkins. It's the reminder that while I keep Margaret squirreled away in safety, life has marched cruelly on for her mother. I can't attribute Hattie's weight loss or short, jagged nails to the nose injury; those are signs of grief alone.

I know what to do for the nose: clamp the ice to it, monitor for bleeding. But what do I do for the woman? Confronted with her pain and finally confident that Margaret will survive, should I tell Hattie what I've done? Hattie could even come with me to get the girl from Coney Island tomorrow . . . but what if she says no?

I force myself to ask the routine questions even as my brain churns in desperation. "How did it happen?"

She swallows, the tendons in her neck tensing. "I walked into the door." Her voice quivers, a slight upward inflection at the end of her words.

I nearly drop the ice again. She walked into a door as much as I talked to my mother over breakfast this morning. No. Michael must have done this to her.

Part of me isn't surprised.

"Is he here?" I ask in a whisper.

Hattie only hesitates for a moment before she nods, wincing. "Yes. But they made him wait outside."

Standard procedure unless the patient is a young child. I've never been as grateful for the rule as I am now.

"But he's mad about being stuck out there," Hattie continues. "I think he's afraid I'm going to say something." She grabs my arm the same way she did when I took her daughter from her arms two months ago. "Don't say anything. Don't tell him I told you." Her voice rises in volume.

I inhale slowly and close my eyes. "Hattie, this is serious. You can't just pretend it didn't happen."

She shakes her head. "No. It won't happen again. This was the first time. I can stop it."

"Hattie . . ."

"I can stop it," she insists again, "because it's my fault."

I wait. She has to be right—for Margaret's sake. Margaret needs a safe home to return to.

"I mentioned the baby, and he told me to shut up. But I didn't listen. She'd be almost two months old now if she'd lived. That's what I said." She begins to cry. "But I shouldn't have. Michael is right. No good can come from talking about her. Not when she's dead."

She's not dead! I want to scream. The very thought of Margaret's body turning cold and lifeless sets my heart racing. But I can't say anything now. Blood is flowing again from Hattie's nostrils, and her tears dilute the stream so it's thin and fast-flowing. In just seconds, her lips are covered in tiny, crisscrossing lines of blood like stitches.

"I need to forget her," Hattie sobs, a red bubble blossoming in her nose. "Then everything will be okay."

I take a deep breath. I can't tell her now. She needs to be sent to Trauma.

Taking my own deep breaths, I hold her shuddering body as we wait for the Trauma nurses to arrive.

"The only good thing," Hattie sniffles, "is that she'll never have to see this."

And then the nurses are taking her from me, leading her away so all I can see is the back of her body. From behind, she could be Mary Pickford, Hollywood's sweetheart. But from the front? I shudder. She's right. From the front, she is something no child should ever have to see.

September 3, 1926. Just one day after Hattie Perkins's hospitalization and two days shy of Margaret's two-month birthday, it is time for the girl to leave Dr. Couney. As the days shorten,

Luna Park is shutting down. Steeplechase closed yesterday; Luna Park will close tomorrow. The babies have to go.

As Louise told me after Margaret's bout of pneumonia last week, Margaret is one of the lucky ones. At five pounds, she is just about ready to leave the incubators by merit of her own health. I am relieved. The nurses tell me that babies have fared worse at the hospitals than the park in years past, and I can't imagine the horror of watching a baby blossom here and then shrivel again at the hospital. Of course, there's another reason I'm relieved. Selfishly, I am afraid of what would happen if Margaret were transferred to the hospital and registered. Would they find her death certificate, signed by an oblivious Ida? I shudder. Here at Luna Park, my word is enough for the nurses to go by.

Margaret is packaged like a gift; Dr. Couney remains a showman through and through. I imagine that my arm could slide under the band of the pink bow tied around the girl's waist, that the stiffly printed graduation certificate Dr. Couney has crafted could cover Margaret like a blanket.

Little does Dr. Couney know that Margaret is not going anywhere she will be seen and admired.

"Bellevue Hospital," I instruct the driver as we climb into the back seat of the automobile. I hold Margaret tight, but her big eyes stare as if from the face of a disapproving grandmother.

"I will take you home," I promise the girl. "But we can't go, not yet. Your mama is sick." My stomach turns to remember the way Hattie looked last night. I'm not sure she's even been discharged by now, and she's definitely in no state to handle her baby.

I've planned as much as I could have in twelve hours. I've

stolen diapers, a bottle, and powdered formula from the teaching rooms, and I'm ready for Margaret to stay with me at the Nurses' Residence tonight. I'll send word to Hattie, and when she's ready to meet with me, I'll take Margaret back.

Until then, I'll have to stay holed up in my room, feign an illness that will use up all of the sick days I've failed to take in my two years at Bellevue.

The lurch of the automobile fascinates Margaret, and her fascination distracts me from my worries. She's been rocked in women's arms, bounced on women's hips—but never carried through the streets of the city. Not, at least, that she can remember. The last time the girl was in a cab was at two hours old, and that was horse-drawn rather than motored. For Margaret, the difference is probably monumental. Even if for me, they are both trips stained like sweat into the corners of my memory. Indelible, the fear and urgency potent. "I suppose you don't remember last time, do you?"

The cabdriver glances back at us, my neck bent as I whisper to Margaret. "Yours?" he asks.

"Yes," I murmur distractedly, then look up in shock. I nearly blurt out the truth—*no!*—but it's too late now. For this ride into Manhattan, at least, I will have to pretend Margaret is my own.

Desperate to avoid further conversation with the driver, I keep up a steady flow of meaningless chatter with the baby. Though she can't lift her own head, I position her so that she is able to watch the people and the streets as we pass them. To her they would appear simply as smudges of light and shadow, but they mesmerize her nonetheless. The ride from Luna Park to Bellevue is a long one, as I know all too well.

"There's Washington Cemetery." I hesitate. I wouldn't tell anyone else, but certainly a baby cannot understand. "My mother . . . that's where she's buried."

Margaret coos in response. I smile softly at her and continue to point landmarks out as we pass. Her wonder is gratifying. "And finally," I conclude, "we'll cross the East River. We're on the Brooklyn Bridge, which will take us back to Manhattan." I usually take the elevated railway, but this is Margaret's second time crossing the river in a cab.

The bridge is only a mile long, and Bellevue's familiar U-shaped outline rises before us. "You were born there." I gesture to Margaret. "And on the other side is the Nurses' Residence. *My* residence." And ours for the night.

Now that the cab has stopped, Margaret's head begins to loll. It rests in the curve of my armpit with a precision that seems very nearly intentional, and I gaze down at her tiny fontanel. What responsibility, to have a baby. So mutable and vulnerable and new.

Someone else's responsibility, I remind myself. Not mine.

I thank and pay the driver and step from the vehicle. Margaret is still so small that I can tuck her into the elbow of my left arm as I approach the building. Though her mouth is shut, a whimper seeps as if from her very pores. "I'm sorry," I whisper, realizing I am the cause of her distress. I release my tight grip. "Nerves. Quiet, okay?"

I carry Margaret up the stairs to the fourth floor. "My room," I tell her as I open the door. I know she doesn't understand what it is I'm telling her, but it seems cruel somehow to carry her silently throughout the city the same way I would an object.

I exhale once we're inside. For the time being, at least, we are safe. Now I have to think about the future.

I settle Margaret gently on the mattress, pull my desk chair to the foot of the bed, and shove my desk so it is parallel to the long edge of the bed. Margaret isn't old enough to roll yet, but I'm not taking any chances.

Once she's set up and content, I stand at my now sideways desk and pull out a sheet of pale blue paper. I run my finger over the embossed crest at the top: *Bellevue School of Nursing.* It's the same as on the pin that graduates like Director Rottman wear, and I'm reminded of my probationary status. If anybody finds me here with an infant, I'll be out on the streets.

But I don't have a choice, do I? Hattie could still be in the hospital, after all. It hasn't even been twenty-four hours.

I close my eyes and think. What to write? I can't tell Hattie everything in the letter. I don't want her to think it's some cruel trick, or be so overwhelmed she never writes back. And most of all, I can't commit my crime to paper. If it falls into the wrong hands or Hattie chooses to report me, being fired will be the least of my problems.

Dear Mrs. Perkins, I begin with a shaking hand. *This is Nurse Althea Anderson, the nurse who was with you for your delivery July 5 and again when you visited Bellevue for a broken nose in September.*

I'm writing for two reasons: first, to inquire as to your health. I was saddened to see you in the emergency ward the night of September 2, and write in hopes that the situation has not re-peated itself. May I be so bold as to ask whether it has?

Secondly, I want to find a time to meet you at your home. I need to talk to you about your daughter, Margaret. I understand that this may dredge up painful memories, but the information I have to tell you is important. In fact, I would dare to say it is life-alteringly so.

With your permission, I would like to come by your house one day when your husband is out. While I'd like to speak with the both of you, I think this is a matter we will be more comfortable discussing first without Mr. Perkins.

Please forgive the cryptic nature of this letter. I simply have things to share with you that are better discussed in person.

Write back with a date that will work for us to meet.

Sincerely yours,
Althea Anderson

I reread the letter several times, tweaking the details until the corners of my eyes twitch with exhaustion. It will have to do. I fold it into an envelope and print Hattie Perkins's name and address carefully on the front. I've had the address memorized since I signed the birth certificate in July.

The return address is trickier. I cannot put my own. Michael will see it, and quite possibly open the letter himself. I finally settle on *Ladies' Home Journal, Philadelphia.* I ink *FREE SEWING SAMPLES INSIDE* on the back of the envelope.

"What do you think?" I look over the desk to the baby hemmed in on the bed and hold up the envelope. "Harmless-looking enough?"

To my distress, she lets out a wail. I drop the envelope onto my desk and clamber over it in my haste to reach her.

I lift Margaret so I can bounce her gently. I have been part of the delivery of countless babies, but never have I stopped to think what the parents do with them after returning home. Oh yes, I could write a textbook on Margaret's physical needs. But concerning how she will spend her time or what I can do to make her happy? We don't cover that in nursing school.

At least I know how to feed the baby. "Look," I say, keeping my voice calm to soothe her. "I have these bottles from the training room, and formula." Using one arm to cradle the baby, I pour the powder into the bottle of water and shake to combine. "Sorry, honey. We can't risk going downstairs to warm it up."

I maneuver the bottle between her tiny lips, and she begins sucking eagerly. I watch with pride. Just two months ago, she was too small to suckle and had to be fed with eye droplets through the nose. Now, look at her.

Margaret suddenly expels the bottle from between her lips with a huff. Her breath hitches, and then she begins to wail.

Sweating, I push the bottle between her lips again. "Drink, Margaret. I know you're hungry."

I hear the sound of her sucking on the bottle's nipple again, and I exhale. Too soon. She spits it out again, her face twisted in fury.

Abandoning the bottle, I shift Margaret's weight into both my arms and bounce her gently. My voice is scratchy with nerves, but I sing the first song that comes to mind: "Amazing Grace."

Margaret's cries soften, and I begin to relax. A drop of sweat rolls down the back of my neck, but I try to ignore it as I sing to the girl.

And then comes a knock on the door.

My knees buckle, and I collapse onto the bed. Sitting here, I am frozen, immobile, unable to move. Sweat pools under my arms, and Margaret squirms like she's considering another cry. The knock sounds again, and I rise. My knees are stiff and reluctant as I walk to the door and open it.

Ida from the next room stands on the other side with her eyebrows high in puzzlement. "A baby?"

"Yes." It's all I can think to say.

"I heard it crying," she explains. "Is it . . . whose is it?"

"*She,*" I correct.

"Whose is *she*?"

I breathe in. "My cousin's daughter. My cousin is out for the day with her husband and their maid had to go home sick and didn't know where to take her. I'm actually—I'm just leaving now. We're having supper at my aunt's."

"Oh!" Ida laughs with obvious relief. "Good. For a moment I thought she was yours, the way you're holding her so tenderly."

I force a smile.

"She's beautiful," Ida coos. "Look at those eyes! So big on such a tiny thing. But . . . she *is* so tiny. She can't possibly be more than a week old?"

I blanch, relieved that at least Margaret has her mother's green eyes and blond hair rather than my darker features. But Ida's right. Margaret is too small to be left with a maid or a cousin. "My family has always had small babies." It's remarkable my voice doesn't shake.

"I can imagine that," Ida laughs. "If they're as skinny as you!"

I breathe out, but my relief disappears when Ida continues. "Can I hold her?"

No, no, no. "Sure," I smile. "Here." My fingers linger on Margaret's skin as I roll her gently into Ida's arms. I don't want to let her go, not after months of being the one to protect her. But when Ida smiles down at Margaret, I have an idea.

"She won't drink her bottle," I say. "Do you mind watching her in my room for a moment while I heat it up?"

Ida barely looks up, tickling Margaret's nose with her finger. "Of course not."

I usher her into my room and close the door, then take the stairs two at a time. In the kitchen, I pour the mixture into a pot and set it to heat on the stove. I force myself to inhale and exhale as I stir the chalky liquid. My heartbeat is just returning to normal when I hear footsteps behind me.

I turn and take an immediate step back, my elbow hitting the pot. The heat stings, but I try to keep my face neutral. "Miss Caswell."

"Nurse Anderson." She nods. "What are you doing?"

I force a cough. "I'm sick," I say. I know I'll have to do better than that if I'm to play sick for the next several days and nights, the number dependent on when Hattie answers my letter. Miss Caswell can't begrudge me an illness, not when I've never taken a day off in my two years here. Not even when my father died.

"Oh?" Her eyes narrow suspiciously.

I cough again. "I'm afraid I need to take the night off. I'm running a fever and have gotten sick several times."

Miss Caswell's face melts in sympathy. "Thank you for alerting me, Nurse Anderson. I'll call Director Rottman so she can speak to your supervisor." She glances behind me. "I think your milk is near boiling."

"Oh!" I look around for a cup, but none are readily available. Cheeks heating, I funnel the formula into the baby bottle and hope that my back blocks Miss Caswell's view.

It doesn't. "A bottle?"

"My hands are shaking," I say quickly. "With chills. I didn't want to spill."

"Hm." Miss Caswell blinks several times. "I suppose that's rather . . . resourceful." She again wishes me a quick recovery and then disappears from the kitchen, leaving me quaking in relief. Thank the Lord it's a Friday and she has supper party planning to distract her.

With the too-hot bottle folded into my pinafore, I run back up the stairs. I burst into my room to find Ida bouncing Margaret, the infant fussing slightly.

"Thank you," I say to Ida. "Thank you, so much."

"Happy to help," Ida says. "She's hungry."

I lift Margaret from the other nurse's arms, relieved to feel her weight against me once again as Ida waves and ducks out the door. I lock the door and sway with Margaret until the bottle has cooled enough to press to her lips.

This time, she gulps eagerly, and my shoulders sag with relief.

I cradle the child close to me and whisper, "What do we do now, Margaret?"

Her bright eyes stare up at me as she drinks, and I smile. We sink into a quiet relaxation on the bed.

Everything is wrong in our world right now, but peace settles over me like a veil as I feed the baby. The outside world can't penetrate the soft, milky bubble that is this moment. I wonder if mothers feel like this all the time.

No. Of course not. It's easy to relax when your duty to a baby is temporary like mine is. I am not a mother. I am not Margaret's mother, however sacred the girl is to me. And I'd do well to remember that as I begin the process of returning Margaret to her parents.

As I begin the process of losing her.

CHAPTER TWELVE

Stella Wright, January 1951

I am desperate for answers, so I leave my mother's things in a heap on the floor, blow out the candles, and run downstairs into the cold to hail a taxicab. "Bellevue Hospital," I say, naming the hospital in Hattie's letter. I don't know what I expect to find, but I must start somewhere.

The traffic is painfully slow. We finally pull up in front of the red brick hospital building, the wind coming off the East River like a whip. *Bellevue.* I shudder. I may not have been here since the day I myself was born in September 1926, but I know about the place. It's a hotbed of filth and sin. Just about the opposite of anywhere my mom would step foot.

I pay the driver and walk inside, cautious of what I'll find as I step through the white-columned door. But the room I enter surprises me. I expect drunk staggering and tortured screams—certainly, those are the stories I've heard of the place—but the people sitting in a sad, uneven semicircle around the room are quiet, if teary-eyed. What stands out is the blinking. Some of the patients blink slowly as if stupefied; others blink rapidly in impatience. I must force my twitching eyes not to emulate their patterns.

I approach the silver-haired receptionist. "Good evening. Does the hospital keep records of its former employees? Is there a place I could find a list of those who worked here in the twenties?"

"*I* was here in those days." The woman winks. "But I have a feeling you're not looking for me."

I smile politely. "I'm actually trying to find the nurses' records. I'm looking for a Nurse Anderson." I swallow and force myself to face the possibility that my mother had secrets. "Possibly a Nurse Althea Anderson."

I don't know why I bother mentioning the name; obviously, this old woman doesn't know her.

"If she was a nurse," the receptionist says, "you should go check across the street at the Nurses' Residence. I know they publish bulletins and such for the members of the graduating classes. They're the ones who'll know."

"Thank you," I say. "Thank you so much."

I pick my way across the street and knock on the door of the old, multistory structure that houses Bellevue's nursing school.

No response. I step back and take the building in, wondering if my mother could have studied here, if I might sense her presence. The address of the Nurses' Residence is carved in stone above the door, faded. It sparks something, and I pull out the thumbprint note.

Michael Perkins
440 East 26th St.

Michael Perkins, here?

My determination redoubling, I knock on the door again. I search without success for a bell to ring, and sigh. Politeness demands that I come back another time, but I've come all this way. What's the worst they can do if I enter uninvited, kick me back out?

I put my hand to the doorknob and test it. To my surprise, the door swings open on well-oiled hinges.

I step in and am met by the suffocating smell of hard work: the sweat of too many bodies, the metal of tools, and the dusty musk of construction. The foyer is stark and empty, but the room beside it is set up to be a lab of sorts: a massive metal table, wooden stools, a skeleton hanging in the corner. I shudder.

I turn quickly and nearly run into a tall, severe woman in a nurse's cap. "How do you do?" Her words are polite, but her voice is as sharp as her crisped pinafore.

"Good afternoon." I extend my hand. "I'm so sorry to surprise you. I am Mrs. Stella Wright. I'm here to inquire about a Nurse Anderson who would have worked here in the twenties."

The woman smiles, her austere face cracking into something beautiful. "Oh, I just love it when young women take interest in our nursing program! We all forget how revolutionary those women were back in that time, what with everything we do nowadays."

Those women. I think of the address on the thumbprint card and interrupt. "Actually, were there any male nurses living here at that time?"

"Oh, no!" The woman's face contorts in horror. "Bellevue did have a small male nursing school, but they never lived in this building. God forbid. Anyway, we've an old stack of annual reports that list each year's graduating class. They're around here somewhere"—she pauses—"though everything's been moving quite a bit in the midst of all the construction. They're razing the building next year."

"I'm sorry to hear that." I look sadly about me, imagining the generations of women who found their calling within these walls. Could my mother have been one of them?

"No." She smiles again. "The place is nearly a century old. I'm sure our girls will be thrilled to be moving somewhere a bit more functional."

I nod without really hearing her, already wondering what I'll find here as the woman escorts me to a library on an upper floor. "Good." She indicates a box in the corner. "They *are* here. Now, if you don't mind—I've got to go get on our cook about supper. I'll come back and check on you in an hour." Her stern expression returns.

"Of course." I'm happy to be alone, to make my discoveries without scrutiny. To find Nurse Anderson. Find my mother? I'm still not convinced it's possible. I'll scan the pages for any Andersons, Althea or otherwise.

I reach into the box the woman has indicated and pull out the pamphlets on either end. The first is dated 1875; the final, 1949. I'm thankful they're chronological.

I take out the entire decade of the twenties.

I run my eyes down each list of graduates. Nothing in 1920 or 1921. By the time I get to 1927 without finding a single Anderson, I'm starting to wonder if I'm wasting my time.

No Andersons are listed as graduates in 1928, nor 1929. I pull out 1930 just to be sure, though no Anderson I may find here could be my mother. I was four years old by 1930, and my mother certainly wouldn't have been in school with an infant straddling her hip or a child tugging on her skirt. Anyway, I remember some of being four: days with Mom at the library, in the park, walking down the street. No hospital visits.

I place the reports back in order in the box and slump back. They reflect what I've known my whole life. My mother was not a nurse. And if she had a family member who was, I may just never know.

Early-winter darkness is falling by the time I leave the Nurses' Residence, but I can still make out the address etched above the door. The very same address on Margaret Perkins's thumbprint note.

Maybe it's foolish, but I'm not ready to go home. I still feel that there's more to discover—and now might be my only chance.

I cross back to the hospital and find the same receptionist on duty.

"Hello." She smiles at me kindly. "Did you find what you were looking for?"

I don't know how to answer her question, so I don't. "I'm looking for something different now," I admit instead.

"Oh?"

"Do you have the birth records of the babies born in this hospital?"

"Not here, I'm afraid. They're at the Bureau of Vital Statistics."

I check the clock behind the woman; it's approaching five p.m. I clench my fists in frustration but thank the woman again for her help before turning to go. As I pivot to leave, I nearly slam into the man waiting behind me. He's wearing a sweater, but it doesn't disguise what's clearly an amputated arm, his left sleeve hanging limply and unnaturally at his side. I know immediately he's a veteran. Jack may carry emotional and mental scars from the war, but no one passing by him on the streets would ever know. He's well-built with shaggy blond hair and the most endearing smile. Women turn their heads when he saunters by.

This man is different, and I don't need to check the service medal pinned to his chest to know he served overseas.

"Thank you for your service," I say. I step around the man and the older woman with him—his mother?—and head toward the door.

I feel his gaze still on me as I turn, and I wonder if he's angry. Until he whistles, long and low, and I stop. I shudder the way Jack does when he hears a car backfire, and my fingers tug at the fabric of my skirt as if I could stretch it longer.

"I'm sorry," the man's mother whispers. "Ignore him, please."

I take a few steps with my head held high. Until the man whistles again, and I turn. "What makes you think," I begin, "you can—"

He jumps forward with a roar, swiping at me. I step back, eyes squeezed shut.

But nothing happens. No one barrels into me.

I open my eyes. The man's mother, small though she is, has him wrapped tightly in her arms to immobilize him as I've had to do with some of my students to stop them from hurting them-

selves or another. I blink at her, not used to being rescued. "I . . .
thank you."

To my surprise, my would-be attacker responds. "*I'm* sorry."
He's crying now. "I'm here for . . ." He coughs. "To address that."

I can't speak past the lump in my throat, so I just nod. I'm not
angry. The man is like my Jack.

The woman releases her son and approaches me to make sure
I'm all right. "Your husband fight, too?" She nods to my ring, and
only then do I realize I'm twisting it.

"Yes. France."

"Be gentle," the woman sighs. "He's seen things he can never
escape."

I'm preoccupied the whole taxi ride home, thoughts of my husband and my mother warring for space in my mind. Jack, because
of the distorted face of the man in the hospital; Mom, because I
can't imagine her in a place that served patients like him. My sensible, even-keeled mother would have been lost in a hotbed of violence and gore like the hospital. And she hated germs; even when
I was sick, she'd treat me at home rather than take me to the doctor's. Nursing would have been my mother's worst nightmare.

And yet. That letter was addressed to Nurse Anderson, and it
landed in my mother's hands. It meant enough to her that she
kept it beside her other treasures for years. I can't leave the city
without trying to find out more. I have to go to the Bureau of
Vital Statistics tomorrow.

I pay the cabdriver and run through the cold into the lobby of
the apartment building. It's hard to believe this is the same lobby
where I played tag with my friends in the building, or where
Mom and I waved Dad off on his business trips. The colors are

brighter now to fit the postwar mood, and floral curtains hang before windows that were bare during the Depression.

The rotary telephone in the corner looks similar to the one we had in the lobby as a child, but I can tell from the oval-shaped base that it's newer. The feedback, I hope, will be less distracting on this model.

I dial our home telephone number and see the maimed veteran's face in my mind as I wait for my husband to pick up.

"Jack."

"Stella!" He sounds relieved to hear my voice, and my shoulders loosen slightly. "I was hoping you'd call—I . . . I'm looking forward to having you home tomorrow."

I appreciate his olive branch and don't want to disappoint him the way he did me, but the questions about my mother are too compelling to ignore. "I'm afraid I need to stay another day."

"What?" His voice suddenly sounds farther away, and I don't know if it's my imagination or the connection. Or Jack himself.

"I'm sorry. I just found . . ." I hesitate. Jack won't understand my need to delve into the past, and knowing I'm running around the city rather than staying safely ensconced in the apartment will worry him.

I also don't want the one person I have left in the world to think that I'm just being rash yet again. I know how Jack feels about my decisions to give Gardner the ultimatum, quit over the straitjackets, and come to the city. I don't need to hear that I'm wrong in staying, or in trying to solve a mystery my mother died without choosing to reveal.

"I just found"—I flounder—"more than I expected. It's going to take longer to go through it than I thought."

"Fine," Jack says. But it's the kind of *fine* that contains unsaid multitudes.

"Jack . . ." I want him to know I'm not staying away to spite him. That I'm hurting, too. That I wish he had offered to come. That I want him to trust me enough to not mind my being in the city, trust me enough to tell me about his past.

"I just hope you get what you're looking for out of this, Stella. I'll see you the day after tomorrow."

And then the line goes dead.

I set the phone down, feeling bereft. I'm not just hurting. I'm afraid. Afraid of losing the man I most love in the world, because however much we love each other, we can't seem to agree on what secrets a marriage can survive.

I remember the words of the Bellevue veteran's mother: *Be gentle.* And I try. I try to understand how such a sweet, goofy man would want to ignore and deny an ugly past rather than relive it; it makes sense that he would fear tarnishing my view of him. But can't he also understand that I don't know who we are as a couple if I don't know who he is as a man?

I trudge upstairs and into the frigid apartment. I gather the many quilts from Mom's old bedroom to put on my own twin, burrowing into them in search of her scent. She used them more and more as she got sicker and weaker; they smell not of the mother I knew and loved but of sickness.

Still, I pull the blankets around me, drowning in them. Sleeping in this place without my mother is wrong, and sleeping in a bed without Jack feels the same way.

CHAPTER THIRTEEN

Althea Anderson, September 1926

The terror of smuggling a baby into the Nurses' Residence is not enough to keep me awake after two months of sleeping so few hours per day. I drift off feeding Margaret, and a knock on the door wakes me with the baby sleeping in my arms on the bed. A thin stream of light glows beneath the door to the hallway. At least that means I can't have slept long.

I extricate myself from Margaret's tiny fingers, which are wrapped around my thumb, and press against the door. "Yes?"

"Miss Anderson."

"Miss Caswell?"

"Please open the door."

"I . . ." I hesitate. "I've gotten quite sick, ma'am. The smell . . . I don't think you should come inside."

"Miss Anderson. Open the door."

My body stiffens. I take two strides across the room and pull the blanket up to Margaret's neck. I don't want to risk covering her face and suffocating her, but I position the pillow so it rests against the back of her head. She'll be hidden from the door . . . as long as Miss Caswell doesn't come in. And as long as the baby stays silent.

"Yes, ma'am," I finally say.

I pull the door open a crack. Miss Caswell raises her thin eyebrows, and I pull it open wider. Without waiting for an invitation, Miss Caswell marches inside, straight to the bed, and grabs Margaret from beneath the sheets.

"I . . ." A strangled, uncertain sound escapes from between my lips.

"Who is this?" Miss Caswell demands. "And don't tell me she is your father's cousin's uncle's niece, either."

"I . . ." I imagine I will be kicked out no matter what I say, but the truth seems most dangerous.

"She's mine, ma'am."

"Yours?"

"Her name is . . ." I flounder. I can't say *Margaret*. Miss Caswell may make the connection to the note with the thumbprint. I comb through my brain for girls' names and, despite living in dormitories full of girls my entire life, come up blank. I cast around for something, anything.

Luna, like Luna Park? The baby opens her eyes, looks into Miss Caswell's hard mask of a face, and begins to wail. I step forward and take her, gazing into her eyes. Despite her size and her ill health, she has a brightness that is hers alone. Her eyes glow like orbs, but it isn't the pale, steady glow of the moon. Her eyes are sparks, blazing like stars.

"Stella." I say it with confidence. "My daughter's name is Stella."

clutch the newly named Stella like a lifeline as house director Miss Hosken, to whom Miss Caswell has apologetically delivered me, details all the ways I have been careless, inconsiderate, feckless, disappointing, and unappreciative. I don't argue with her; I knew as soon as Miss Caswell asked me to open my door I would be dismissed. Bringing the baby home at all was a risk that I didn't fully appreciate at the time. My life as I knew it is over, and the career I have been building toward my whole life is gone. On top of that, my small inheritance is wasted, and I've nowhere to go.

I don't know what comes next, and it is only the weight of Stella in my arms that keeps me from falling apart.

Miss Caswell, at least, is concerned about me; she brings me a glass of water and frets about my health. "Is the baby all right?" she asks outside Miss Hosken's office before watching me disappear inside. "Do you need anything else?"

Her kindness is no comfort when in the span of an hour I've gone from nurse to unwed mother. I focus on Stella's sweet face to tune out Miss Hosken's lecture. While I nod and murmur my apologies at all the right moments, I'm not listening. I'm planning. I need to pack, find a way to get Stella—Margaret—safely back to her parents, and find a job for myself. The mental to-do list is all that keeps me from collapsing into a heap on the floor, for I'm afraid that if I collapse, I'll never rise again. It feels as if my entire life has been stolen from me.

At the end of the lecture, I'm exiled to my dormitory. They won't make me move out until daylight tomorrow, but I'm not to leave my room or interact with the other nurses. I suppose I'm a corrupting influence now.

I pore through the want ads as I pack, but there are few live-in positions available, and even fewer in parts of the city I'd consider safe. Many of the advertisements don't look for workers at all but wives. I'm nauseous at the very thought of meeting a man through an advertisement in the paper. It seems impossible, but I wonder if such a thing could explain some of the strange and often dangerous pairings I've encountered at the hospital. Does a woman ever respond to one of these and end up, like Hattie, in a marriage that is abusive?

No, not abusive. Hattie said Michael hit her only once, and I must believe that for their daughter's sake.

Unnerved, I put the papers aside and focus on my packing. I fold my clothes and press them into my valise under a handful of medical texts too valuable to leave and Evelyn Scott's *Precipitations*. I resist the urge to open the book and read the verses I know will calm my mind. This is not a time for reciting poetry or for fanciful imaginings. This is a time to find a place to live, a job.

"I'm so sorry." Ida sticks her head in. Her face is tear-stained. "Someone asked why you weren't at supper, and I told them you were with your cousin's baby. I wouldn't have said anything if I'd known Caswell thought you were sick."

I force a smile. "It's my fault, not yours."

Ida continues with her awkward apologies and then, as she seems about to go, hesitates. "Do you know what you're going to do?"

I keep my faux smile affixed to my face. "We'll figure something out."

"I only ask because I may have a place for you," Ida explains in a rush. "My grandmother's dear friend is looking for a caretaker. Her son and daughter-in-law are moving outside the city, so they won't be able to check in on her as often. She asked me if I'd be interested, but . . ." Ida trails off. "I'm here."

I should be here, too.

Ida fumbles in her pocket. "Here, let me give you her name." She gives me a handwritten note with the name Mrs. Wallace and an address in Times Square alongside a job advertisement. "She hasn't sent it in to the papers yet, so you have a good chance. Though, of course . . . well, it's probably best you don't tell her your situation. You could be a widow, perhaps?"

"Thanks, Ida." I scrutinize her face, taking in her watery eyes. "Actually . . . I have one more favor to ask of you."

Ida shifts her weight slightly, and I shake my head. "It's nothing to do with the baby."

I return to the letter on my desk, pull it out, and add a postscript asking that Hattie's reply be sent care of Mrs. Wallace, Times Square. I don't know if I'll be there when she responds, but I do know I won't be here. It's my only hope at this point.

I seal the envelope and hand it to Ida. "This goes to Hattie Perkins in Trauma. It's important."

Were I in Ida's place, I'd question the letter and its contents. But mercifully Ida doesn't. "I'll make sure she gets it," Ida promises. "I owe you."

And then she is gone. I turn to the baby, who is oblivious to the chaos she's just caused.

"Stella." I whisper her new name. It fits her far better than Margaret ever did. Margaret is a name from my own generation, from Hattie's. The name of a woman whose husband hits her and whose friends look the other way.

Stella is the name of a new generation of women. Women like suffragist Stella Benson or Victor Hugo's muse. Women who will grow up to shine like stars.

I sit with Stella on the edge of the bed. She has a new name. I need a new story. I'll apply to Mrs. Wallace's as a widow, and leave her when I've returned Stella and my story no longer holds.

I take a shuddering breath. My whole life has been built on the foundation of solid, long-term plans; I've always known what I'd be doing the next day, the next month, the next year.

Now, I hardly know my next step. And once I return Stella—*Margaret*—I'll have to figure it out alone. I am walking in faith, and as I look down at Stella beside me, I know that even if I can't see the future, this, now, is the right path.

've been told to leave by six in the morning, but I don't want to face the other nurses. Stella and I leave at five a.m., when the only soul awake is the groundskeeper snuffing out the gas lamps outside the hospital. He is a small, shriveled man the same height as the lanterns he tends, and I made an effort to speak to him each morning. Today, I just give him a wave from afar, praying that Stella is masked in the darkness. I don't want even him to know I'm leaving in disgrace. Ashamed, I turn my face and run. Away from the river and the hospital.

I turn back when I'm at a safe distance. I would cry if I weren't so numb. I've spent two years and four months in Bellevue's halls. Just two more months and I would graduate, a crane pin affixed to my bosom and a degree in my hand. I could work at Bellevue forever, take my pick of any hospital in the country. And now it's all gone. Everything I've ever worked for.

But I can't sink into despair. I have Stella to take care of. God knows how I'll cope once she's gone; I'll have nothing.

I clutch her to me, grateful that she is part of my story for now. Our first stop as mother and daughter is a pawnshop. I've rehearsed my story time and time again, and Stella has heard it enough in our journey across the city that I hope she's come in some primitive place to believe it as true. I am Althea Anderson, widow. I trained at Bellevue but left to marry, only for my husband to fall gravely ill of tuberculosis. By the time he passed away, our daughter Stella was born, and I could no longer return to the hospital.

But to sell my story, I need a ring. The pawnshop is squeezed narrowly between its neighbors, filled to the brim with other people's jewelry and furniture. It smells of rust, like blood.

It is hot even so early in the day, and the metal scent seems to seep into my clothing and rise from under my arms. Despite my own discomfort, Stella is alert and fascinated. Her eyes are wide at the shine of metal and the bump of the door shutting behind us.

I breathe in deeply through my mouth and instantly regret it. My throat feels coated as if with polish. "Excuse me, sir?" I approach the man at the counter. "I need a ring."

His gaze shoots immediately to my bare left hand and then back up to the baby at my breast. But the revulsion I expect does not come. Instead, the man's face stretches slowly into a smile like the cut of a scalpel. "Rings are expensive, I'm afraid," the man shrugs. My toes clench. He knows that Stella and I are desperate—an unmarried woman and her illegitimate child. Shame rises hot within me, making my head feel as if it will float up and away while my feet stay leaden, rooted to the floor. Through this sensation of being stretched apart I hear the heavy thud of a box; the man has lifted an array of rings onto the counter for my viewing.

They overwhelm with glitter and gold, relics of the rich Edwardian years and even the decadent time of Queen Victoria. Relinquished to the pawnshop by families who once had the wealth necessary to adorn their fingers like kings. Perhaps sold by brides left at the altar or families short of a working man after the Great War, these rings are studded with green emeralds and red rubies, then welded to resemble hearts or stars or even doves. They are more than I need. I want something subtle, and more importantly, inexpensive. I don't have enough of my father's inheritance left after two years of school to pay for anything more.

I don't have anything now, except for Stella. And she won't be mine for long.

I finally select a pair of simple gold bands. The pawnbroker undoubtedly overcharges me for them, but the situation would replicate itself anywhere else in the city. An unwed mother is pure, distilled desperation, and no man would be foolish enough to keep from capitalizing on it.

"At least we are now above suspicion," I tell Stella as I slide the rings on outside the building. "Regardless of the fact that the rings are a bit too large and the man who sold them was perfectly horrid."

Something in my tone must belie my disgust, for Stella makes a noise in response. "Stella." I shake my head even as I smile. "That was not funny. In fact, it was quite unkind."

I become aware of the slick, heavy sweat beneath my gown. I carry Stella in one arm and all my belongings in the other, and my body sags under the weight of my wool dress. "Well," I relent. "I suppose we do deserve something to laugh about." I lift her to kiss her face. "I think," I whisper to the girl, "that we are doing the right thing." My new rings slide to the base of my finger. "Or at least"—my voice drops—"I hope that we are."

Breathing deeply, I look down at my list. I cross out this errand as though I'm doing my Sunday shopping.

Except today's list tells a story. The details I invented last night are printed in careful script; in this new world, I cannot afford to forget that though I am still Althea Anderson, I earned the name by virtue of my deceased husband. I am, for all intents and purposes, the widow of Joseph Henry Anderson. *He died*, I rehearse, *six months ago*. Recently enough that Stella is legitimate; long enough ago that the lessened state of half-mourning is appropriate. Accordingly, I am dressed in a high-necked gown of gray wool, and the few pieces of jewelry I own are tucked away and hidden.

I pull out Ida's note, the address scribbled alongside a not-yet-advertised job description. *WANTED for an invalid widow suffering from weak heart, but not otherwise disabled; must be accustomed to nursing; duties light, chiefly at night; age from 25 to 35; good reader preferred. Apply by letter, to M. Wallace, care of Charlotte Wallace.* I pray that Mrs. Wallace will like the look of us as I trudge the two miles to Times Square.

"Please, dear God," I pray. "I don't know whether I deserve this chance, but Stella does."

And then I knock.

The inhabitants are slow to answer, and I pull back slightly to take in the building, which lines Times Square on 43rd Street. I am accustomed to living in dormitories, and this two-story town-house will seem large in comparison. Stella's eyesight will sharpen as she gazes out the window and sees the bright lights: *The Rose of Stamboul*, Macy's, Columbia, the King of Pizza. How she will learn to sleep through the night with trolleys and motorcars rumbling below her, I am less sure.

The door finally begins to pull open, and I stand straighter. It folds in slowly, and I wiggle my toes in apprehension.

"Oh, dear." The woman who finally appears is frightened. "You aren't my daughter-in-law." She begins to slide the door closed, but I step forward and speak quickly. "Mrs. Wallace," I begin, "I am . . . . *Mrs.* . . . . Anderson. I was sent by Ida Berry as a potential caretaker."

Relief subtracts years from the woman's face. "I didn't know I requested a woman with a baby."

"Oh." I wrestle briefly with the desire to lie. "You didn't, I'm afraid. But my husband—her father—is deceased, and I was hoping you would appreciate her . . ." Stella begins to whine and squirm. ". . . vibrancy." *Stella*, I beg silently, *quiet*. "She sleeps well and cries little."

I could have said she cries all night, and I'm not sure Mrs. Wallace would have heard me. Her gaze is fixated on Stella. As if Stella has rehearsed her part the way I have, she stares solemnly back at Mrs. Wallace, green eyes wide open and imploring.

When Mrs. Wallace sighs, I begin to hope. *Please*, I pray again as Stella and I cross the threshold, *please give us this job*.

Mrs. Wallace leads us to her small kitchen. A counter lines one wall, the icebox beside it. She sits us down at the cluttered table in the center of the room.

"My daughter-in-law gave me a script . . ." Mrs. Wallace fumbles around until she pulls out a handwritten sheet of paper. "Let's see. I have a weak heart and a history of heart attacks, and I need significant help with meals, cleaning, taking my medications, and going up and down stairs." Mrs. Wallace squints. "Well. I sound utterly helpless." She places the sheet down. "My daughter-in-law has been helping me, God bless her, but she is as high-strung as they come. All I really need to know, if you're friends with Ida, is that you have experience as a caretaker."

I smile. I approve of this daughter-in-law. "I'm a trained nurse," I assure Mrs. Wallace. "I was unable to graduate due to marriage and my husband's subsequent illness, God rest his soul, and then we had Stella. But I've experience in surgery, obstetrics, pediatrics, palliative care, emergency and trauma . . . and just about everything else."

Mrs. Wallace raises her eyebrows. "So you can read, I take it."

I smile. "Yes, ma'am. I adore to, in fact."

"Have you read anything recently that you would recommend?"

"Evelyn Scott," I respond immediately, though honesty is not part of my script. I recite a line about shadows and snow, one that feels particularly applicable to my own current existence of secrets and subterfuge.

Mrs. Wallace waves her hand. "I've lived many decades of

146

sadness and prefer happy poetry, but you have a melodic voice. You will do."

God must harbor some special love for Stella (who couldn't?), because Mrs. Wallace enlists me to begin immediately. After feeding Stella, I unload my toilette into the small upstairs bathroom that is to be ours. I set the one framed picture I have of my mother and father beside my bed and then sit on its edge. Stella is cradled in my arms, her eyes wide open. New sights, new sounds, new home. Two new homes in as many days, I realize, but Stella seems unfazed. All morning, her unblinking eyes have taken in the city's chaos and grime as if she is as eager to observe New York's many corners as I am a surgery or a birth. "Funny"— I smile down at her—"that we already seem to have some things in common."

Especially, I do not add aloud, *as you are not truly my own.*

I bite my lip. For the last two months, Stella has been my confidante. I have gone to her when the doctors have belittled or ignored me, when the long days and hours have seemed too much to handle on my own. I have had Stella as my secret keeper, as a listener who will not and cannot judge.

Now, our charade can continue just a little while longer.

Is it wrong that part of me is grateful?

CHAPTER FOURTEEN

Stella Wright, January 1951

I wake early in the dark apartment, eager to get to the vital records office and put this whole matter to rest. My face is puffy from sleeping so poorly. Though I remember my bed being comfortable in my childhood, I tossed and turned last night. I realize only now that it was the first night Jack and I have spent apart since we married, and the timing unnerves me. As if sleeping apart is a product of our discord and not just distance.

Pushing my fears aside, I do my makeup and hair as usual in the weak morning light, not because I expect the staff at the Bureau of Vital Statistics will spare me a glance but because a set face proves I am ready to meet the day. I wash and rinse with freezing water. I apply powder and blush and then eyeliner and mascara. Red lipstick, a pillbox hat atop my curls.

The subway is chaotic at this time in the morning. I stand and clutch the ceiling straps, grateful that I'm wearing gloves to keep the grime off my hands. My mom was more conscious about germs than most women of her time, and I can't help but wonder now if it was because she had a background in medicine.

If she had a background in medicine.

Reaching the Bureau of Vital Statistics before opening, I pace up and down Worth Street to keep warm: from records office to city clerk's office to courthouse. Men in suits bustle past, and I envy them their purpose.

I'm at the front of the line for the records office at 8:59, and I hop up the marble steps and open the door just as the bell chimes for 9:00.

"Good morning," I chirp. The man behind the desk looks up, and I take in his thick eyebrows and receding hairline.

"I'm here for a birth and death certificate," I announce. "For Margaret Perkins."

"Just fill these out." The man slides two forms across the counter to me.

"Thank you." I record what I know and the man takes the forms without expression, disappearing into the back room.

I retreat to one of the uninviting chairs that lines the room and wait. As my back grows sore and the minute hand makes its turn round the clock, I start to regret this trip. What do I expect to find, anyway? What does it matter when Margaret Perkins died, if I don't even know who she is?

Just as I'm starting to think I've been foolish in staying an extra day in the city (could Jack be right again?), another man appears with my documents. I keep myself from reaching out and snatching them as he drones on about the rules—no food, no drinks, no leaving the building with the records.

"Of course." I have a pen in my pocketbook so I can take notes if I need to. "Thank you."

Margaret's death certificate is on top. My eyes flick quickly across the first few fields: borough, hospital, file number. I confirm the name, Margaret Ann Perkins. Female, white, and single. Instead of an age being marked for the girl, a sloppy checkmark dominates the field reserved for babies who died after less than a day. The death date is July 5, 1926, which would make her birthdate the same.

How could she have died in July 1926 when the thumbprint and note serve as proof that she survived until August?

Puzzled, I continue down the left side of the certificate. Father: Michael Perkins; Mother: Hattie Perkins. The place of death is Bellevue Hospital, and the cause is listed as "Born early, two months," signed and sworn by a Nurse Ida Berry.

I press my lips together. I have as many questions as I did before. More.

I look next to Margaret's birth certificate. The information matches what I know about Margaret: her name, her parents, her birthdate (again, July 5, 1926)—but my lips part with shock when I see the signature in the bottom corner. Ida Berry may have watched Margaret die, but she isn't the nurse who delivered her.

That was my mother. Her measured hand is as familiar to me as her voice, and the fourteen letters of her name march across the line: *Althea Anderson.* Below is the signature of a physician supervisor scrawled in cursive that is impossible to read.

Part of me is tempted to dismiss it all. Didn't I just ascertain at the Bellevue Nurses' Residence that my mother was never a nurse? Surely there's more than one Althea Anderson in the world.

Except for the handwriting. I've read a thousand notes in my mother's firm script, from those tucked into my lunch pail in grade school to the letters she'd write me weekly after I moved away. I'd recognize her handwriting anywhere.

I look up to the ceiling. Something else tugs urgently at the back of my mind, and I squeeze my eyes shut in frustration.

Then it hits me.

My mother couldn't have delivered a child in July 1926, because I was born just two months later. September 5, 1926, to Margaret's July 5.

I wait my turn at the counter again, foot tapping impatiently. "I need another birth certificate form, and also one for marriage licenses. Please."

This time, I eschew the hard chairs and pace back and forth until the worker returns. "I have the marriage certificate," he tells me, "but I couldn't find the birth certificate."

I stare at him in shock. I requested my own—do I not exist?

He must sense my rising panic, because he makes an effort to reassure me. "It's not uncommon. Hospitals were rather slapdash in their approach to record keeping back in the day. But again"—he waves the sheet in his hand—"here's the marriage license."

"Thank you." At least he's given me something to hang on to.

I look at my parents' certificate of marriage.

I see their names, the place of marriage, the witnesses, and the celebrant. Finally, there's the date: *July 1927.* I blink and nearly drop the paper in surprise. My parents weren't married until nearly a year after I was born?

My mother was never anything but even-keeled, and my older father never seemed the passionate type. He and Mom didn't act particularly loving toward each other; they didn't even kiss each other on the cheeks, for God's sake. He would give her a chaste kiss on the forehead sometimes, more like a father than a lover. It's impossible to reconcile the parents I knew with the story this paper tells, of two people too overcome by passion to wait for marriage and a child born out of wedlock.

I grip the sheet tighter. I have more questions than I did an hour ago. I get a new story from every new source, and none of them add up. My mother was a nurse, but she wasn't. Margaret died at birth, but she didn't. I was born in September 1926, but my parents didn't marry until 1927. Mom was a nurse in July, and I was born in September.

I take a deep breath and try to calm my thoughts. Does any of it matter? I know who my mom was. She was kind and patient, caring and generous. She held my hand and listened to my stories for so many years; does it matter what she did before all that?

Yes. The answer is clear and final. Without my job and my kids, without my parents, and with tensions with Jack bubbling to the surface, I hardly know who I am anymore. I need the knowledge of my mother to be an anchor. She made me who I am, and I need her help to figure out who I can become after losing both her and my job in one fell swoop.

But I don't even know which revelation to focus on: my parents' marriage date, Margaret's death, or my mother's apparent time as a nurse.

I press the heels of my hands to my brows. It's like I'm back at my mother's place gathering her treasures—but they keep slipping out of my hands.

Mom, who were *you?*

CHAPTER FIFTEEN

Althea Anderson, September 1926

"'I must learn to be content,'" I read, "'with being happier than I deserve.'"

I nod along with Elizabeth Bennet's final words. I, too, am happier than I deserve with Stella at my side. Only during the night do I dream of what my world will be once I have to let her go.

I push the thought aside and smile at Mrs. Wallace. "With that, I do believe it is about time we get you into bed." She grumbles, but I am firm, and I assist her as she mounts the stairs and changes into her nightdress. I've learned this past week that her mind is sharp; she merely needs help with the physical tasks that have stretched into impossibility with age. Right now, that means standing behind her to slide her coat off her stiff shoulders and bending to retrieve her nightclothes from their drawer. "Arms up." I slide the gown over her head and lead her gently to bed. "Your medicine." I hand it over with a glass of water, which Mrs.

Wallace accepts with gratitude. "Is there anything else you need?" I ask her, setting the glass atop a coaster so that it does not stain the late Mr. Wallace's mahogany table.

"No, Althea, thank you."

"Of course." I exit the room, smiling softly to myself. Though I prefer the hustle and bustle of a hospital ward, I have enjoyed serving Mrs. Wallace more than I expected. I'll be disappointed to leave her after returning Stella to the Perkinses, perhaps because spending prolonged time with a single patient cultivates a bond that is oft impossible to forge in a place like Bellevue.

Well, I laugh to myself, *prolonged time with* two *patients, really*. I let myself into my room to find the latter breathing heavily, ready to let out her signature cry. She is hungry, and now, after Mrs. Wallace has gone to bed, I am able to feed her. "Here, sweet girl," I coo as I tilt the bottle to her lips. "Is that better?" She drinks greedily, and I close my own eyes as I lean back against the bed's headboard. Between feeding Stella every three hours at night and attending to Mrs. Wallace as she rises to use the bathroom, I get very little sleep.

As if on cue, a thump sounds from the direction of Mrs. Wallace's bedroom. Oh, dear. Has she tried to get up on her own? With her joints, the task of climbing out of bed is a daunting one.

I place Stella in her bassinet. "Mrs. Wallace," I call, "do wait for me!"

But she is already on the floor when I appear in her doorway. The lamp beside her bed is on, casting a garish light across her empty bed. Her face is enshrouded in shadow, and I go closer. "Mrs. Wallace?" Her eyes are closed. "Mrs. Wallace?"

I reach out and place a hand on her forehead. It is cool, nearly clammy, and I pull back in alarm. I remember her history of heart attacks and clench my toes. Could she have gone into cardiac arrest?

I put my ear to her chest. No. Her heart is beating, and quickly. But she will not wake up when I call her name.

I run downstairs and pick up the telephone receiver. "Operator," I gasp, "I need to be connected with Dr. Gregory Shelton." Mrs. Wallace has coached me carefully on her physician's name. The operator puts me through to his line, and I keep my voice as measured as I can. "Dr. Shelton, I am Mrs. Wallace's new caretaker." I recite the address. "It's quite urgent."

"I'm so sorry." A sleepy woman's voice surprises me at the other end of the line. "But he is out. A patient called half an hour ago."

My voice threatens to spiral into panic, but I pull it in. "Does he have a colleague I can call? It is rather an emergency."

"One moment."

I flinch at the click as the doctor's wife sets the phone down. Moments later, she returns. "Dr. Charles Morrison. Much younger, but highly recommended."

"Operator . . ." But the line has already clicked. The operator has been listening in to our conversation, but I cannot fault her when efficiency is so critical to Mrs. Wallace's well-being. She connects me quickly to Dr. Morrison's line, and I launch again into my request. "Dr. Morrison. I was referred to you by Dr. Shelton." Again, I recite Mrs. Wallace's address and the nature of the call. "How quickly can you be here?"

After arranging the doctor, I run back upstairs to find

Mrs. Wallace's condition unchanged. "Circulatory shock," I mutter to myself. But what caused it? People don't just keel over with shock for no reason, and I don't see any blood loss. I flick the ceiling light and kneel beside Mrs. Wallace. There it is, nearly imperceptible on her knobby skin. A small lump above her left shoulder signifies a fractured clavicle.

Wincing, I lift Mrs. Wallace's feet gently and place a stack of pillows beneath them. Pulling the blankets from her bed and tucking them under her sides to keep her warm, I am reminded of Stella in her incubator, the temperature set at a perpetual ninety degrees. "You will survive, too," I promise Mrs. Wallace. "Just as Stella did."

I have done all I can for the shock, but I can begin treatment of Mrs. Wallace's clavicle while waiting for the doctor to arrive. I grab the copy of *Pride and Prejudice* Mrs. Wallace and I read from just half an hour earlier and place it solidly on her shoulder. The book is not heavy enough to truly do its job, but it is better than nothing. I press her arm to her side and pray the doctor hurries. I do not have the necessary materials to treat her injury myself, but this will help it set when the doctor arrives with the bandages she needs.

I release Mrs. Wallace's arm as an urgent knock at the door sends me dashing back down the stairs. I am grateful that I remain in my jacket and skirt; I have not yet changed into my nightdress.

"Dr. Morrison." I pull open the door and mask the shock of looking up at such a young face. The other doctor's wife warned me the man would be youthful, of course, but I didn't expect someone practically my own age. Dr. Morrison's hair is nearly as dark as mine, and it frames thick brows and deep gray eyes. I have to step back to take him in, as he's at least a head taller than me.

"Thank you for coming. I am Mrs. Anderson." I nearly say *Miss* in my preoccupation but stop myself. "Mrs. Wallace is upstairs. Shock and a fractured clavicle. I hope you have a Velpeau bandage? Or a Sayre's dressing?"

As I lead him up to the woman's room, I recount the care I've given. "I have lifted her feet and covered her in blankets for the shock. There was little I could do for the collarbone, but I've weighted her arm."

The doctor throws an astonished glance back at me as he slips past into Mrs. Wallace's room.

He then crouches at the side of Mrs. Wallace's bed where I stood just moments before, his own dark hair and gray suit the mirror image of my own. After a moment's study, he turns to me. "You are exactly right." His lips twist into a smile. "But how on earth did you know?"

I stiffen. This is what I do not miss from Bellevue: the doctors' continued disbelief that a woman can grasp the medical profession as they do. "I am trained as a nurse." I provide no further explanation, waiting for the disdain to flit poorly disguised across his face.

Instead, he smiles again, the movement casting off the shadows the lamp had projected onto him. "Come, then. Help me with the bandage."

I mask my shock and hold the arm in place as he rolls the muslin around Mrs. Wallace's left shoulder. He loops it under her elbow as I pull the skin back gently to make room; deftly, he crosses it back up her arm, over her chest, under her right axilla, and back to the left shoulder. When he has repeated the pattern six times, he leans back. "You know how to do that on your own, I trust?"

I nod.

"Excellent. She will need it replaced every five to six days, the skin cleaned with alcohol between each resetting. I'll leave you the muslin."

He does not ask again whether I am capable, and for that I am grateful. "Of course."

My words are accompanied by Stella's rising wail. "Oh." I straighten. "My daughter." The lie, however temporary, feels more and more natural with each passing day. "If you'll excuse me."

Dr. Morrison nods. "Of course."

I am not one to share personal information unbidden, but I rush to clarify. I do not want to lose the respect of the one man who does not seem distrustful of my knowledge. Do not want him to think me a loose woman. "Her father was consumptive."

I gesture down at my stiff gray dress to signify my state of mourning. Though the untruth leaves me hot with shame, I have little choice. And I have grown accustomed to guilt.

"My condolences."

"Thank you." I smile slightly and retrieve Stella. When I return with her to Mrs. Wallace's bedroom, the woman's eyes are open.

"She is beginning to regain consciousness." Dr. Morrison grins widely.

"And her blood pressure?"

"Better."

I slip to my knees beside her. "Mrs. Wallace." I put my hand to her cheek. "You're safe." I talk to her until she herself can speak, though I know not what I say. I slide easily into the litany of comfort giving and soothing; my voice, supervisors used to tell me, is like a lullaby.

"She is lucky to have you." Dr. Morrison's voice is low and cool, and I push aside the guilt that I won't be with Mrs. Wallace for much longer now. It's just a matter of time.

The doctor continues. "You could be working in any hospital in the city."

I should be. But I cannot, not anymore. "I am not registered," I confess. "I left school early to marry and then my husband fell ill." I manage to get the lie past the lump in my throat.

"And now?"

I dip my chin to draw his attention to the infant in my arms. "I cannot. Not with Stella."

"Forgive me." Color spreads across the man's cheeks like a port wine stain.

I smile. "No need." I smooth Stella's wispy hair and say what I imagine a mother would say. "My daughter is enough."

"Is she?"

I look up, startled.

"I mean no offense." He looks unsure of himself for the first time. "I have overstepped."

"No, no." I ought to be offended. For myself and for Stella. But this doctor has seen something in me that even those who know me have not: that in leaving the medical profession, I have lost something of my very self. "You are quite nearly right. She is enough. But only." I find that, though I am not her mother, my words are true. Saving Stella makes this all worth it, whatever the outcome. But I will never stop missing nursing.

He nods. "You always wanted to be a nurse?"

"I always wanted to deliver babies," I confess as we lift Mrs. Wallace back into her bed. She is asleep now, rather than unconscious; her heartbeat is regular, and her skin is warm and alive.

"And now you have your own."

"And now I have my own." I look at Stella. *Though she isn't mine forever.*

"Well." Dr. Morrison wipes his palms on the front of his pants. "I am glad that I will be leaving the lovely Mrs. Wallace in good hands."

"Thank you," I gasp as Stella appears to smile at the man. "Her first smile!" I want to freeze the moment, watch Stella beam forever—even if, as a nurse, I know Stella is too young to smile intentionally.

To my surprise, the doctor grasps Stella's fingers between his own. "Are you going to help your mother?" he asks. "Surely you're old enough to have some medical training," he jokes.

I chuckle. "She's just past two months." I regret the words as soon as they're out of my mouth.

But it's too late. Dr. Morrison blinks. "She can't be more than six pounds."

"Close to. She was born two months early," I admit, unable to lie anymore to the doctor. "Two and a half pounds."

His eyes widen. "Yet she survived?"

I should just nod and move on. I should smile and pat Stella's head and let the doctor marvel over her strength. But for more than two months, I have kept the entire world of Luna Park hidden inside me. I am desperate to share it, and whom better to tell? I will never see this doctor again.

So I tell him. "She's a fighter. The Luna Park nurses saved her, and Dr. Couney. Out on Coney Island."

"The showman. The one with the incubators."

I nod. "More than a showman."

"Thank the Lord. How terrifying it must have been, to risk losing the one piece of your husband that remained."

I cannot help but shake my head as I think of Michael Perkins. "I do not love the girl for her father. I love her because she is my Stella. My star."

I gaze into her gemstone eyes as I say it. It's a dangerous thing, to love this girl. But the danger doesn't make it any less real.

"Well, she is lucky to have such a qualified, devoted mother." Dr. Morrison smiles. "Good-bye, Stella." He bows. "Good-bye, Nurse Anderson."

I bite my lip, pleased to be addressed again as the nurse I wish to be. "Good-bye, Dr. Morrison. Thank you for your assistance."

Only when he is gone do I question my manners. Should I have offered him coffee, tea? What is the etiquette for engaging with a man who has made a doctor's house call in the dark of the city's cavernous night? And worse, what had possessed me to tell the doctor about Luna Park? My natural reserve has always suited me, and here I am blurting out things that would better stay secret. I sigh, reassuring myself that Dr. Morrison will forget about us. He won't see us again, this almost-nurse and almost-daughter. We'll fade into the back of his mind; we'll disappear. If he ever returns to Mrs. Wallace's, Stella and I will surely be gone.

"Well," I murmur to Stella. "I suppose there's nothing to do for it now. The next time we need a doctor it will be Dr. Shelton." I put Stella down and change into my nightdress. "We won't see Dr. Morrison again."

But I am wrong. The doctor calls in the morning, and I assure him that Mrs. Wallace is doing better. When I mention the pain in her collarbone, however, Dr. Morrison reacts as if I have told him she has had a heart attack. "I'll be over this afternoon," he promises. "Can you wait that long?"

"Surely some pain is natural?"

"Oh, yes," he apologizes. "I didn't mean to alarm you. But don't you think she would like to take something for it?"

"I suppose so."

"Unless"—a laugh rises in his throat—"Mrs. Wallace has some bootleg whiskey tucked away in those cabinets of hers."

I smile, though he cannot see me. "We will see you later, then. Thank you."

When I hang up, Mrs. Wallace clucks her tongue. "That doctor," she sighs, "acting just like my daughter-in-law."

"Pardon?"

"All aflutter. Charlotte is sweet as honey and about as sensible, too. Not a calm bone in that girl's body."

I stifle a laugh as I gaze upon Mrs. Wallace's indignant face.

"You," she specifies, "are not like that. You told me what happened last night as if we were taking a stroll through the park."

This time, I do laugh. "Perhaps. But not every woman has had the training that I have." I shrug lightly. "I am merely fortunate."

Mrs. Wallace waves her hand as if to dismiss my claims. She grimaces, and I place my hand on her good shoulder.

"Aflutter or not, Dr. Morrison will be your favorite when he brings that medication." I grin.

And he is. He's Stella's favorite, too; she doesn't take her eyes off him the entire time he's here.

"Good afternoon, little star." He thumbs her forehead gently. Few men would be anything other than wary around my daughter, and I smile at Dr. Morrison.

"Are you in obstetrics?"

"No," he admits, "though perhaps I should be."

"It was my favorite ward."

"Remind me where you trained?"

I hesitate, loath to give more clues to my past, but his warm eyes disarm me. "Bellevue."

"I'm sorry you couldn't graduate," he says.

I open my mouth to thank him and then shut it again, suddenly uncertain I've heard him correctly. "Pardon?"

"The hospital. I'm sorry you weren't able to finish your training. It must have been hard, to get so close and then to leave. Whether it was your choice or not."

"I . . . yes. Yes, it was." Of course it was. The doctor's words should not come as a shock after our conversation last night, but I know of no other person who would say the same. God knows the other women who dropped out to marry or raise children were looked at with a faint modicum of relief, as if they were only finally fulfilling their true and natural purposes. To the rest of the world, the only tragedy is the death of my supposed husband; the thought that I might miss nursing is impossible to fathom.

Except, apparently, for this man. This strange Dr. Morrison, who seems less like the doctors I know and more like—well, I don't know who. The doctor is not sad enough to remind me of my late father. He is passionate, not bitter and disappointed to be teaching women like the profe ors at Linden Hall. I look away from Stella and up at the man. "It was very hard. Thank you for your sympathy." The words sound trite and generic, but I mean them. *Thank you*, I am saying, *for seeing me.* "Would you ever leave it? The medical profession, I mean?"

He shakes his head. "Never. So many people are sick, so many people are dying . . ." He breaks off. "How horrible that sounds." He smiles wryly. "But I only mean that there are so many reasons for this job."

"To save people."

"To save people," he agrees. "I think I would like delivering babies, too. Serving someone so vulnerable and dependent."

His words remind me of Hattie. Stella's—*Margaret's*—delivery, Hattie's vulnerability in the face of her husband's control.

Stella falls into crying as if she can sense the change in my mood. "Oh." I pat her tiny nose. "She's hungry." We are upstairs outside Mrs. Wallace's bedroom, and I nod to the stairs. "Her bottle is in the kitchen."

I readjust Stella in my arms as I near the staircase. "Here." Dr. Morrison reaches out. "Let me."

I hesitate only a moment. "Thank you," I say as I carefully pass Stella over and then run downstairs. I'm back quickly, and return to find Stella humming happily in the doctor's arms. "Hmm." I squint at Stella. "Maybe you weren't so hungry after all!"

Dr. Morrison laughs as he passes her over to me. "She just knows there's no point in crying to the strange man in the house.

No milk." He holds his hands up to show Stella. "All I've got on me is whiskey."

"They gave her a drop every day at the island." I quickly look down at Stella and away from Dr. Morrison. That's the second time I've offered information about Stella unbidden. I must be even more desperate to share the miracle of Stella than I realize. Or perhaps the doctor is just that type of listener, the type to make you forget you're talking at all.

Dr. Morrison raises his eyebrows. "I suppose it worked for her."

"Everything did. The incubators, the nurses, the feeding spoons . . . it's an amazing facility."

Dr. Morrison wrinkles his brow. "I would have thought . . . well . . ."

I laugh. "You would have thought it an unsavory place, you mean."

The doctor shrugs in a way that turns his shoulders inward, and I see him suddenly as he must have been as a boy. "I'm sorry."

"No." I realize too late that contradicting him so is rude. "I would have thought the same, had I not been there myself. It's sandwiched beside a roller coaster and the Lilliputian Village, after all! And it's a dime to get in and ogle at the infants as if they're mere sideshow freaks."

He blinks with wonder. "How incredible. I'll have to visit"—he smiles—"and perhaps I can convince you to give me a guided tour?"

My nurse's training is all that keeps my face from dropping into abject terror. This is why I never should have mentioned the incubators to this man. What is it about him that made me do it?

I settle on a neutral answer. "Unfortunately, the facility does not reopen for another eight months." Noncommittal.

"Hmm." Dr. Morrison's voice is low, as if he is actually disappointed. "I really would like to see it. Do you know, by any chance, whether Stella's success is typical?"

"Oh, yes!" I hug Stella to my chest. I can talk about this: general statistics and procedures that have nothing to do with Stella herself. "Eighty-five percent of the babies survive, ones that wouldn't make it a day at the hospital."

"How?"

I am so eager to share the wonder of the place that saved Stella that it all spills out despite my slight sense of misgiving. I describe their filtered oxygen and temperature regulation, the nurses and their love and cleanliness, the way that babies too young to suckle drink through the nose using pipettes and folded spoons. "He's been there succeeding with these babies for over twenty years"—my characteristically smooth tone rises into something sharp—"yet the hospitals still refuse to do the same!"

The doctor, leaning against the wall outside Mrs. Wallace's bedroom in a way that makes him look less like a doctor and more like a man, shakes his head. "I've had little experience in hospitals," he admits, "always having served privately. But it seems to me that the benefit of the institution is to house the equipment that a physician such as myself cannot cart around, equipment such as those incubators."

"I completely agree!" Why do I, normally so calm, blink as if about to burst into tears? "Bellevue does have the newest equipment in all the other wards, you know. But the babies get neglected, even though we had the first obstetrics ward in the nation. But it's primarily for the mothers, and certainly not for the early babies. I gather they're viewed as too much of a risk to spend the money on."

Dr. Morrison opens his mouth and then closes it again.

"What is it?"

"Nothing," he assures me, "nothing, really."

Again, it is not my place to question a doctor. But I keep my gaze fixed on his face for just a moment. Long enough to tell him that I still want to know.

He relents. "I've also heard tell that others, other medical professionals even, don't *want* to save the babies who come early. Some of them are of the opinion that they won't turn out . . . right. Or that they'll pass their"—he coughs uncomfortably—"weakness onto their children. I'm sorry, I shouldn't have even begun."

I brace myself as if on the deck of a boat, my legs tense and rooted. "They're 'undesirable.'" I've heard the word at Bellevue whispered under the breaths of doctors reluctant to serve the drunkards, the mentally handicapped, the cripples, the patients in the new psychiatry ward that is the first of its kind.

Undesirable is the word used to describe the ones doctors view as burdens on society. The ones they are reluctant to save. Yet matters are worse in nearly every other corner of the medical world. Bellevue alone is revolutionary in its willingness to serve anyone and everyone who comes through its doors. They didn't turn a soul away even during the Spanish flu, though I've heard beds lined the hallway like toy soldiers.

"They aren't." Dr. Morrison's response is instantaneous. "They aren't undesirable. Just look at your daughter."

"No. No. Of course not. *I* know that. But to know there are so many people who could think such a thing . . ."

"I'm sorry I ever mentioned it."

I shake my head. "I'm a nurse, Dr. Morrison. It's my job to see the nasty side of things. And then it's my job to make them better."

CHAPTER SIXTEEN

Stella Wright, January 1951

I need an action plan. Something to do, somewhere to go. I can't sort out this mess sitting still in this stuffy office, but it's hard to think of answers when I hardly know what questions to ask. I need more information about my mom, need to explore the world she inhabited before I came along. I think again of my parents' marriage certificate and march outside to find a pay phone.

"Operator?"

"Number, please."

I recite the number of Ann Leslie, my mother's closest friend. Well, her closest friend as far as I know. I'm beginning to wonder how well I truly knew my mom. Maybe she had a secret stash of friends hidden away somewhere.

"Mrs. Leslie." I nearly cry at the sound of her voice. Her Midwest drawl is a relic from my childhood, a near extension of my mother herself. "It's Stella. Stella Wright."

"Stella!" Mrs. Leslie sounds as overcome as I. "Oh, Stella. How are you, darling?"

"I'm managing. And yourself?"

"The same, dear. The same."

I pause a beat. "I'm calling because I actually have a question for you. About my mom."

The woman laughs gently. "Let's see if I can answer it."

"Do you know if she was ever a nurse? It would have been before I was born."

"A nurse? Althea? Oh, no, dear. Absolutely not. She hated blood, don't you know? Couldn't volunteer at the hospitals with us because of it. Remember when the rest of us went in and helped at Bellevue in the early forties during the war?"

"Of course," I murmur, though I don't. Presumably because Mom didn't go along.

"We invited her every week, but she always went pale and told some story about needles and blood. She couldn't stand the sight of it. Surely you knew that?"

"Yes, yes. How could I have forgotten? Thank you for reminding me."

Though Mrs. Leslie cycles through all the required niceties, she must be able to tell I'm distracted. When the telephone interrupts us to say we are running out of time and to put in more coins, she lets me go. "Take care, dear. You go ahead and call if you need anything." After her merciful farewell, I set down the receiver with a hard click. All these new discoveries have been strange and hard to decipher, but this single conversation threatens to be my unraveling. My mother, afraid of blood? Far from it! My mom always took charge in the case of an injury. She was the one to deftly wrap my arm when I fell from the curb into the road as a child, unfazed by the angle of the bone in my shoulder. She was the one to pull out my splinters, quiet and dogged in her determination.

And when I cut myself making vegetable lasagna at age fifteen, my mother slept in my room so she could change the bandages soaked through with deep red blood. She sang to me so I wouldn't cry looking at the gash, but she didn't need to sing to keep herself calm.

My mother lied to Ann Leslie. That, more than the letter or the legal documents or the thumbprint, convinces me she had secrets.

But what were they? And why?

Overwhelmed, I put my head back and breathe deeply, summoning all my energy to keep from crying. I want so desperately to be able to call my mom. Without her, who do I have to talk to?

Jack, she would tell me. She was so happy when I married him. I suppose she'd feared that I wouldn't meet a man who'd accept me and my headstrong ways.

"You'll never find a husband," I recall a well-respected professor telling me my freshman year at Vassar. She'd pulled me aside after a class in which I'd snapped back at a male student who'd claimed the Brontës weren't worth studying, and I didn't know whether to be offended by her remark or honored by it. Herself unmarried in middle age, the woman had ended up a professor of female literature. Didn't seem so bad to me.

I met Jack three days later. Against all odds, he had ended up at Vassar as one of just thirty-six male students admitted that April: three percent of the student body. Roosevelt's Servicemen's

Readjustment Act of 1944 had sent so many G.I.s into universities free of charge that there was no room left for them in traditional schools. Driven by patriotism, women's colleges such as ours, all-female since its founding in 1861, began opening their doors to the men. Our thirty-six were local Dutchess County men recently discharged with honor, and though I was curious about these boys, I was not impressed by them. The whole lot seemed to be shameless flirts—and while I could not blame a veteran for craving a woman's companionship, I feared that their pleasure-seeking would disrupt the haven that Vassar had become for us girls.

And the bragging! Everywhere the men gathered were choruses of bravado and self-proclaimed heroics. Yes, we supported the G.I. Bill. Yes, we welcomed these men into our fold. But there was only so much swaggering hubris I could handle. Jack has told me since that the majority of the soldiers were not truly as self-important as they seemed; rather, the men lacked confidence after the war and feared ostracism in a world of women. At the time, however, I considered the lot of them pompous fools.

Except for Jack. He was different. When I first stumbled upon him, he was tucking into a signature Vassar Devil: ice cream, chocolate cake, and fudge.

Sitting alone on a bench outdoors, he looked up as I passed. "This," he mumbled with dark crumbs pasted on his chin and caked in the corners of his lips, "is the best part of being discharged."

A laugh escaped me. "I can tell."

His face reddened, incongruously childish for a man who had

been through war. "Sorry." He searched in vain for a napkin. "Battle wasn't great for our table manners."

My laugh came out like a bark. "I can tell that, too."

He'd merely groaned in response, offering his half-eaten dessert as a token of peace. "Here. Help me make up for it."

Now, I can nearly taste the chocolate we shared. Rich and decadent, warm fudge and cold ice cream.

Maybe I should call Jack. My fingers brush the smooth curve of the telephone as I start to lift it. Perhaps my husband would see these mysteries—the letter, Margaret's death and thumbprint, my mother's late marriage and her apparent lies—more clearly than I can.

Or perhaps he'll tell me to forget it all. To come home and focus on our future instead of the past. And part of me . . . part of me is tempted.

I crash the phone back into its receiver. I won't call him. Something in me thinks I owe it to my mother to find out who she was before I came along. And I owe it to me, too. I can't return home as listless as I was when I left. Here, I have a goal. A goal that matters.

I finger the letter in my pocket. Hattie Perkins to Nurse Anderson. *My* Althea Anderson. I don't know where this road is taking me, but I have to follow it. I miss my mother too much not to claim everything that's left of her.

I reread Hattie's letter and then close it back up. No more clues. I look again at the envelope addressed to Michael Perkins and flip to the return address. *1208 Surf Ave., Brooklyn.*

Brooklyn. What on earth would a tiny, premature baby be

doing away from both the hospital and her parents—not even in Manhattan but across the river?

I pick up the phone again and ask the operator for 1208 Surf Avenue. After a brief pause, she informs me that Coney Island's Luna Park is closed for the winter. I thank her and hang up, bouncing on my toes. Coney Island seemed strange enough, but Luna Park? What were infants doing at the amusement park?

Just because the park is closed in January doesn't mean I can't find out. The public library in Bryant Park has a local room; surely, I'll find something there.

I hail a taxicab to take me back toward Midtown. When I'm half a mile away from 42nd Street and Fifth Avenue, I ask the driver to stop, and I get out. I've missed the city, and I want to walk its streets again. I crane my neck as I walk beneath the massive steel bars that crisscross the sky, wondering at the construction men perched with their sandwiches atop them.

A sigh escapes me as I reach the library and gaze upon its stone pillars. My mother loved this place like a second home, and we would spend hours curled up in its polished corners. She used to read to me in her steady voice: nursery rhymes, children's books, and sometimes the poetry she loved so much.

Climbing the steps now, I remember the days I spent hopping up them, the year I christened the lion statues my special friends. "Hi, Joe. Bill." I whisper their old names as I pass them and step inside.

I give my coat to the attendant and stand in the grand Astor Hall lobby for a moment, gazing up at the detail on the walls. Just being here makes me feel as if I'm closer to my mother. She had a full-time job keeping me safe as I skipped around the lobby, grazing the other visitors and, several times, nearly knocking over the candelabras underneath the arched doorways.

I make my way to the local room, my heels clacking against the tile floor, and approach the librarian.

"This might be an odd request," I begin, "but do you know anything about Luna Park and the treatment of premature babies?"

I keep my head high, though I can't help but feel ridiculous, and am surprised when the librarian smiles. "Oh, yes. The man who ran the place, Dr. Couney, died just last year. There was a big buzz about it."

"The man who ran what place, exactly?"

"The incubator ward! He ran them on Coney Island and out in Atlantic City, too. Saved thousands of lives."

I shook my head. "I knew there was a hospital on Coney Island, but I didn't realize it was part of Luna Park. How unusual."

"Oh, no, dear. It wasn't a hospital. They were part of a show."

I shake my head, struggling to understand.

"Listen. The doctor died in March of last year, so I'd recommend his obituary if you want the overview. You can find it in the periodicals room."

Thanking the librarian, I fade quietly into the periodical stacks. I pass over the microfiche in favor of the more recent paper newspapers. As the woman predicted, I find Couney's obituary on the first page of the March 2, 1950, *New York Times*.

> Dr. Martin A. Couney, 80, a specialist in the care of prematurely born infants, who for a number of years conducted a baby incubator station at Coney Island and

who also exhibited such babies to the public at fairs, died last night at his home, 3728 Surf Ave., Sea Gate.

Surf Avenue again. The man lived close to his babies.

A pioneer in incubator methods of treating premature babies, Dr. Couney is credited with having saved the lives of more than 6,500 infants placed under his care.

Six thousand, five hundred infants? I nearly drop the paper, I'm so taken aback.

He was born in Alsace shortly before the Franco-Prussian War and studied medicine in Breslau, Berlin and Leipzig. He did post-graduate work in Paris under the late Pierre Constant Budin, noted French pediatrician, and then came to the United States.

Dr. Couney started exhibiting the "incubator babies" more than fifty years ago. After conducting exhibits in London, Berlin and at the Pan-American Exposition in Buffalo he had shows at both Dreamland and Luna Park, Coney Island. The night Dreamland was destroyed by fire, the babies were saved by a speedy transfer to the Luna Park incubators.

The "Incubator Doctor" was a physician first and a showman after. It was his boast that he did not receive fees for the infants he cared for, but used the exhibition method to pay the excessive costs of treatment in the days before hospitals started to give specialized care to premature babies.

Babies were sent to him from hospitals and clinics from various parts of the country.

I shiver. Bellevue was one of those hospitals, and Margaret was one of those babies. But Hattie never saw her daughter again; was she one baby Dr. Couney wasn't able to save?

His wife, Mrs. Anabelle Maye Couney, died in 1936. A daughter, Hildegarde Couney, who was Dr. Couney's principal aide, survives in his home.

Funeral services will be held at 1 pm tomorrow at Kirschenbaum's Westminster Chapel, 1153 Coney Island Ave. Interment will be in Cypress Hills Abbey.

I read the obituary again. *A daughter, Hildegarde Couney, who was Dr. Couney's principal aide, survives in his home.* I copy down the address and tuck it beside the letter and the thumbprint in my purse.

"Find what you needed?" the librarian asks politely as I leave.

"Oh, yes." I thank her with a smile. "I know where I'm going next."

My mother and father never took me to Coney Island as a child. I never questioned it. I couldn't picture my calm, collected mother on a roller coaster or parading around in a bathing suit. We did other things together instead. The nights I got restless and wished for a sister or a brother, Mom always knew what to do, whether it was dressing up like Nancy Drew and Bess Marvin or letting me stay up late to catch fireflies.

"Bioluminescence," Mom taught me, pointing with her thin fingers to the end of the bugs' abdomens. We'd put our little friends in jars and set them on the windowsills for night-lights. By morning, they'd always escaped. I wonder now if my mother let them go.

Now, as I sit in the taxi on the way to Brooklyn, I remember it all: catching fireflies, baking cakes, playing dress-up. So many cherished memories. What will I find out today? Will whatever it is taint the recollections I have of my mother?

I'm relieved when my thoughts are disrupted by our arrival at the Couneys' home. It's the pale yellow of a melted candle: skinny at the top and with widening layers beneath.

I knock on the door before I can doubt myself. Before I can think too much about what I'll discover.

The woman who opens the door cannot possibly be Dr. Couney's daughter. With lines disappearing into the folds of her neck, she is decades older than my mother. Heavyset and with hair that used to be dark, the woman fills the door like a shadow. "Yes?"

"Good afternoon." I reach out to shake her hand. "I'm Mrs. Stella Wright. Is Dr. Couney's daughter in? I'm hoping to learn about a girl who was one of your incubator babies back in the twenties."

"She is." The woman nods. "But I'm Nurse Louise Recht. I worked with Martin for forty-four years. You can talk to the both of us."

"Thank you."

Nurse Recht leads us to a sitting room that, like the outside of the house, is a cross between decadence and decay. Dim lighting reveals a red velvet sofa slumped alone along one edge of the room. No carpet covers the floor, and the cold radiates from the hardwood through my shoes and into my toes as I cross the room. I look around as I sit. Where are the trinkets? The paintings and vases that go with such rich fabric and dark mahogany furniture?

"Hildegarde will get you tea." Nurse Recht aims the comment at the woman who has just appeared from the stairway. Like the nurse, she is sturdy and dark-haired. Though younger than the other woman, she wears a set of glasses that sit uncomfortably atop her nose.

"Of course," she murmurs, exiting the room. She returns with a teapot and three chipped china mugs.

"Thank you." My voice is painfully loud as I take the cup.

We sit in a lopsided triangle. I am on the depressed sofa cushions, Nurse Recht sits in an armchair nearby, and Hildegarde is set farther back on a streaked wooden chair.

"How do you do?" I nod at Hildegarde. "I am Mrs. Stella Wright. I'm here to ask about Margaret Perkins, one of the Luna Park babies back in the late 1920s." The woman's face remains impassive, no quirked eyebrow or tightened lip suggesting even a flicker of recognition.

Nurse Recht intervenes. "Hildegarde here mostly ran the Atlantic City location, but I was at Coney."

"Do you remember her? Margaret?"

"We had thousands of babies." Nurse Recht purses her lips at me as if I suggested otherwise. "I don't remember the names of each one."

"What about my mother's name, Althea Anderson? She was a nurse at Bellevue."

I think. My mother didn't graduate from Bellevue, according to the school's reports. But she signed a birth certificate there.

"Bellevue didn't usually send us their babies." Hildegarde frowns.

"No . . ." Nurse Recht holds up a finger. "But there was the one time. I don't remember the baby's name, but the nurse who brought her was here every day for two months. Althea." She looks up at me. "Your mother?"

"Yes." Barely able to contain my excitement, I pull out the portrait of my mother I keep in my pocketbook. "She's quite young in it, but I imagine she would have looked much the same when I was born." I pass the image to Nurse Recht, who startles. The photograph was taken when my mom graduated from high school, and she looks worlds younger than I recall ever having seen her. In the photograph, her collarbones jut out below a string of pearls, and her slightly pointed chin is tucked toward her shoulder. Dark hair like Nurse Recht's or Hildegarde's is pulled back in plaits atop her head, and the tip of a bouquet is revealed at her chest. She isn't beautiful, but she is mine. I reach back for the image. "You recognize her."

"Yes." Nurse Recht smiles. "We became good friends. Like I said, she was here almost every day."

"And it paid off. Look at you now!" Hildegarde raises her eyebrows. "The spitting image of Marilyn Monroe."

"What do you mean?"

"You're like me." Hildegarde points to her own body. "Proof of the incubators' success. Dad told reporters how much I weighed till the day he died. But he would have loved to have a pretty girl like you in the papers instead."

"Do you mean to say you were one of the incubator babies?"

"Six weeks early, 1907."

My head swims. "But wait. I wasn't—I mean, I'm not—"

"The baby Nurse Althea Anderson brought to Luna Park was not *her* baby," Nurse Recht interrupts. "The mother was recovering from birth and couldn't come herself."

I breathe out with relief. "That's right. *I* wasn't the baby. Her name was Margaret, and the mother's Hattie. Do you remember what happened to her?"

"I can't tell you if she was a Margaret or not, but Althea's girl made it just fine. Althea took her home that September, when we were closing down the park. She was probably—I don't know, five pounds by then? Big enough to survive. Althea was taking her back to her parents, and I never did hear anything else about her. Never saw Althea again, even, which surprised me."

I shake my head. "Are you sure it was September that she took the baby home?"

"Most definitely. I know Althea was with us that whole summer, till Labor Day."

My next question is indelicate, but I have to ask. "Do you recall whether my mother was expecting her own child at the time?" It would explain why she didn't graduate—she was pregnant with me, dropped out of school, and married my father.

Though the timeline seems off, since I was born September 5. Just days after Labor Day, when she was still working and ferrying babies back and forth across the boroughs.

Nurse Recht laughs, interrupting my thoughts. "Oh, no. They

wouldn't have kept her on at Bellevue if she were. And she was skinny as a rail, that Althea. Looked more like a preemie all grown up than Hildegarde does."

The two nurses are still talking, but I miss what they say. Part of me is scrambling to piece everything together; part of me is resisting. I don't snap back into the present until Hildegarde plunks a thick album in front of me. "Here are newspaper clippings and photographs from over the years," she says. "You might find them interesting."

I pull the album toward me and flip through the pages.

INCUBATOR MAN SAVES 2,750 LIVES!

**STRANGEST PLACE ON EARTH FOR HUMAN TOTS
TO BE NURSED, FED, AND CARED FOR:
YET THE SYSTEM IS PERFECT.**

**INFANT WEIGHING POUND AND A HALF
MAKES BID FOR LIFE.**

SAVES 10,000 LIVES.

PLEASED WITH BABY PLANTS AT CONEY.

SMALLEST BABY IN THE WORLD.

**HOME RUN AFTER BEING BORN
A DUBIOUS 2 POUNDS.**

The articles range from 1903 to the late 1930s, and a few clippings even hail from outside the state of New York. I stop flipping when I reach one with a picture. A younger Hildegarde stands in a nurse's pinafore, her gaze steady toward the camera. She has an infant in each hand—not in each arm, but each *hand*. An empty milk bottle sits on a table beside her, and the babies are the very same height and even width as the narrow glass pitcher. Unintentionally, I gasp, and Hildegarde smiles slightly. "I wish I remembered their names. Cute little things."

Nurse Recht shakes her head. "It's so hard. We fought for those babies day and night, but they all grew up and left us eventually. Too many names to count."

"Of course." I think of her words. *We fought for those babies.* "I imagine it was hard work."

Nurse Recht smiles wryly. "Hard work in and of itself—the machinery, the hours, the feedings, the diapers. But harder was the outside world and its clamor. No one else thought these babies could survive. No one else wanted them to."

I think of James, whose parents doubted he could read. Of Mary Ellen, who Principal Gardner is convinced will never be more than an oversized baby doll.

"But you did it anyway," I breathe.

"Of course we did, all the way through forty-three, when the incubators finally made it into hospitals. Until then, we had to. These babies could survive. Look at Hildegarde! The people who called us devil worshippers, freaks, circus acts . . . the ones who accused us of being liars and frauds and con artists . . . they couldn't save you. But we could. So"—she shrugs, no-nonsense—"we did."

"And my mother was part of that. Saving those babies."

Both women nod. And to think my mother never let on, that I never knew she was a nurse at all. Why did she never tell me?

I look back down at the scrapbook. I gaze upon those tiny babies, froglike in proportion and antlike in scope. Even with Hildegarde sitting before me, I can hardly believe they survived.

"No one else at the time treated them?" I clarify.

"No." Nurse Recht's voice is hard. "You have to remember, many babies were born at home at that time, and the eugenics movement was not yet associated with Hitler."

I cringe at the man's name.

"The field of eugenics still had many scientific proponents here in America, Mrs. Wright, and they did not think anyone born with any disability should live. Thank God for the men who helped Dr. Couney change things"—she nods reverently—"men now at Bellevue and in Chicago."

"Your Dr. Couney obviously had a different mind-set. Maybe it was his European education. Where did he train?"

It's an innocent question, but Nurse Recht and Hildegarde exchange a tense look and our triangle dissolves. "He studied under Pierre Budin." Why is Hildegarde's voice so stilted?

Nurse Recht lifts her chin. "And his nurses were highly trained. I graduated from la Maternité de Paris. Europe remains the leader in natal care, but I am glad America is changing. Glad we are finished with the eugenics movement and its dangers."

"It has not changed enough." I lift my own chin. "I teach—taught—the disabled. Most of the school administration thinks they should just be institutionalized. Institutionalized! But they're just kids."

Our triangle connects again as Nurse Recht leans forward. "And ours were just babies. Strange, isn't it, what men will do to hide their weakness?"

I've been flipping through the clippings as the nurses and I talk, and I stop now. "This bow." I point to a wide velvety bow wrapped around an infant's concave stomach. "Was that something you did?"

"Blue or pink," Hildegarde smiles. "Every one."

My shoulders rise so that my elbows lock, hands still framing the photograph. "My mother kept mine," I whisper.

"Yours?"

If my mother was telling the truth all those years, if the bow really was mine, yes. *I* was there at the island. I myself existed in that strange scientific world of metal and tubes.

"It could have been Margaret's," I try, more for myself than for the nurses. A blurry truth is starting to surface, but I can't let my mind go there, not until there's proof.

"She was devoted to that girl." Nurse Recht shook her head. "The same way a mother would be."

I close my eyes as I pull the thumbprint card from my envelope clutch. "Did you all send these out, too?"

"Yes." Hildegarde smiles softly. "My father was quite the showman. Knew exactly how to tug at parents' heartstrings. We did holidays from Father's Day to Chanukah, anniversaries, birthdays."

"This card was in my mother's things, but it's addressed to Michael Perkins. Margaret's father."

"I suppose he gave it to your mother as a token of thanks."

I shake my head. "The address is Bellevue's Nurses' Residence."

The women exchange a look. "Interesting. She must not have known the Perkinses' address."

"And there's one other thing I don't understand. This same Margaret . . . she is listed as having died at birth."

"That's not too hard to explain," Nurse Recht admits. "Hospital record keeping was really quite haphazard until the forties. They may have signed the death certificate before they brought her here, not expecting her to survive."

Easy enough to believe. But if it was merely an administrative mistake, and Margaret survived to return to her mother, why did Hattie never know the color of her eyes? Everything—all of this, my missing birth certificate at the bureau, my mother's slender figure in the summer of 1926—is impossible to ignore, but the very thought of what it might mean terrifies me. "The thing is, I was born September 5, 1926. Two months to the day after Margaret, and that same week my mother took Margaret home."

The nurses exchange a quick, nervous glance. "A coincidence."

"Unless—" I am desperate to share the theory that has sprung up with a terrible, sudden clarity: that I am Margaret, that my mother raised me unbeknownst to Hattie and her husband. I am desperate to share because I am desperate to hear a plausible alternative. "Unless . . ."

CHAPTER SEVENTEEN

Althea Anderson, October 1926

Stella becomes the calendar of my days. Her feedings and naps mark the minutes and hours, and her slowly growing weight charts the passage of days and eventually weeks until September has passed. Mrs. Wallace and Dr. Morrison, whose frequent visits to check on his patient I find myself looking forward to more and more, seem to take almost as much pleasure in Stella's progress as I. Each milestone—Stella's sticking out her tongue in mimicry, turning her head to reach her bottle—is both a joyful celebration and a sobering reminder. While my guilt at Hattie's not being here to see her baby's development is omnipresent, it isn't strong enough to keep me from dreading the day I hear from her.

Each day that passes without her letter feels like a pardon, but still I await my sentence. Ironic, since losing the baby will free me. Without her, I will be able to get a better job, stop wearing all black, sell my pawnshop wedding bands.

But I don't care about being free if it means losing Stella. I didn't birth her, but I watched her come into the world. I watched her fight for life and win—first when she was born, then when she came down with pneumonia, and then again when she was taken from the incubators before Labor Day.

And she watched me. Stella was with me as I ventured into Luna Park's crowds for the first time, as I discovered the oasis of calm within Dr. Couney's incubator wards. Stella was with me as we crossed back into Manhattan and as I stood shamed before Miss Caswell and Miss Hosken; she was with me as I held my head high before the pawn seller's smug smile. She was with me when I knocked on Mrs. Wallace's door and with me when Dr. Morrison entered into our lives.

When Hattie takes back her baby, I'll lose Mrs. Wallace and Dr. Morrison, too. They've both become so dear so quickly. I bask in the warmth of Mrs. Wallace's delight when she holds Stella, her smile taking years off her face. I relish Dr. Morrison's visits and companionship and the way he talks to Stella like she's a tiny adult. As for his conversation with me, I feel a thrill when those gray eyes look into mine like I matter.

A tear slips from my eye, but I brush it away before it can fall to Stella's cheek. She's nestled in the crook of my elbow when we hear a metal clink outside, the low whistle of the postman.

Every day I collect the mail with fear and anticipation in my heart. Now, breath short, I force myself to move.

A letter for Mrs. Wallace from a friend in Colorado. A letter from her late husband's sister.

And then my heart stops. An envelope from the Perkinses' residence in Washington Heights.

I swallow. I don't want to open it. A panicked thought swiftly crosses my mind, that I might dispose of the letter and none would be the wiser. But of course that's not true.

The time has come for my sentencing. I have to know what Hattie says.

I pull the sheet from inside the envelope. The note is surprisingly brief, but I suppose all I requested was a date and time. I sit down to read.

Miss Anderson,

I close my eyes. How quickly I've been demoted from "nurse."

Do not write to my wife again. The grief is making her hysterical as it is. She does not need new details to dwell on and drag her back into the past. Neither she nor I wishes to hear from you. My wife is in no condition to be a mother, and we are better off without the baby or her memory.

Thank you in advance for acting in accordance with our wishes.

Sincerely,
Mr. and Mrs. Michael Perkins

Mr. and Mrs. Michael Perkins! I don't believe that for a second. Whether Ida delivered the note to Hattie and Michael found it, or whether he took it before his wife could ever read it, I don't know. But I don't believe Hattie had a hand in this response.

My anger at Michael boils, and I breathe deeply to keep it

from bubbling over. Michael Perkins is controlling and demanding, but perhaps he is trying to protect his wife from further heartbreak. Grief does strange things, and both he and Hattie are suffering. When I bring them their baby, everything will change.

Dread sits heavy in my belly. I can't imagine my life without Stella. But her parents need her, and I must take her home.

Today.

I claim a medical emergency involving a cousin, and Mrs. Wallace gives me permission to take the afternoon off. With my heart in my throat, I contemplate returning without Stella. I'll tell Mrs. Wallace we have to move in to help said cousin, and that I've left Stella napping there until I can get back. That is, if my grief doesn't fell me before I make it back to Mrs. Wallace's. I feel remorse that I won't be giving the kind woman two weeks' notice, but there's nothing that can be done.

Because it's a Thursday, I pray that Hattie is at home and her husband at work.

For the first half of Stella's and my ride to the Perkinses', I force myself to point out the buildings and parks we pass. These are my last moments with my darling and I make the most of them, holding her close and taking in her scent. Kissing her downy cheek. A subdued panic beats in my chest, mixed with heavy sadness that weights my limbs. I am the only one who has been with her from the moment she was born. I am the only one who knows her true story.

After a time, I can no longer summon the energy to feign

excitement over the landmarks that signify Stella's exit from my life. "Sorry, Stell," I breathe.

Margaret, I remind myself. Her name is Margaret. How silly, that the name seems to me to change her very being. When she is Stella, she is vibrant. She is a fighter. She is mine. But as Margaret, she is another woman's baby—one that, like a fragile object, I must handle with care. One that, like a package, I must deliver to her rightful home.

I shift away from the window and rest against the back of the bench, clutching Stella—Margaret—the baby—to my chest. Dizzy, I breathe in her milky scent, let it flood my body with calm. In, out. In, out.

If only I could make the inhale last forever.

The most notable feature of Michael and Hattie's row house is its four large windows. Stella will like those, I imagine. She's a curious baby. The curtains on the ground floor are pulled back to let in the last fading rays of autumn's light, and I cannot help but peer through them as Stella and I approach the building. I have lied to my employers and the Luna Park nurses, stolen from the hospital, deceived an innocent old woman, and kidnapped a baby. What is snooping compared to the rest of my crimes?

My sins, when listed, seem so much greater outside the context in which they have been committed. All I've meant to do is protect the baby.

Stella squeaks, and I squeeze her in response. Michael is home. The figures of Stella's—Margaret's—parents move quickly

behind the glass panes that separate us. Though Hattie is gesticu-
lating wildly, Michael stands still and erect. I had hoped to see
Hattie alone, but I can't prolong this any longer.

Still, my feet don't move. Stella and I stand back, watching
the scene through the window play out like a silent film. Michael's nostrils flare, and I just have time to wonder whether they
are fighting before his hand lifts. But he doesn't slap her. Instead,
he holds his hand up, fingers spread. *Stop*, it says.

Hattie doesn't. She takes a step closer, face contorting to hold
back tears. It is Stella who first senses what is about to happen.
Stella cries out as Michael grits his teeth and shoots his hands
around his wife's neck. Circling both palms around his wife—ten
fingers spread like flowers on a grave—the man shakes her violently before releasing her, pushing her hard enough that she
stumbles back. "Oh," I cry out, instinctively shooting my own
hand over Stella's eyes. "Oh!"

Hattie is on the floor now. I search her face for signs of shock
and find none. Pain, yes. Hurt, undeniably. But no surprise. Hattie's husband has nearly strangled her, shoved her to the floor—
but she doesn't widen her eyes or bring a fluttering hand to her
mouth.

She's accustomed to this. That time in the hospital on September 2 may have been the first time Michael hit his wife, but it
wasn't the last. And this is more than just the second.

I can't help but wonder what role I've played in this violence.
Should I have left well enough alone? Would the two parents
have retreated together into their grief had I not prodded it, poked
it, reminded them of the daughter they believe is lost?

Tears leak from my eyes even as Michael returns to the room and hands Hattie ice for her neck. His expression does not change; his mouth does not move.

Holding Stella, I fight the urge to retch. I've seen women battered nearly to death in the hospital, but I've never watched it happen before my eyes. And oh, God, the act is far more horrible than the injuries resulting from it.

I back away, shaking. I can't risk Michael looking out the window and recognizing me—or, God forbid, his daughter. Who knows what he would do? Kill Hattie? Unleash his violence on the infant?

"We're leaving, Stella." I look down at the innocent little girl and say it again. There's no other choice, is there? Not when Hattie herself told me how grateful she was that her baby didn't ever have to witness this. Not when I don't know what further harm my waltzing in may cause. Not when Stella deserves better.

And off I walk, clutching Stella to my chest and hating myself nearly as much as I hate Michael Perkins. Because under the layers of fear and revulsion and grief, I am relieved.

I don't have to give her up.

We walk, Stella still cradled to my chest. What else is there to do? We walk until Stella is fussy, and I find a patch of sun-mottled grass to stop. I sit beside Stella, who is captivated by the feel of the grass and dirt. "You haven't been outside much, have you?" I laugh. I am awed I can laugh under the circumstances, but Stella's face is the picture of wonder. Her eyes open and shut rapidly as the sunlight bounces off her pupils, her expression somewhere between that of an irate elderly man and a puppy. I resolve to take Stella to Bryant Park more often.

A shiver runs through me. A whole new world is opening before my eyes: a world in which Stella and I can go to as many parks as we want, spend the rest of our days lying in the sun-dappled grass.

The weight of the decision to keep Stella settles upon me. This is a whole different crime—not just medical malpractice or insubordination or deception but *kidnapping*. Pulling Stella from certain death and promising to return her was one thing. But taking another woman's child and raising her as my own is an entirely different one. Now I really could end up in jail, me and my dark plaited hair and nurse's pinafore among the drunks and the murderers and the thieves.

But I would rather be put in jail than condemn Stella to life with a father who belongs in one.

I refuse to subject Stella to the violence of a man who never wanted her.

Especially when mothering Stella these past three months has been as natural as if she were mine alone. Loving Stella is like breathing. I couldn't stop if I tried.

But as I walk through the streets of the city, I recall the myth of Althea, the legendary Greek woman for whom I was unwittingly named. Althea, a woman warned by a prophet that she would kill her own son by fire. Althea, who locked away a burning log to save her son and then, years later, knew exactly where it was when the time came to kill him.

Is that what I am doing for Stella, saving her from a violent home and then plunging her into one built on secrets and lies? Merely prolonging the girl's suffering rather than alleviating it?

You are being absurd, I tell myself. I have based my life on logic and science, and I know that a name is nothing more than a string of symbols and sounds.

But I still can't help but wonder. Am I truly saving Stella, or am I saving myself?

CHAPTER EIGHTEEN

Stella Wright, January 1951

Nurse Recht cuts me off. Her face has closed at the mention of my birth and the timing of my mother bringing Margaret home. She suddenly appears cold and emotionless. "I'm so sorry, dear, but we simply cannot remember that far back. Especially at my age. I am eighty-seven years old, you know." She's a terrible actor; she was as sharp as I just a moment ago. "And actually," she suggests, as if it has just occurred to her, "I do need to get my rest."

Hildegarde stands. "I will help you upstairs, Aunt Louise." She looks to me. "You can see yourself out."

I sit in Hildegarde Couney and Nurse Recht's sad, deflated living room alone and grit my teeth. I can't face the idea of sitting still in a taxicab, new discoveries clamoring for air in my brain all the way back to Manhattan. I refuse to look straight on at the truth that has taken shape.

Instead, I pick up the album the nurses left downstairs. I flip through the pages again, scrutinizing each baby's face for something familiar. It's hard to differentiate their features in the old, grainy photographs. Most of them are girls, their tiny faces prunelike and pinched. But I can't see their eye colors in black and white or tell whether their heads are topped with blond or black. And I'm fooling myself if I think I would recognize my own smile or my mother's thin face in any infant.

I thump the album down and sigh. The ground is shifting beneath my feet; more than anything, I need certainty. And there is only one more person to whom I can think to reach out if I want to find it.

I stand, intent upon leaving and finding a pay phone. As I pass through the kitchen on my way to the door, I spot an old-fashioned telephone half-hidden behind a bowl of softening fruit. I glance behind me. The women are nowhere to be seen.

I dial 411 and ask for Mr. and Mrs. Michael Perkinses' number in Manhattan.

"Please stay on the line." The clipped voice of an operator crackles through the earpiece. I chew my lip in impatience as I wait. The woman returns briefly with a number, its exchange WA-7. So, the Perkinses live in Washington Heights. Their daughter's death certificate already confirmed they are white like my own family, and their residence adds that they are likely middle- or lower middle-class.

Burr, burr. I wait anxiously as the telephone rings and suddenly feel this was an idiotic thing to do. What will I say to whoever picks up? That I have a twenty-four-year-old thumbprint suggesting their dead infant may not have died after all?

I don't have time to deliberate. A quiet "Hello?" on the other end of the line shocks me nearly into dropping the telephone. I wasn't prepared to face a real voice, a real woman.

"Mrs. Perkins?"

"This is she. May I ask who is calling?" The woman's voice is soft like my mother's was, but something in it sounds different. Perhaps it is the timbre of their voices: My mother's was like the old corset I found in the attic yesterday, delicate but laced with steel. This woman speaks as if she is treading across the frozen surface of a pond, as if speaking too loudly will send her crashing into its icy depths.

I shiver. "My name is Stella Wright. I believe you knew my mother, Althea Anderson."

"Oh!" Hattie's voice is high-pitched in surprise. "Oh!" She repeats.

"Who are you talking to?" A deeper voice in the background, harder to make out. Michael?

"Oh," Hattie says for the third time, her voice muffled now. "A—a magazine publisher." The woman's voice is clear again as, I assume, she transfers the receiver back to her lips. "No, thank you," she tells me. "We won't be purchasing a subscription today."

Click.

"Mrs. Perkins?" I am met with the low hum of the dial tone and flap my arms in frustration. She'd recognized my mother's name; that much was clear.

I resist the urge to immediately call the Perkinses again. Obviously, they aren't going to talk to me right now—and I've trespassed long enough.

I hear a foot on the stairs and jump. Slamming the telephone down, I run outside and walk, fighting tears. I feel woozy, like my head's going to float away from me and disappear into the foggy winter sky. I almost wish it would, so everything I've learned wouldn't clamor so loudly within it. The pink ribbon, which means I was a Luna Park baby. The fingerprinted note, which means Margaret was.

My mother, skinny as a rail. Hattie, whose daughter never came home.

Light-headed, I almost think I'm imagining the words on the sign as I approach a dilapidated bus station: *To Luna Park.* I know the park burned nearly to the ground in '44, and then again in '46 and '48. But past and present are colliding in strange and frightening ways today, and the sign almost convinces me that I've found myself in the twenties. That Luna Park is in its heyday.

I collapse onto the bench and wait for the bus to come. It's nearly empty when it does, but I take a spot in the back. I'm not in any condition to talk to the driver.

Instead, I lean back and grapple with what I've learned. Here I am at Coney Island, twenty-three years after I was apparently here as a newborn. But I wasn't here as Althea's daughter.

I was here as Hattie's.

I suddenly feel nauseated and place my head between my knees, breathing deeply.

I feel the woman across the aisle look at me, then reach across to gently touch my shoulder. "I was the same way with my first. Congratulations."

Congratulations?

Oh. I cringe as I realize her mistake. Jack would be thrilled were the woman correct, but no. I am not with child, merely sick with uncertainty. I lack the energy to explain the real source of my nausea, so I smile weakly. "Thank you."

In awkward silence, we drive a mile or two down Mermaid Avenue before the bus stops with a sigh. I step out, thanking the driver, and follow the signs that send me a block south to Luna Park. I know better than to expect grandeur, but the ruins of the place take my breath away. The ground is the same gray as the wintry sky, rubble and ashes still littering the landscape. Here at the entrance, only a stone wall remains, its painted heart faded almost to nothing. In the distance, a minaret still stands, and there are remains of a wooden roller coaster that looks like the curved skeleton of a dinosaur.

A cat appears from underneath a metal scrap and scurries off silently. I can see its ribs, and I press a fist to my mouth. *We fought for those babies day and night*, the nurses said. And now look at the place. The place that saved me, a field of ashes and debris.

This time, I can't stop the tears. My mom is gone, and I don't know what to believe about who she was. And now, even this—this place that made my life possible, this place that the nurses hailed as a bastion of strength and healing—even this is in ruins.

I can't help but see it as a cruel allegory for my life. I've lost my parents and no longer know who they were, I'm jobless, I'm on rocky footing with Jack.

Was it just yesterday morning that I took the train into the city? It feels like a lifetime ago, and suddenly I'm desperate to talk to my husband—the man who's always been willing to serve as a listening ear or a shoulder to cry on. The only person left in this world who knows me and loves me.

I recall seeing a pay phone at the bus stop and I practically fly back, then dial Jack at work.

"Jack!" I cry out when I hear his voice on the other end of the line. "Oh, Jack." I hadn't anticipated the rush of gratefulness I'd feel just hearing his voice.

"Stella? What's the matter?" His voice is urgent with worry, not distant like I feared.

I attempt a laugh, but it sounds more like a sob. "Is it that obvious?"

"Stella, honey, what is it?"

"Everything." I hardly even know where to start, but once I do, the words don't stop. Funneling more and more coins into the machine as the operator interrupts us, I tell Jack everything: about the letter from Hattie and the fingerprint note, my mother's signature on the birth certificate, discovering the year of my parents' marriage, the conversation with Louise and Hildegarde and what I learned about the pink bow. "And now I'm here at Coney Island, Jack, and I don't know who I am anymore. I mean, who was my mother? Did I really almost die at birth? There's so much I don't know about. I *lived* here, Jack, at Luna Park. My life started *here*, and I didn't know I'd ever set foot south of the parkway!" I pause, trying to explain why I'm in tears. "It's just that I don't know who I am all of a sudden. And I have no idea who my mom was, anymore. She wasn't even my real mom." My voice breaks, and I know I'd fall to the ground if I weren't leaning against the phone booth. "It's like everything was a lie, Jack, my whole life. And I can't ask my mom about it." Another sob. "I just feel so . . . alone."

"Honey, you're not alone. You're never alone."

I take a deep breath to calm myself down. "I know," I whisper. "I guess I just forgot."

"Forgot?"

"The way we left things. I didn't know what it meant." I'd felt so far away from Jack, been so afraid that our disagreement when I left had festered in my absence. My obstinacy has burned bridges before.

"Oh, Stella, no. I love you no matter what. You know that. We will work through this"—he pauses—"through all of it."

I grip the phone. "Promise?"

"Promise. I'm just worried about you, Stella. I need to hold you, see that you're safe. I can't wait to see you tomorrow."

I hesitate.

Jack's tone shifts slightly. "Aren't you coming home?"

"I—I think I need to stay another day. I need to visit Hattie."

"Stella, honey, do you really think that's a good idea? Just wait a bit. You called me in tears after making all of these crazy discoveries. I'm not sure now is the best time to go see this stranger when you have no idea what she's like. Stella, please, come home."

"Stranger? She might be my mom, Jack. I can't just stick my head in the sand. I can't come home and sit around day after day wondering about this. Sure, finding out the truth might be hard, but it's not as if ignoring your problems is any better." Overwhelmed, my voice comes out sharp and loud.

"And that's what I do? Just because I don't tell you everything I saw and did in the war?"

My stomach drops. "No, wait, Jack, that isn't what I meant. I was talking about me, saying that I can't leave and just forget any of this happened."

Jack doesn't respond.

"Are you mad?" I finally manage.

"No." Jack's voice is quiet. "Not mad."

"What's the matter, then?"

Jack sighs. "You don't want to come home."

"It has nothing to do with you—"

"I know," Jack interrupts. "I know that. But Poughkeepsie was my decision. And now that you're down in the city, you don't want to come back to this boring life, to sit home alone day after day."

"Jack, honey, that's not it. I just need to figure this out. I can't get my mom back, you know? But I can at least do this one thing. It's like—well, I'm going to the places she went, meeting the people she met. Learning who she really was."

"And who you are."

"Yes." I nearly burst into tears again. "You get it."

"No," Jack says. "I'd do anything to escape the past." His voice hardens. "To figure out who I am without it."

I bite my lip, afraid he'll take offense at my next words. "But you can't." I rush to clarify. "Our pasts are always there. You already know yours, but I need to understand mine."

He takes a slow inhale, a long exhale. A bit of humor creeps back into his voice as he says, "You never do make things easy."

I smile softly and exhale.

"No laugh?"

"The closest to a laugh anyone could get out of me right now."

"I wish I could hold you."

"Me, too. Very soon," I promise.

"I love you, Stella."

"I love you, too."

I hang up and wrap my arms around myself to warm them, smiling softly. Jack and I are going to be okay.

But it's not time to go home yet. I stand up straighter. WA-7, I dial.

Please pick up. My hand clenches around the telephone like I'm going to shatter it. One ring, two rings, three rings. *Please.*

Finally, I hear the click of Hattie lifting the phone on her end. The ringing stops, and the air crackles between us.

I take a deep breath, light-headed. "Hello, Mrs. Perkins. This is Nurse Anderson's daughter again. I understand if you are unable to talk, but—" I'm saved from having to figure out where to go from here by a deep roar, only the beginning of which reaches me before the line goes dead. I jump back in alarm, and the phone cord yanks me forward again. "Mrs. Perkins?" I speak with the hope that my words can somehow disrupt the steady hum of the dial tone. "Ma'am?"

I call one more time, but the phone rings and rings with no answer. They're home, obviously. They're just avoiding me. Or worse.

I place the receiver back in its cradle. *"A magazine publisher"*— Hattie didn't want Michael to know she was talking to me. That last roar echoes in my mind.

And yet she clearly knows something. Hattie recognized either my name or my mother's.

I must find her.

Back at the library, I track down Hattie and Michael's address in an old city directory. The only book I can find is dated 1934, but the address listed is in Washington Heights. I don't think it's too much to hope that it is the same one.

Then again, I have a tendency to let hopes fly away with me. Last year I was certain Mary Ellen's utterance of "hello" meant she would repeat words I said, and I expected to get her speaking fluently. I flush now to remember my eagerness, unfounded and embarrassing in the face of Principal Gardner's skepticism. Jack calls me the Keeper of Grand Ideas, but he's only half right. I'm the Releaser of Grand Ideas. I catch them, entertain them briefly, and then watch them drift away from me when my foresight proves lacking. I do not always, as my father was prone to remind me, "think things through." In that way, I was different from both him and my mother. Though she was always calm, she encouraged my own spontaneity. "Don't settle. And don't you ever stay silent."

I won't. I'll figure this out—who Margaret is, who my mother was, who I am—no matter how many abruptly ended interviews I must endure to do so.

I copy down Hattie and Michael's address. I'll go first thing tomorrow. It being a weekday, I'm hopeful that Michael will be at work and Hattie will be home alone.

I don't know what I'm going to ask her, but she has to have the answers.

CHAPTER NINETEEN

Althea Anderson, November 1926

The phone rings as I set Mrs. Wallace's porridge on the kitchen table. I send up a quick prayer that, whoever is calling, it isn't Mrs. Wallace's son. If he cancels dinner tonight, she will be brokenhearted.

"Hello?"

"Mrs. Anderson?" The deep voice is not that of Mrs. Wallace's distracted son but one I have come to know even better. Dr. Morrison has continued his visits to check on Mrs. Wallace's collarbone throughout the two months I've been here, but I've never known a collarbone injury to last longer than eight weeks. It pains me to think our time with the doctor may be drawing to a close; he provides me my only window to my old life in the medical world. My only window, really, to the world beyond this townhouse. My only connection to someone my own age, to someone who sees me as a peer rather than a caretaker.

"This is she. Is something the matter, Dr. Morrison?"

"No," he says hurriedly. "I simply wanted to ask your permission for something."

I am intrigued. On paper, my life is a wild adventure: subterfuge, secrets, and lies. But my reality is more mundane. I spend my days washing diapers and preparing meals. "Go on." I perch on the balls of my feet, curious.

"I have a meeting tonight with some other physicians from the AMA."

The AMA, the American Medical Association. They are the group responsible for promoting preventive health care, the group currently working on a list of hospitals approved for residency. What could Dr. Morrison possibly be asking me in regard to these illustrious men? My heels quiver.

"It's not an official AMA meeting," he clarifies, "but a group of us meets every other Saturday evening of every month." He laughs. "A thrilling way for a young man to spend his nights."

I can't help but smile. "I am the same. My idea of fun is curling up with a medical text. And who knows? Perhaps I'll get a chance tonight—Mrs. Wallace's family is coming for supper, and I'm off." I laugh. "That is, if Stella cooperates."

A pause. I fear I have made the doctor uncomfortable, spilling my thoughts so. It is not my place as a woman or as an inferior. My heels hit the ground as I open my mouth to apologize, but Dr. Morrison's voice filters through the receiver before I get the chance. "Would you like to come to my meeting tonight, then?"

"Pardon me?"

His voice grows stronger. "I was calling to see whether you would allow me to recount your experience at Dr. Couney's incubator ward. I think my friends would be fascinated. But it would be even better to hear it from you, the true expert. If you aren't working tonight."

Expert. I glow, even as my automatic response echoes through the telephone speaker. "I can't."

And it's true. I can't, can I? I'm a mother, not a nurse. I have secrets to hide, not stories to tell.

I pick the easiest truth to share. "I can't leave Stella here without me."

"Bring her."

"Pardon?" It seems all I can do is ask Dr. Morrison to repeat himself, and I feel foolish. But I cannot possibly be understanding him correctly. Me, bring Stella to a meeting of medical men? I'd be more likely to marry President Coolidge himself.

"It's a very informal meeting, at one of the men's homes. His wife is there with their infant, and I can't imagine your bringing Stella would be any different."

I can. The wife will excuse herself politely after appearing briefly in her most becoming gown; she will set supper on the table and then disappear to care for her child as a woman should. The men will be left commenting on the comeliness and domesticity of their host's wife; the man will bloat with pride.

I, on the other hand, will not be excusing myself. I will be there, crying infant in my lap, as I insert myself into a conversation they are convinced I have no right to invade.

"Unless"—Dr. Morrison corrects himself quickly—"unless there is another reason you do not want to come. Perhaps you would not find it interesting. I apologize if you feel that I am pressuring you."

Perhaps you would not find it interesting. I have worked with doctors to deliver dozens of babies at Bellevue, spent months at Luna Park learning the ways the early ones can be saved. I find the topic of their preservation more interesting than anything else on earth, save my daughter herself. And I suddenly cannot bear Dr. Morrison's thinking I do not. He is the only man who has ever appeared to respect me. I cannot have him believe that his respect is unfounded. Even if it is risky to link myself to the incubators or give the world a trail to follow. I've given up my career for Stella; I can do at least this for myself, and for other babies like her.

And so, closing my eyes, I answer the doctor. "No. I would love to be there. Thank you."

H e arrives to escort me to his friend's at six. Rightly, he assumed that I would be uncomfortable appearing on my own. *Not even on my own,* I chuckle drily, *but worse. With a baby on my hip.*

"Have a good evening, Mrs. Wallace." I bid the woman farewell and cast one last look at her in her finery. I've spent the entire afternoon ensuring that she looks her best for her son and daughter-in-law's visit, and she wears an old-fashioned but beautiful dress of deep magenta.

I feel guilty leaving her. Though the job comes with an evening off each week, I've never taken advantage of it but for that fateful day I went to the Perkinses'.

I pour Mrs. Wallace a glass of water before I go. "I'll be back by nine thirty," I promise her. "Have a good night with your family."

"And you at your meeting," she says.

"Thank you."

I shift Stella slightly in my arms. And then, flexing my toes, I step out onto the stoop.

Dr. Morrison is waiting, and he takes my arm gently as I nod my permission. In winter, six in the evening is well past the night's chilly threshold, and the world is gray and black around us. It wouldn't be safe for Stella and me alone.

I sink into the night in my gray woolen dress, the only one in which Dr. Morrison has ever seen me. The alternatives in this half-mourning charade are white and lavender; the first, too likely to be stained by Stella's spit-up milk; the second, too frivolous in a room of learned men. I have done all I can to ensure that they will take me seriously. I'm grateful I never bobbed my dark hair, and I've parted it and pulled it back into a braided knot.

Still, the doctor's light touch on my arm reminds me I am a woman. He guides us gently, Stella and me on the inside of the sidewalk. He purchases our subway fare, ten cents in total, and escorts me to the car. The conductor opens the door to let us in as we approach, ringing the bell to signal our entrance. "Thank you," I whisper as Dr. Morrison offers me his arm to step off the platform. I cringe as my ring reflects the light in the car. Dr. Morrison is escorting me, touching me, under the assumption that I am a widow. But I am not a widow. I am a girl of twenty-four years old, and I am out for the first time with a man. I imagine the other subway patrons assume us married, Stella our daughter.

If only I could give that gift to Stella. The gift of a real family: husband, wife, baby girl. Instead, she is here with a mother who is a liar and a criminal, a man who is but the emergency physician of her mother's employer. A stranger.

I shouldn't have come.

"Please, take my seat." Dr. Morrison lifts his hat and stands to allow a boarding woman his spot; I nearly follow him, eager suddenly to get off this cramped subway and back to Mrs. Wallace's. The doctor, Stella, and I are a dangerous parody of a family, and my stomach lurches in shame as the subway begins to move. Stella coos. Perhaps the motion of the car simulates the rocking of a mother; I don't know. To me, despite the fabric-covered seats and the wood paneling, the subway is an uncomfortable place. We passengers are strangers, and both our silence and our noise are awkward. It is different at the hospital, where a layer of vulnerability renders a stranger an intimate acquaintance.

The woman sitting beside me watches Stella. I smile politely as I take in the woman's appearance: a working girl. Her hair is bobbed, and a cloche hat sits atop her head. She eyes my rings with envy, and I pull my sleeve in a nervous attempt to hide them. The more people I lie to, however indirectly, the more intense my shame. No wonder I never lied even as a teenager at boarding school: I did not sneak off to smoke or miss my curfew necking with boys in the yard. Even then I would never have described myself as weightless, the way my mother's death hung heavy on my shoulders like a too-big dress—but now, I feel the palpable heaviness of untruths like stones.

At Grand Central, we transition onto the Harlem line that will take us to Scarsdale. Though this is Stella's first time out of the city proper, I scarcely hear the announcements for the train stops we pass. I am so wrapped up in my own thoughts that Dr. Morrison must tap my shoulder lightly to get my attention when it is our turn to alight. I stand with an embarrassed dip of the head.

I lift it as we approach a grand Colonial Revival home. I am determined, despite the baby in my arms, to make a respectable impression on the men within the mansion. I want them to see the fruit of my difficult work, my single-mindedness, my studying and years of practice. I want them, unlike the doctors at Bellevue, to see me with the respect with which they see one another.

A woman swings the white door open when we knock. She wears a pale pink tea gown of crepe de chine, lace fins falling across her otherwise bare shoulders and down her back. I resist the urge to tug self-consciously at my own dress.

"Mrs. Burns." Dr. Morrison bows slightly as he turns from our hostess to me. "Mrs. Anderson. A fellow medical worker."

"How do you do?" Mrs. Burns smiles graciously. "Come along inside. Dr. Burns and the others are in the sitting room." Her expression registers no surprise at my presence or my baby's, and for that I am grateful despite the pallor her shimmering gown casts over my own.

"Thank you," Dr. Morrison and I chorus in unison as we traipse through the doorway and left to the sitting room. Unlike the entryway, enshrouded in floral wallpaper and dotted with porcelain urns, this room is entirely devoid of pink or lace. Unless the men's cigar smoke merely clouds such elements from view. Already uncomfortable, I press my lavender handkerchief gently to Stella's nose.

"Charlie." The men nearest the doorway turn to greet the doctor, removing their cigars from between their lips to smile.

"Dr. Reynolds." Dr. Morrison nods. "Dr. Mason. May I present Nurse Althea Anderson."

"How do you do?" I echo Mrs. Burns's words even as I notice the shift in my name. Thirty seconds ago, I was Mrs. Anderson; now I am Nurse Althea Anderson. "I appreciate your letting me be here tonight."

The smiles drop from each man's face; they exchange uncertain glances.

"Althea"—Dr. Morrison steps in—"has valuable medical experience that I think we would all be interested in hearing."

"Certainly, certainly," murmurs the first man, his hair thick and dark. Dr. Reynolds? Dr. Mason? I cannot recall. Especially not now, as my name has just gone through yet another reincarnation. Althea, he called me. Althea.

"What of the baby?" The other man interrupts the beating of my heart. "Does the baby have unique medical knowledge as well?"

I flush as the first man, who is at least attempting politeness, disguises a snigger as a cough.

"In fact"—Dr. Morrison's voice takes on a nearly physical presence, the word *fact* falling heavy from his mouth like a foot planted on a step—"yes." He is about to continue, but I speak before he is able.

"Don't worry about it, Doctor. Your friend was just teasing." Teasing, ridiculing, provoking. But they won't get a rise out of me. Challenging them will merely set them more deeply against me, and showing my distress will weaken me in their eyes. I know the way these things work. Dr. Morrison—Charlie, tonight—does not.

"Let's go introduce you to the others, then," Charlie responds gruffly. A compromise.

He leads me to a larger, louder cluster of men. I see as we approach why they congregate here on the far side of the room; behind them stretches a dark walnut bar. A few of the men lean laconically against it, and I wonder whether Prohibition has changed the contents of the cabinet. I doubt it. I study the men. The tallest of them is clearly the host of the evening; he is relaxed in a way that can only mean this is his domain.

"May I present Nurse Althea Anderson." Charlie's voice has an edge to it that was not there the first time he uttered this phrase. "Althea, this is our host, Geoff." He indicates the man I had pinpointed: Dr. Geoff Burns.

"How do you do?" The phrase is becoming quite tiresome, and I am regretting already that I have come.

"Grace!" Geoff bellows. His wife comes striding in, rushed but unharried.

"Geoff?"

"You sent Mrs. Anderson into the lion's den." Geoff chuckles. "And the little one, too."

"Stella," I answer reflexively. "Her name is Stella."

Grace turns her sparkling smile to me. "I'm so very sorry! I was under the impression that you were joining the men in here for the evening. Our little Joseph will be delighted to have a playmate. Come along!"

"Oh." I pause, searching for a polite way to correct her. "You were actually quite right. I *will* be joining the other doctors this evening."

She turns a questioning glance to her husband, who, in turn, looks askance at Charlie. "Charlie, old horse, you finally settling down?"

I close my eyes briefly and then open them. "I am a nurse, Dr. Burns. Geoff. And I have experience that Charlie"—I stumble over the use of his Christian name, so improper in any other situation—"thought you would all find fascinating. But if you would prefer that more modern medicine stay entirely in the hands of nurses—bedpans and bedsheets do, after all—I completely understand. I can go."

Grace Burns's eyes are narrowed in what is either admiration or fury; perhaps both. Charlie is covering a smile. And Geoff Burns is laughing. "Well, well! We've got ourselves a guest to remember."

Perhaps it is amusement crackling in his voice rather than respect; certainly, I am a novelty more than I am a peer. But I have made my point and carved out my space, and so I smile and play the part I have created. "Charmed." I extend my hand. "Truly."

The medical talk starts up over supper. Stella has been exiled to Grace and Joseph's nursery—so that she doesn't get any ideas like her mother, I suppose—and my fingers itch without her. Surely any mother would be nervous to leave her baby with a stranger, but I am terrified. Though I am committed to Stella as if she were mine, I feel always as though the world may come and snatch her from me. "Jig's up," they say in my dreams, where kindly nuns are just as likely to spirit my daughter away as are men masked in black. In reality, it would be Hattie or Michael, or perhaps the police. Certainly not Grace Burns, and certainly not her six-month-old son. But still I fret. Still I listen, anxious to hear a cry, a laugh, even a rustle from the nursery above.

"So, Althea." Geoff looks over his china plate to where I sit gratefully next to Charlie. "Tell me about your . . . expertise." He cocks his eyebrows as if awaiting the punch line of a joke.

"Certainly." I clear my throat. "It actually concerns Stella, in a way." I put down the olive I grip gingerly in my fingers.

"So your experience is from being a mother, rather than a nurse." The man who utters these words says them kindly, with relief. As if he has been released from the burden of distrusting me; as if I have been freed from the pressure of real knowledge.

I roll my shoulders back until I feel the stretch in my neck. "My first experience was as a nurse. At Dr. Couney's incubator park on Coney Island."

"The freak show?"

I take a deep breath. I may be putting myself at risk, but these doctors are part of the AMA. They hold sway in the medical world, and my words to them might be able to save the lives of other premature infants.

"Yes, the freak show. The one that saved my daughter's life."

The men quiet at that.

I breathe in. "Couney is able to save the vast majority of the babies brought to him, despite the fact that most of them weigh but two pounds. Bellevue, where I trained, could do none of that." As I continue, I forget to whom I'm speaking, lost in the wonder of the ways to save a life. "These babies struggle to breathe, to suckle, to regulate their body temperature. And

Dr. Couney *saves* them, using European technology that our hospitals refuse to adopt."

"Where did he get his degree?"

I don't let the men see me falter. "He studied under the Frenchman who invented baby incubators. Budin." Dr. Couney spoke little of his past in my time at the island; in fact, he often deflected to discuss that of his nurses. I must confess I've wondered since what Dr. Couney was trying to hide. But I don't think it matters. What matters is that he saved my baby's life, and many others.

"Incubators . . ." The man across from me at the table furrows his brow. "So they work the same way a farmer's do? For eggs?"

"Similarly." I smile patiently. "But more sophisticated by far."

"Heating, then." One of the men inserts himself as if afraid that I will otherwise assume he does not understand the concept of temperature. How insecure man can be when threatened by an intelligent woman.

"Certainly. The incubators are thermostat-regulated so that they replicate the temperature the babies were accustomed to before birth, and the air pumped into them is heated through hot-water coils. It's filtered as well, passed through absorbent wool over antiseptic solution and then filtered again to remove large particles—dust and the like."

"So that's it?" Dr. Burns asks. "All the little guys need is heat and air? I've seen babies put in hatboxes and sandwiched between hot water bottles, and that works just fine. What makes Coney Island so different?"

"That does work for some." I don't want to alienate my host. "But many babies who are as small as my Stella was, two and a half pounds, they cannot even eat yet. They cannot suckle. And Couney's nurses are uniquely able to feed them regardless."

"What, with magic?" This from the man to whom Charlie and I first talked as we entered the room. The man who likened my having any expertise whatsoever to a baby having the same.

I stretch my face into a smile. "With a gavage to the stomach through the throat, or with a specially manufactured spoon that allows the nurses to drip the milk into the nose."

"Their mother's milk, I hope."

Not for the first time, I think about my inability to feed Stella the way a real mother could. The nurses at the island tut-tutted over the babies who had to turn to the wet nurses for milk. I myself wondered if they were less devoted—what else would keep them from their children? But now my stomach churns, for I did the same thing. I kept Stella from her mother and her milk. I close my eyes briefly and then return to the conversation. *Focus, Althea.* "It depends," I tell the man. "Some mothers do bring their milk; mostly, it comes from wet nurses."

"Kids that can't even eat." The man who is either Dr. Reynolds or Dr. Mason—whichever one it was whom I found less hateful—shakes his head sadly.

"Makes you wonder," says his counterpart, "whether God even wants them to survive."

Makes you wonder whether God even wants them to survive.

Makes you wonder.

"We will follow," Michael Perkins vowed, "God's plan."

"Excuse me." I scoot back in my chair and place my napkin on the table. All my energy goes into setting it down gently rather than breaking down. And then I flee, the sound of each man's chair grating along the glossy floor as he stands. Funny, that they're willing to adhere to such archaic forms of respect yet unwilling to treat me with the decency afforded any other human being.

Charlie catches up to me just as I am emerging with Stella from little Joseph Burns's nursery. "Althea." Charlie reaches out to touch me and then thinks better of it. "I am so, so sorry. I gave him a good talking-to, Althea, I did. I had no idea they would say such horrible things."

I keep walking. I have perfected the demure silence; I will use it tonight to my advantage. Stalking into the dining room, I approach the man who has so gravely insulted my daughter. "Hold her," I command him. "Hold her and then look me in the eyes and tell me God didn't want her to live."

He chuckles uneasily, but the other men don't join in. "Go on," Geoff Burns urges him. "Put this to rest."

The man takes Stella uneasily. "Sorry to offend you, ma'am. Of course your little girl is God's own gift."

I hug Stella close as he hands her back to me. "Indeed. And you would do well to remember it."

I turn and glide from the room, using the silent walk I have adopted in the years of caring for sleeping patients.

"Women," the man hisses to his friends as I go. "Damned hysterics."

I pause. I want to leave, escape this dark enclave of thick curtains and covered windows. I know Charlie would be willing to take me home; likely, he would be eager to. Even as I stop moving, my knees point forward over my toes toward the door. But those men in there are going to tear me apart if I go, and Charlie, too. And I am tired of being underestimated. I am tired of keeping quiet and meeting the low expectations of men who consider themselves superior.

I look down at Stella. She is unaware of the cruelty around her as she tugs happily on my brooch. She was lying so sweetly next to Joseph when I ran to find her, both babies grinning slightly as Grace sang over them.

Gritting my teeth and clenching my toes, I turn toward the staircase. I carry Stella carefully up them and return her to Grace's care. "Thank you," I murmur, not trusting myself to say more. And then I return to the table downstairs, taking my seat and folding my napkin primly on my lap. "So"—I smile brightly—"where were we? Had I told you yet about the woolen clothes?"

CHAPTER TWENTY

Stella Wright, January 1951

I wake up with Hattie's name on my lips. Now that I've talked to the incubator nurses, I can't leave without reaching her. I need to know for certain that she is my mother, need to answer the questions that still remain. Why did she give me up? Did she think me dead? How did my mother—Althea—end up raising me as her own? Why?

And who does it make me?

I examine my face in the mirror as I make it up. Full lips. Long lashes. Blond curls. So different from my mother, Althea, differences I had always dismissed.

I wonder what Hattie will look like.

Taking a deep breath, I knot a scarf around the base of my neck—no perky victory rolls today—and put on yesterday's dress. I didn't pack for a third day in the city.

I hail yet another Checker cab and sit in silence until I thank the man when he pulls up in front of the Perkinses' modest row house.

I take a deep breath. What will I say to Hattie when she opens the door? I had all night to solidify a plan of action, but I came up blank. There's no script for such a unique situation. I will see what Hattie says to me, and go from there.

I knock on the door.

A light is on in the house, but nobody comes to the door. "Come *on*," I mutter. I'm resisting the urge to turn and run almost as strongly as I'm resisting the urge to grab the door and enter uninvited; I am equal parts terrified and excited.

But still no one answers. I bang loudly on the door. "Hello?" I call, craning my neck in an attempt to see through the windows. The lowered blinds cast impossible shadows, but I do finally hear a noise inside. Nervous, I straighten my dress and wait for the door to swing open.

But it doesn't. "Hello?" I call again. For the second time comes that rustling sound and the faint accompaniment of a voice. I wrestle only a moment with indecision. I have not come here to leave with nothing.

I try the door handle, but it catches. Locked. I press my ear to the wood.

"Please . . ." A voice, faint and frightened.

"Hello?" I position my mouth so that it lines up with the crack between the door and the wall. "Is there someone there?"

"Please," she repeats. "The back . . . the birdhouse."

My legs shake so intensely that I can barely walk. Once, I fall, stumbling over a rock in the backyard. But I find the birdhouse. With streaked red paint and rough wood, it is a homemade thing, but it serves its purpose. The key is hidden deep inside, and I pull it out and take it around to the front door.

"Hattie?" I call once I've opened the door. I am prepared to explain who I am, but I find her in the living room and stop abruptly. This woman does not need to know my name; what she needs is my help. "Hattie," I whisper. I have never seen the woman before, but I know this must be her. Even purpled and leaking blood, her lips are plush and soft. They're Cupid's-bow lips, a perfect indent between them, and they match mine with uncanny precision.

My mom's lips were thin, like the rest of her. Nothing like my curves. Nothing like Hattie's.

But there's no time to dwell on any of that now. Now, I must do something for this woman, whose face is little more than a footnote to the rest of her body's destruction.

"How long have you been here?" I whisper.

Her lips—those punctured, puffy lips—mouth a response I cannot make out. "Don't talk," I amend. "Just . . . lie still."

I squeeze between Hattie's limp form and the side table upon which the phone she'd answered sits. I call the operator. "I need an ambulance."

"One moment." Her voice is infuriatingly calm.

I bounce on my toes as I wait for the line to connect. "Station Thirteen." A man's voice. I tell the man about Hattie's injuries, our location. "Please," I add uselessly, "please hurry."

"They will. Stay on the line. Is the patient conscious?"

"Yes." I ought to stay calm, but I cannot. Not when confronted by the destruction of a body so similar to mine. A body that throws my entire life into question. "Yes, she's conscious. But how can I help her?"

"Assess her injuries. Is there anything hurt other than her face?"

"I can't tell."

"Remove her clothing. Gently."

I unbutton the top of Hattie's dress gently and pull it to the side. A yellow stain blooms across her chest—an old bruise—and in the center is a large purple blotch like eggplant. Nausea rises in me again. I wish my mother were here. She was never fazed, would have stayed calm even in the face of this desecration.

I pull the two sides of the dress farther apart, finding a stained-glass mosaic of red, purple, and blue. The marks track up Hattie's neck and become hard, round circles like thumbprints. I think of Margaret's small ink thumb on the note in my clutch. Did that thumb come from the man who left these prints? Did mine?

Don't think. I realize only now that I'd failed to notice the unnatural angle at which Hattie's arm is twisted above her head. It lies askew, her light hair underneath it like the lining of a coffin. I am awed that she had the strength to pull herself toward the door so I could hear her from outside. The strength, or the desperation.

"Her chest is bruised, and I think her arm is broken," I tell the emergency operator.

"Don't touch her arm," he instructs. "Is there blood?"

"On her chest."

"See what you can do to clean it up without moving her. You need to see where it's coming from, and whether the wound is still bleeding."

I swallow as I set the phone aside. "I'm going to go get a

cloth," I tell Hattie, "but I'll be back." I return with a wet wash-cloth pulled from the small bathroom off the kitchen. "Here." I dab gently at Hattie's lips first to remove the blood that has dried. *You're just cleaning*, I assure myself. Just like wiping Mary Ellen's legs or washing my own body in the shower. Just cleaning.

The blood from her lips has stopped flowing, and the cut on her chest is scabbed over. I alternate between the window and Hattie until the ambulance arrives fifteen minutes later. "Thank God." I run outside. "She's in here. Please, hurry."

Two young men, dark-haired and silent, traipse inside with a stretcher. "Are you the doctor?" I turn to the older man.

"Yes, ma'am. Who are you to the patient?"

"Her daughter," I blurt, determined to stay with Hattie.

Her daughter. I fall to the ground as the doctor follows his assistants inside. *Her daughter, her daughter, her daughter.*

Is it true? *Am* I that woman's daughter? Did I come from her curved body, battered and bruised? I run my hands down my own skin.

If Hattie is my mother, am I going to lose her, too?

CHAPTER TWENTY-ONE

Althea Anderson, November 1926

"How did you remain so calm?" Charlie asks me on the way back to Mrs. Wallace's. Already we've ridden the train and IRT subway in silence, the eerie half-light in the car discouraging any attempt at conversation.

I shrug. Certainly I felt anything but calm. "Practice."

"I would have lost my senses."

I look at him and smile. "I somehow doubt that." But perhaps he is right. There is a certain quiet intensity burning beneath his surface. He is not one to stand for injustice or to stay silent on it.

"Althea . . ." He hesitates. "I'm sorry. Mrs. Anderson."

"No." I shock myself. Stella is asleep in my arms, and I am very nearly able to convince myself that I am still the young girl I was three months ago. I am tired of being a Mrs. "Althea is all right."

"Althea. Then, of course I am Charlie." He hesitates. "I never anticipated that they would react the way they did."

"I know."

"I want to make it up to you."

I should laugh, thank him, offer up a flirtatious suggestion. Wasn't I raised to be a cheerful conversation partner? But I do not laugh. Instead I sigh, and tell the man the truth. "Oh, Charlie. If only it were that easy."

"You're mad, then."

"No. Well," I amend with a wry smile, "not at you. It's just . . ." How to explain? It's just that a lifetime of disrespect cannot be corrected by one man's kindness.

"It's just that you don't want to associate with me anymore. Not if I'm friends with that crowd."

Now I nearly do laugh; his words are so far from what I was thinking. And what associating does he plan to continue? Mrs. Wallace is nearly well, and I certainly won't ever attend another one of those AMA meetings. There is no reason our paths should cross again.

The thought makes me suddenly lonesome, and I pull Stella closer into my chest. Perhaps my dismay stems from having no one else with whom to truly talk or laugh. I am not Charlie's maid or his mother, and so I am able to speak to him freely. Or as much so as I will ever be able to speak with any man; never can I confess the truth of Stella's origins.

"You aren't them," I soothe Charlie now. "I know that." Certainly, I know that living among a group does not make a person part of it. Even after twelve years of living chest to chest and shoulder to shoulder with bright young girls at boarding school, I am not one of them. I was and remain too serious, too detached, too focused.

"Well, then." Charlie exaggerates his sigh of relief to make me smile. "Good." He pauses. "I will hope to see you again soon, then."

"Likewise." Does he mean it? Do I? "And thank you for walking us home." We have arrived at the door to Mrs. Wallace's, and the Times Square laid out before us is not a place I would relish walking alone. The street pulsates brightly under the dark sky, signs and buildings lit up like the red tip of a cigar.

"Of course." Charlie bows slightly and begins to turn away. I watch him, his tall, dark figure a solid silhouette against the busy backdrop of Times Square. The crackling bulbs of Broadway's noisy signs send Charlie's profile into sharp relief: cheeks whittled into chin, eyes in the shadows of his brows.

I think of his first visit, my telling Stella we'd never see him again. He'd surprised us the next morning with a call.

"Charlie."

He turns.

"Coffee. Would you like some coffee?" We had left the Burnses' just after dessert and fruits, as soon as the finger bowls had been distributed for washing. Charlie had not retreated into the smoking room with the others for the traditional coffee and cigar, and I wonder if perhaps he would appreciate the drink now. Does he smoke too, I wonder? Miss Hosken would not have heard of it in her nurses, but a private physician can do as he pleases.

"Of course, if it's too late . . ." I trail off.

"No. I would be delighted."

We each pause for a moment, uncertain as to the next move. Finally Charlie reaches past me to hold open the door; I skirt past him into the kitchen and ask him to sit. "I'll take Stella up," I say. I do so, tucking her into her bassinet, and then go check on Mrs.

Wallace. She is asleep, her blankets pulled up to her chin. I smile. However hysterical Mrs. Wallace claims her daughter-in-law Charlotte to be, the girl obviously loves Mrs. Wallace dearly. I imagine Mrs. Wallace feels the same way in return. "Good night," I whisper. I know she can't hear me, but it's a tradition I began at Bellevue when leaving sleeping patients' rooms. I was always afraid they would be gone when I returned, that my last words to them would have been "Lie down" or "Don't let that bandage slip."

I return downstairs and start the coffee. The routine is a comfortable one: I slip the filter into the Tricolator, spoon the coffee grounds on top, and press them down with the lid. Steam condenses on my face as I pour the boiling water over it all, and I wipe my forehead with my sleeve. Keeping an eye on the stove, I sit gingerly across from Charlie at the table. The house is silent, and I am acutely aware of each movement of my own body: a bead of sweat rolling slowly between my breasts, the slight tremor in my legs beneath the table. The silence is punctuated only by the occasional splinter of ice in the icebox. I am afraid to move, any sound of my skirts rustling or my shoes tapping against the floor a foghorn in the silence. Light-headed, I realize even my breathing is shallow and silent. *You must be tired*, I scold myself. *Go up to bed.* But it is early still, not yet time for sleep for any but the oldest and the youngest in the city. The Mrs. Wallaces and the Stellas.

I wonder whether Charlie is sleepy. The shadow of hair along his jawbone, faint like a sketch, lends his face a weary air. But his smile is warm.

"Althea . . ." he begins.

"Yes?" I lean forward in my seat. We're close enough that our foreheads would touch if we angled our heads just so; close enough that Charlie would need to scoot only an inch closer to kiss me.

I watch his lips as they move. "Thank you for coming tonight."

"Thank you for inviting me."

Does he move a bit closer, or am I imagining it? "I'd like to take you out to a real dinner one day," he whispers. "If Mrs. Wallace doesn't mind my kidnapping you again."

I jolt back, severing the connection between us. *Kidnapping.* What a terrible, violent word—a word to describe violence and desperate grief. I've kept Stella as my own when she is not—isn't that the definition of kidnapping?

No. I try to calm my breath. I didn't kidnap Stella, I saved her. I saved her from her father's violence, from a home plagued by cruelty and aggression. *I didn't kidnap her.*

Charlie senses my shift in mood. "Thank you for the coffee." He stands, and for one crazy moment I think about confessing everything.

Then he is gone, the crisp nighttime air rushing into the kitchen as if to fill a hole.

"Good-bye," I whisper.

Stella has fallen asleep immediately after the night's excitement, but I cannot. My skin still buzzes the way it did with Charlie sitting so close to me at the kitchen table, and I pinch myself in an effort to stop thinking of him. We can't be anything more than friendly colleagues, as tonight's AMA supper reminded me. It's too dangerous. It was right to let Charlie disappear into the night. Wasn't it?

The reckless urge to tell him the truth possesses me. He's a doctor; he knows that our mission is to save our patients at all costs. Surely he would understand. Surely he would forgive me.

I stare at the ceiling and imagine Charlie's face. I move my mouth in the shape of the words: *Stella was not born to me. I took her.*

No. *Stella was not born to me. I saved her. I took her to Coney Island against her father's wishes, and I was going to take her back.*

But what if, at that point, Charlie was already on the phone with the police? What if he sounded the alarm before I explained why I kept Stella as my own?

A new start, then. *Stella wasn't born to me. Her biological father was abusive. He didn't want her at Coney Island, so I took her myself. She wouldn't be safe with him, so I chose to raise her as my own.*

I picture Charlie's deep gray eyes. He isn't one to jump to conclusions or judge, not like those men at the AMA meeting who were ready to discard me without a thought. Charlie is different: a good listener. The type of man who seeks to understand. And, oh, imagine a world in which he knew and understood Stella's and my truth! I know he has felt the same connection that I have. Maybe one day he would want to be a family the way we seemed to be on the train today: Charlie, Stella, and me. It's almost too fantastical to imagine: a stable home and two parents for Stella, enough money to live comfortably and go to school. A time when I wouldn't be alone.

I'm still fantasizing when Stella cries for a feeding at one a.m., and I lift her from her bassinet to give her a bottle. We curl up together the way we did that night at the Nurses' Residence before Miss Caswell knocked on the door and caught us. And finally, with Stella's soft body nestled in mine, I fall asleep.

As I wait to see if Charlie will be in touch again, my days take on the quality of that sleepless night: impossible to track and both endless and forgettable. I read aloud to Mrs. Wallace for hours at a time, pausing only to feed Stella and prepare Mrs. Wallace's meals. When the woman tires of books, we lay Stella on a blanket on the floor and watch her play. She is beginning to react to our sounds and faces with squeals, and both Mrs. Wallace and I can't help but laugh at her noises. She still can't weigh more than ten pounds, but she can scream!

Every time I laugh at Stella's expressions or clap after she masters something new, I feel a pang of guilt. Hattie will never know of these moments. And though I'm used to guilt, I no longer can rely on tasks to occupy my mind and distract me. Just over three months ago, I worked twelve-hour shifts six days a week. I was taking notes, cleaning sheets, changing bedpans, soothing children, delivering babies, bandaging wounds, attending lectures, monitoring charts, aiding operations . . . and now I barely leave the triangular prison of kitchen, bathroom, and bedroom. Meanwhile, Dr. May Edward Chinn became the first African-American woman to graduate from Bellevue Hospital Medical College. And I dropped out of even its nursing program.

I pray for Dr. Chinn each night. The road won't be easy for her going forward.

But at least she has her degree. I have nothing to show for my two years of work. Meeting Charlie's AMA acquaintances has reminded me of how much I miss medicine. I'm newly aware of what I gave up, though also of what I have gained.

I gaze at Stella beside me on the floor and can't help picturing Charlie sitting beside her. Charlie: his tall, lean frame. His large hands, one of which had spanned from Mrs. Wallace's wounded shoulder to her well one. Laid flat against my back, it would easily span one side of my waist to the other. I shiver.

I hold my own hands in front of me, fingers outstretched. My skin has a softness to it that it never used to have, and I don't like it. I'm accustomed to skin rubbed raw from soaking bandages in antiseptic. While I was expected to remain calm and composed as a nurse, my hands gave away the reality of the hard work. Now, they just remind me of the static nature of my days.

I need to take action. I never planned for this life to be permanent, but now that it is, I need to move forward. I can't get my daughter a birth certificate, but I can get her the next best thing. And I can make Charlie a part of it.

I broach the subject over breakfast. "Mrs. Wallace, Stella was never baptized. I've been thinking about doing it near Thanksgiving, and I wondered if you would like to be Stella's godmother?"

Mrs. Wallace throws her hands up with such gusto I'm afraid she'll refracture her collarbone. She hobbles her way over to me and scoops us into a hug. "I don't know if I'll live to see a grandchild"—she squeezes me—"but this is almost as good."

I find myself smiling as widely as she.

"And what do you think," I ask carefully, "about having Dr. Morrison serve as Stella's godfather?"

Mrs. Wallace's wrinkled face contorts into a smirk that makes her look ten years younger. "I think that's an excellent idea."

I excuse myself from the table to hide my blush. "I suppose I should call him to talk about it." I pick up the telephone.

"Charlie?"

"Althea!" He sounds delighted to hear from me, and I readjust my sweaty grip on the receiver.

My usual confidence flags a bit. This is utterly improper. Who am I to be calling a man on the phone?

"Good morning," I begin as if I'm about to give a lecture. "I . . . Are you going to the AMA meeting this weekend?"

"Depends on why you're asking." A smile creeps into Charlie's voice, and my lips turn up in response.

"I'm . . ." I falter. "It's just—"

"If I didn't know better," Charlie teases, "I'd think you were asking me on a date."

I cover my eyes, mortified, but don't deny it. "I just have something I'd like to talk to you about. In person. Would you like to come over for supper?"

Charlie doesn't even hesitate. "I'll be there," he tells me.

"Wonderful. Six o'clock on Saturday."

Charlie arrives promptly at six. He first attends to Mrs. Wallace, asking after her arm—less because he thinks it necessary, I believe, than to save me from having to jump into discussion immediately. I have never courted before, and I know not what to do with myself. Is this even courtship? I don't know. A better question: Do I want it to be?

Fortunately, Mrs. Wallace keeps conversation flowing throughout supper, engaging Charlie for me when I must rise to bounce a screeching Stella. With the four of us there at the table, it feels like a Sunday brunch or supper at the Nurses' Residence; I am among peers. Only after supper do I begin to itch with apprehension. At her pointed request, I assist Mrs. Wallace up the stairs and into bed; then I give Stella her bottle and put her in her bassinet next door.

I creep back down the stairs, embarrassed. Charlie had come over for what is ostensibly a date, and here I am reminding him of my motherhood. As far as he knows, I've been married before. Though I've never so much as kissed a boy, I'm soiled goods in Charlie's eyes. The empty bottle I carry downstairs to wash in the sink simply reminds him of it.

"Sorry for all of that." I rinse the bottle quickly. "I imagine you're wishing you had gone to Dr. Burns's."

I lift my arm to turn off the faucet and encounter a slight weight on my shoulder. I turn. Charlie's hand is on me, and his face is creased into a deep frown. "Althea." He directs his pale gray eyes on me. "I do not wish that I were there, not when I could be here with you."

"Why?" I can't help but laugh, water dripping down my arms and onto my drab woolen dress. I smell of milk and antiseptic, of which I am all too acutely aware.

"You would never dream of disrespecting those men the way they did you, Althea. And, despite the fact that they did, despite the fact that by all appearances you are *accustomed* to such cruelty, you persevere."

"I persevere." I am ashamed at the edge of bitterness that creeps into my voice. "Charlie, I never even completed my degree. I am not a nurse."

"I saw you when Mrs. Wallace fell. You are a nurse, Althea. And you're a mother. A mother who believed in your daughter

even when the doctors didn't. That sounds to me like perseverance."

I duck my head to hide the red creeping of pride that surely
flushes across my neck and cheeks.

"Althea." He tips my chin up and opens his mouth as if about
to speak. I hope he doesn't; there's no hope for my gathering the
words for a sensible response, not when he holds my face so. His
fingers are colder than I would have expected, and they fill me
with the same invigorating burst of urgent energy as watching the
color fade back into a patient's pale cheeks or seeing their fingers twitch after a bout of unconsciousness. Tightly coiled. Ready
to leap.

He doesn't speak, not yet. Instead, he closes his mouth, his
gray eyes a soft flurry of snow, and leans gently forward.

I am poised like a bird cupped delicately in his hand, and I
know as water soaks lukewarm into the waist of my dress from
the sink behind me that Charlie is going to kiss me. I still clutch
Stella's bottle in my right hand, but I raise my left to Charlie's
shoulder. My rings clang tinny beside his ear as I do, and he startles. He jerks back.

"I'm sorry." He wipes both his hands on his trousers as if
needing to cleanse them of me. "I'm so sorry."

I straighten. "Quite all right." More than all right, by God. I
wanted that as much as he did, maybe more. But my rings have reminded us both that I am a widow. Allegedly. And I am still in
mourning. And they've reminded me of all the lies I've told Charlie.

Charlie backs away to sit at the kitchen table. "You had something you wanted to discuss?"

Refusing to let myself cry, I sit in the chair across from

Charlie—as far as I can be from him at the small, round table. "Yes. Stella is going to be baptized in a few weeks, and I was wondering if you would be willing to be her godfather."

I sound stilted and formal, but Charlie leaps up. "Stella's godfather! Oh, Althea, I'd be honored."

I grin, almost forgetting my disappointment. "I'll call you when the date is set," I promise him. "Thank you."

With our business done, Charlie leaves. I don't try to stop him. But when I go up for bed that night, I do not immediately collapse back onto my mattress. Instead, I pull off my two thin gold rings and drop them gently into the drawer beside my bed.

When Charlie returns days later, he notices. He is a doctor, after all, trained to observe the body and its changes. And though he says nothing, his eyes widen almost imperceptibly. His head tilts ever so slightly on its axis. A dark strand of hair slips to brush his eyebrow, and my stomach tenses.

"Come in," I say to him. "You look like you have something on your mind."

Now he is the one to beam as I pour him a cup of coffee and sit across from him at the table. "You'll love it, I think. No." He laughs. "Not I think. I know you will. Trust me."

I do.

He takes a deep breath. "I've been visiting every hospital in the city with an incubator." He pulls out a notebook bloated with use. "Look." He passes it to me. Inside are diagrams labeling the incubators' dimensions and components, statistics on the number of children saved at every weight from a pound and a half to four.

I flip through the pages the way I would a Bible. With reverence, for it is the power within these sketches that saved my baby girl.

As I reach the center of the book, the drawings change. Almost as if we have gone back in time, steel replaced by wooden slats and water coils by hot water bottles. "What is this?"

"For those who don't have incubators. The mothers who give birth at home, in fall or winter or spring. I'm trying to determine the most foolproof way to keep them alive, too."

I point to one image. "This one, the hatbox. A man brought his child to Dr. Couney once in one of these. The girl was surrounded by feathers to keep her warm."

Charlie reaches out and grabs the notebook from me with the energy of a little boy. Pulling a pencil from its binding, he adds a note and then passes it back to me. "What else have you seen, Althea? What do you think works?"

He wants to know what I think. I am sitting, but my legs want to leap, carry me up through the ceiling and to the sky. Instead, I curl my toes in excitement as I search through my memory. "Clothing should be wool, certainly. Warm bricks are used sometimes, from the fireplace. But perhaps more important than the incubator is the feeding, Charlie, for the babies too small to suckle. Dr. Couney's nurses used special spoons, but I don't suppose those are common. Perhaps babies could be fed through the nostrils with an eye dropper. And for those that cannot do even that, would you be able to acquire rubber catheters small enough to use?"

He again snatches the notebook and scribbles furiously as I talk. "Yes." He looks up at me, sweat collecting on his smooth brow. "Yes."

With the incubator sketches before us, I can't help but think again of telling Charlie the truth. Look at his passion for saving these babies, his conviction that it is right. Surely, he couldn't blame me for rescuing Stella from death.

"Some parents refuse to let their newborns go to the island," I begin with forced casualness. "They don't want the babies to be part of a freak show."

Charlie looks up, brow scrunched. "That's not right. Maybe we should think about how we can change the public opinion about Dr. Couney, in addition to the practicalities of providing incubators to families too far away." He's flipping pages again as he talks, jotting down his thoughts as he shares them. I'm caught on the first part of the words: *That's not right.* If it's not right for a parent to refuse treatment, surely Charlie thinks it's right for a nurse to require it. Surely Charlie would agree with me.

I give him one more test. "Or we could focus on changing hospitals' perceptions. Then, regardless of what the parents think, the doctors will recommend the babies for care."

"That's true," Charlie muses, chewing on his pencil. "Thank you, Althea."

I close my eyes, draw in a deep breath, and get ready to form the words that may change my life. But when I open my eyes again, Stella's name on my lips, Charlie has stood. His notebook is tucked under his arm. "I'm afraid I have an appointment in half an hour," he apologizes. "I just couldn't help but stop by first."

"Right." I swallow. "Good-bye."

CHAPTER TWENTY-TWO

Stella Wright, January 1951

The doctors won't let me in to see Hattie until visiting hours this afternoon. Each second of waiting seems impossible. I can't just sit here in the lobby, antiseptic smell soaking into my skin.

I use a hospital phone to call Jack.

"Jack."

"Stella, sweetheart. Are you okay?"

"Jack, I don't know what to do."

"What's the matter? Did something else happen?"

Haltingly, I tell Jack about calling Hattie after we spoke and going to her house this morning. I know he didn't want me to go, and I fear his disappointment. But I need him, so I tell him all of it. "I found her beaten nearly to death, Jack." I take a deep breath. "And I'm afraid it's my fault."

"No, Stella." Jack's voice is confident, reassuring. "You might have scared her husband or angered him, but that's not an excuse for violence. Listen to me. Michael Perkins did that to his wife, not you."

"But if I hadn't called . . . Jack, she must be my mother. The resemblance . . . it's undeniable. My mother . . . and I may have gotten her killed." The next words burst out of me, though I try to keep them tucked away. "What if she dies before I can even ask her for answers?"

"Oh, Stella. Do you want me to come to the city tonight?"

I'm so surprised by his offer that I don't answer right away.

"Where are you, what hospital?"

"Jack—"

"You aren't supposed to be using that phone." A nurse appears glaring at my side.

"Please." I attempt a smile. "I'm almost done."

"You *are* done," she corrects me. "I need to make a hospital call."

I put my mouth back to the receiver. "Jack, I'm sorry. I have to go."

The nurse snatches the telephone, and I back away, defeated. I wonder at Jack's offer and what it means. I'm touched, and of course part of me desperately wants him here—but another part of me fears he'll convince me to leave my past well enough alone.

They still won't let me into Hattie's room. Facing this interminable wait, there's only one place I want to go.

I run outside, coat flapping, and hail a taxicab. I give the driver the address for Evergreen Cemetery. Like most of the active cemeteries in New York City, it's outside Manhattan in

Queens's Cemetery Belt. The drive is long, and I bounce my knee the whole way there, my fingers ripping at my nails. When we arrive, I pay the driver and walk through the gates. The frost on the ground crunches under my shoes, and I pull my coat tighter around me. I find my parents' shared headstone and crouch before it. My mom brought flowers to Dad's grave once a month, and I'd sometimes come along. But this is the first time I've been since Mom's funeral.

Cold spreads damp circles across my skirt where my knees meet the ground, and I shiver. The names on the tombstone are as clear and precise as the days they were carved, and I almost wish moss and lichen would weave through the etchings. I hate the sharp-edged clarity of my parents' death dates, the finality of my father's 1945 and my mother's 1950.

Chin up, Stella.

"I can't help it, Mom. I hate that you're gone."

I pull my fingers from my glove and trace the A of her name. *Who were you, Mom? Who is my father? And who am I?*

Losing my mother opened a crevasse in me that will never be refilled. Already there was a missing piece of me, a phantom limb that reached to call her when she could no longer be reached. But to think I may lose her all over again—to think she may not have ever been mine—how will I survive it?

I let out a sound that is primal and raw. The wind whips my voice toward the river.

Althea Anderson. My mother. But who was she, really? Why did she raise me if I wasn't truly hers?

I cradle my head in my hands, one gloved and one bare. I know my mother—or the woman I thought was my mother. She didn't do anything recklessly. She didn't do anything selfishly. If she stole away with me, she had a reason.

I trace the letters of her name and then my father's.

I rest my forehead on my parents' grave marker and sob. Frost seeps into my skirt and my bare palm grows red from cold.

No one is here to see me.

I am utterly alone.

My skirts are wet and my eyes are puffy when I return to Bellevue in the afternoon. But Hattie looks far worse than I. She looks as if she is suffering even in her unconsciousness.

Out by Coney Island, the thought that Hattie might be my mother made me nauseous. I'd hoped this morning I would present her with my evidence and she would provide me with an alternative. If she had told me I was hers, I'd have fought. Argued. But after seeing her lying on the ground, blood-spattered and bruised . . . my fight is gone. This woman with her round face and Cupid's-bow lips resembles me as only a mother could.

"Mrs. Perkins." I kneel beside her bed. "Hattie. Can you hear me?" Her eyes are open, and they slide toward me. The bruising on her face has worsened, but at least the blood has been cleaned. Her arm has been set and is in a cast.

"Margaret?"

I gasp, and Hattie's brow convulses. Afraid she won't stay awake long, I skip the small talk. "Yes, Margaret. Tell me about Margaret."

She knows immediately what I mean. "We didn't take her to the island." Tears well in Hattie's eyes, though she hadn't cried when I found her body ravaged on the floor or when the ambulance men lifted her roughly onto a stretcher.

"To Coney?"

"Michael said no."

"And you?"

Her nostrils flare as her head tremors slightly. For a moment, I fear she is having a fit—and then I realize she is shaking her head. *I didn't say anything*, she is telling me. And she is ashamed.

I hear my mother's words in my head. *You have to speak out.*

I always thought she was talking about bullies at school or boys who doubted my brains. Later, I associated the advice with the war, and what the Nazis did to the Jews and the homosexuals and the disabled. And recently, I thought about it in terms of protecting my students.

But maybe my mother's advice came from somewhere else entirely.

I don't press Hattie on what she did or did not say to her husband. "What happened?"

"She died." Hattie hiccups. "We let her die. There was no doctor here for the early babies, not like now—"

"Did you *see* her die? Did you see her body?" My voice is too demanding. I am asking too much of this woman, who lost her child twenty-four years ago and now lies broken in a hospital ward with a stranger.

Hattie shakes her head, and I pull out the thumbprint card. "What if she didn't die, Hattie? What if someone took her to Coney?" I press the thumbprint note into her hand. "Look."

"Margaret," Hattie whispers. "Margaret. But where . . . ?"

"Right here." I shudder even as I volunteer myself as this

woman's daughter. "I . . . I think I am Margaret. And you . . ." I reach up and trace the outline of my pert nose and bow-shaped lips. "That would make you my mother."

That nausea again. I refuse to let it rise and overcome me, breathing slowly through my mouth. I start to become aware of another feeling as the nausea subsides. A strange sort of tenderness. Not love for this woman, but something approaching it.

Hattie stiffens, and a spasm of pain twists her lips. "It can't be. You can't be."

Oh, how much I want to believe her. For just a moment, I decide not to argue. "Really?" I cannot disguise the hope in my voice.

"Go." Hattie's voice quakes even as her jaw hardens. I watch the purple bruise shift and stretch as she clenches her teeth. "My daughter is dead."

"But . . . but what if it isn't true?" I can't help but press.

She asks me a question rather than answering mine. "Who raised you?"

"Althea Anderson and—"

She looks up sharply when I say my mother's name. "You know her!" I exclaim.

Again, Hattie doesn't answer. "Did she ever hurt you?"

"Of course not."

"Did you love her?"

"Yes." My answer comes without a moment's thought, and it's true. Whatever my mother's lies mean, I decide it doesn't change the fact that she was the best mother I could have hoped for, my best friend. The woman who made me *me*.

Hattie lets out a wrenching sob and reaches for me. I hesitate and take a step toward her. But I'm not ready to embrace her. I can't put my pale skin against her pale skin, let my blond curls brush hers.

I'm still frozen when footsteps enter the room. I turn, hoping it's a nurse so I can ask about Hattie's condition. But the footsteps belong to a tall man about Hattie's age. His eyes are hazel, and his hair is darker than Hattie's or mine.

"My husband," Hattie murmurs. Her eyes are wide, as if she did not expect to find her own husband at her bedside. And no wonder. He's the one who hurt her, isn't he? The roar I heard on the phone?

My nostrils flare. The mom who raised me was obedient and quiet. The mother who birthed me is scared and submissive. But I'm none of those things, and I want to send Hattie's husband reeling.

Stupidly, I only now realize what Hattie's husband would be to me. *My father.*

But he doesn't transform before my eyes to some sort of sympathetic figure; he stands before me at once a stranger, a monster, and the man who made me.

The fight seeps out of me. I don't want to hit him. Look at Hattie—that's what he would do, and I don't want to make myself anything like him.

I step forward and then back again, not sure whether to introduce myself to the man, condemn him, or run from him.

Hattie speaks, making my decision for me. I turn to her with desperate hope. For what, I can't say. "This nice lady"—she gestures to me—"is . . . an intern at the hospital. She was checking to see if I needed anything before going home. Isn't that sweet?"

I suspect I look anything but sweet. My face is contorted in

246

fury as I gaze upon the man who's landed his wife in the emergency ward. My legs shake, and I fear I'll fall if I try to take a wobbly step in my heels.

"Very." Michael is dismissive, striding to his wife's side. Surely he notices her cringe as he approaches. Does it bother him, or does he relish it? Perhaps it reminds him of his power. "Did you—" he hisses as he reaches his wife, lowering his voice so I cannot hear the rest of his question.

Whatever it is, Hattie assures him that she did not. Then she looks up at me. "Good-bye, nurse," she calls. "Thank you for the care." She is crying unabashedly now.

"I can stay," I offer helplessly. "Do you want me to stay?"

"No!" I hear the urgency in her voice.

"You want me to stay," I repeat.

"My *wife* said *no*." Michael turns, and in his eyes flashes confirmation that he is the reason Hattie is here in the hospital at all.

"Indeed. The hospital is really not a safe place for someone healthy like you." Hattie looks at me imploringly.

"Make sure you get out too, then." I hope she understands my meaning. "You need to stay safe, too."

And then I turn and flee.

I do not want to return to my mother's, Althea's. I'm afraid of what else I may find when I am confronted by her ghost in the apartment. I'm afraid of what anger toward her I may unleash within me alongside the grief. She never told me the truth, and now I'm left with so many questions and no way to find answers. I feel unmoored. So I gather myself and focus on what I *can* do.

I find a nurse and ask for the baby doctor. "The incubator man," I clarify. It's a tenuous connection, but Hattie mentioned that the hospital has a ward now. If the doctor is an expert on premature babies, perhaps he can explain to me the chances I had of surviving, give me reason to believe that my mom did the right thing when she stole me away from my birth mother.

And from my birth father. Certainly, he was another part of the reason my mother kept me for her own?

The nurse gives me directions, and I am knocking just moments later on an office door. "Doctor?"

He appears quickly, disheveled but handsome in middle age. He's younger than I expected. Close to my mother's age. But his polite smile drops when he sees me. I can't decipher the expression that replaces it. "Are you . . . ?"

"Stella Wright." I stick out my hand.

"Stella . . . you're Althea's daughter. Oh, my God."

I freeze. How does this man, whom I've never even laid eyes on, know who I am?

Yet another surprise, another revelation that raises more questions than answers. My skin is hot and flushed, and tears press behind my eyelids.

My overwhelm threatens to send me into hysterics, and I shake my head. "I'm sorry," I say. "I shouldn't have—I have to go."

CHAPTER TWENTY-THREE

Althea Anderson, January–April 1927

By January of the new year, Stella is beginning to roll over, reach for me as I work, and even babble. Charlie visits most Sundays after church, taking almost as much joy in her progress as I do. Our eyes often catch over Stella's head or our fingers brush as I pass her to him to hold, but we are rarely truly alone with one another. We talk medicine, debating recent progress such as the development of an intradermal tuberculosis vaccine and setbacks like the court's decision that Carrie Buck could be sterilized against her will, both of us hopeful that the Supreme Court would overturn the decree. We spend hours together with Stella, and by the time the girl is eight months old, or six from her due date, she is covering her eyes with fists for peek-a-boo whenever she sees Charlie. He plays with her in a way that I can't, throwing her into the air and tossing her with an abandon a mother lacks. With the arrival of spring in April, the three of us take regular trips together to picnic in the park, after which Stella and I take home an assortment of flowers for Mrs. Wallace to press into an old leather album. Daffodils are her favorite. "They make me feel like a girl again," she declares, pulling one from the pile to stash behind her ear. "Oh, how I could dance! That was the only way I knew to help Mr. Lincoln and the war, to dance with the soldiers home on leave and transport them into a world of gay ladies and fine dresses." She chuckles lightly. "Transport ourselves there, too. It wasn't so pretty even up here in the Union states, you know. But I can't complain." Her smile now is soft. "Met my husband in Lincoln's militia."

"There was fighting in New York?" I am surprised; never had I heard of a battle nearby when in school.

"No," Mrs. Wallace laughs, "except to protest the price of bread under inflation. My husband was sent in to keep the peace during the Draft Riots of sixty-three." Her voice softens. "We were married fifty-two years."

Unbidden, my thoughts drift back to Charlie. The sunbursts of witch hazel he picked for me to press alongside Mrs. Wallace and her daffodils. Would I be so happy now without him? No. I love his laugh and his eyes and his calm, steady hands; his eagerness and his passion and his recognition of a like mind despite its trappings. I love the time we spend with him, as if we're a family instead of a complicated mess.

It's exactly this that has stopped me from telling Charlie the truth. I saw sense after I almost told him in my moment of hopeful fantasy in November. No matter how many tests I might set up for Charlie, I can't know how he would react. This current existence can't last forever; nothing does. But I want it to go on as long as it can, and the fear that Charlie will reject us after learning the truth is too strong to let go. One day, I'll have to make a choice—but not yet. Not now, when things are too perfect to destroy. We are happy, now; why ruin it?

I released myself from half-mourning a year after my husband's alleged death. I once again wear colors and patterns, and I take off my rings unless I am out with Stella among strangers.

"I didn't love my husband," I confess to Charlie after we've returned to Mrs. Wallace's on a bright spring day. The lie feels like a truth; I had no husband, after all, to love. Stella is upstairs, her tiny ears unmarred by my decrial of the man who I claim is her father.

"I'm sorry," Charlie murmurs, but I barely hear the words. I stare transfixed at his lips, dark red against fair skin, and those gray eyes. His words are gentle and sympathetic, and he does nothing to belie that anything more lies beneath the surface. Then again, neither do I, my hands folded demurely in my lap. Is it possible that he is as hungry as I? Does he crave so desperately the touch of my hand the way I do his; does he break out in sweat at the very thought of my skin?

Althea, I demand, *control yourself.* But I cannot. Charlie has moved to sit beside me at the table, and he caresses my cheek gently. "You have been through so much, Althea."

I lower my eyes. I have, perhaps, but not in the ways he thinks. I am not a widow. I am merely a woman who has torn herself from her world to save a girl who isn't hers, a woman who has suffered by her own hand.

"Althea." He lifts my chin and brings his lips to mine. For a brief moment I feel nothing. I am too stunned.

But then God almighty, there it is. I feel it. I know now why

I have lain awake every night, know now what it is my body somehow knew I wanted.

I kiss Charlie back. *Forget about my husband*, I try to tell him, *forget that I am a widow*. I'm twenty-four, after all, and right here is exactly where I should be. "Charlie," I say aloud instead, whimpering as his hands alight like feathers on my waist.

He pulls back after a minute, his breath heavy and ragged. I stare back at him and try to calm my own breathing. Neither of us speaks.

"I've been waiting for that," I finally confess.

"Me, too." Charlie's nostrils flare with honesty. "Me, too."

Mrs. Wallace's voice cuts into the momentary silence. "Althea?" She is upstairs resting, tired from the time outside in the sun and the grass. "Althea?"

"Oh," I whisper. "Mrs. Wallace needs me."

"Of course." Charlie dips his chin. "I will see you tomorrow?"

"Please." I smile as I lead him to the door.

He tips his hat and disappears, the outline of his broad shoulders receding amid the car horns and horses. I watch him go and then close the door, wobbly, both giddy with joy and anxious for more. "I've been waiting for that," I'd whispered, and I had. But now I know too that I was waiting for so much more.

I go upstairs and pass my bedroom, heart rate increasing. Stella sleeps beside my bed, and I allow myself a brief moment of indulgence. What if Charlie and I were married, curled up beside her bassinet? Desire wraps around me, nostalgia for a family I've never had.

I force myself past my own bedroom and into Mrs. Wallace's. "You called?"

Her wrinkled face pulls into an apologetic smile. "I just need a glass of water, dear."

"Of course." *This is my job*, I remind myself. I cannot fault her for needing me. I fetch her a glass of water and then return downstairs alone. Birds chirp outside the window, and I press my forehead to it. Charlie, Stella, Mrs. Wallace, and I ate our midday meal out in Central Park, basking in the fresh air and the sun. Like a proper family. I again let myself picture things as I wish they could be: Charlie leaning over the picnic blanket to kiss me lightly, Mrs. Wallace bouncing Stella on her lap. Stella perched atop Charlie's shoulders. Wedding bands on his hand and mine.

Stella lets out a cry, and the image dissolves. "Coming, darling!" I call to her. I run up the stairs to quiet her before she wakes Mrs. Wallace. "Here, sweet girl." I cradle her and nudge her bottle gently between her lips. When she's done, I carry her down to the kitchen. She glances around the room quizzically, fuzzy eyebrows furrowed. She wriggles until I place her on the ground, and then she rocks in an attempt to crawl toward the door. I laugh lightly. "He's not here anymore, baby girl. But don't worry." I smile. "He'll be back."

Indeed, Charlie calls on our household the next morning. I am aiding Mrs. Wallace with her knitting when he knocks on the door, and I nearly trip over Stella in my haste to answer it. "Good morning!" I greet Charlie warmly, taking in the irresistible dusting of stubble along his chin. "Come on in."

He stoops to pick up Stella as he enters and swings her around. "How's our little birthday girl today?"

My eyes widen. "Charlie, you're right! She's nine months old today!"

He doesn't hear me. Stella is giggling with delight. Her choppy chuckle makes me laugh too, and Mrs. Wallace peeks her head around the doorframe to see what all the ruckus is about. She too smiles to see Stella's joy, and the four of us return to the sitting room to visit.

"I can't believe she'll be a year old soon." I shake my head as I gaze upon my daughter. Nine months. Seventy-five percent there. "And to think she'd be just over half a year had she been born full-term!"

Charlie whistles. "A miracle." I smile. Charlie's frankness is one of my favorite aspects of his demeanor. He doesn't dilute his thoughts or beliefs for the sake of propriety or comfort. He is passionate and intense, and he never falters. He continues now. "Do you have any plans for her real birthday in July?"

I grin. "Perhaps we'll simply tell her the fireworks the night before are hers."

"Nonsense!" Mrs. Wallace drops a stitch. "You must give her a proper party. I'll have my son and daughter-in-law come into town, and of course the good doctor." She points at Charlie with a knitting needle, and he shrinks back slightly. "Althea, you ought to bake her a cake."

"Mm." I close my eyes and breathe in. "I have a lovely recipe for the Ritz lemon pound cake. Or perhaps I ought to make the butterscotch penuche. Lemon may be too sour for our little star." I sweep her into my arms.

"I suppose she's too young for one of Nathan's famous hot dogs," Charlie jokes. "But a trip out to Coney Island would be fitting."

Stella squeals as I grip her upper arm tightly.

"Sorry, darling." I lower her to the floor so she can play and then look up at Charlie. "I'm not sure . . ." I cough. "It might bring up traumatic memories for her." A weak excuse, as there's no chance of Stella remembering the first few weeks of life. But the best I can invent. "The incubators, the pneumonia . . ."

"Of course. I'm sorry if I was being insensitive."

"No!" Guilt forces the corners of my lips into a stiff smile. "It's a wonderful idea. I'm just a paranoid mother." I attempt a breezy laugh that comes out as a bark. Well. I'm not one for breeziness even at my best.

I must steer the conversation from Luna Park. Absurdly, all I can think of beyond Stella's birthday is Charlie's crimson mouth. The winter of his face: snow-gray eyes, berry-red lips, the dark shadow of his scruff.

I swallow. Now is not the time. Not with Mrs. Wallace's knitting needles clacking beside me and my daughter skirting under the table in an imagined game of peek-a-boo. Charlie takes pity on her and covers his eyes. "Where's Stella?" he coos. "Stella, Stella, Stella Star? Where are you?" He draws the words out so she laughs. "Aha! I hear her!" he cries, ducking his head underneath the table to meet her eyes. "I found her!" He pulls her up and tickles her belly.

My thoughts darken with envy. My father never played with me so, wrapped up as he was in grief and anger. *But perhaps Stella's life can be different*, I think as I look at Charlie. What a lovely father he would make. Never would any daughter of his fear speaking up or speaking out. She would have his authenticity.

And how lucky his wife would be, too. I feel my face flood

with heat, and I lecture myself sternly. *Adenylyl cyclase*, I remind myself. *Vasodilation of the blood vessels in the face. That is all.* I repeat the steady, unchanging science to myself until my blush fades.

But what of the rest of my body, flushed and eager? I shake my shoulders slightly to remind myself where I am. The formal sitting room of my aged employer and with my infant daughter.

I smile as that very daughter's face shines with glee. Perhaps we are an odd group, arranged here around the sofa with the knitting and the milk and the medicine. But my daughter is happy. My daughter is happy, and so am I.

As long as I can forget how Hattie must feel today, how she must feel on the fifth of every month. She's spent nine months grieving while I've been gifted Stella's first smiles and laughs and watched her learn to roll over and learn to crawl. Hattie has spent nine months sleeping beside a dangerous man while I have spent nine months curled beside their precious baby girl.

Almighty God, I pray silently. *Watch over Hattie. And forgive me, dear Lord, for all my sins.*

Stella laughs loudly, and my gaze jumps to where she rocks on her knees in front of Charlie. He's tickling her belly and she's wrapped up in that deep, gurgling laugh I am so in love with. The sound is pure joy, and I take a deep breath.

Stella is happy. I have done nothing that needs forgiving.

I am eager to see Charlie alone again, as we haven't had a moment without Stella and Mrs. Wallace since our kiss. But when he bounds through the door in the early morning two days later—early enough that I am the only one awake—he is so excited I nearly forget what's happened between us. His eyes appear translucent in the morning light, and his lashes sparkle as with dew. Stella will be delighted to see him when she awakes.

"Althea," Charlie crows, "I've done it."

"Done what?" I laugh, too surprised to even help him with his coat. "What have you done?" I imagine mornings like this one in our future, set alight by his passion and fire.

"You know I've been meeting with doctors from hospitals across the city. Interviews, tours, just preliminary things. But now I've partnered with Julius Hess, Althea, the pioneering neonatologist." The excitement in his voice sounds like a child's, and I wonder what Stella's passions will be as she turns two and five and ten. "Hess and I are going to study, improve, and then publicize Couney's incubators, Althea, and we aren't going to stop until every hospital in this city has an incubator ward for its babies, Althea. Every last one."

I am filled with a cocktail of elation and hopelessness more potent than any drink banned by law. "So you'll work," I clarify, "with Couney?"

"Yes." Charlie grabs my hand eagerly. "And you started it all."

But I no longer hear him. His hand on mine sends electricity rocketing through my body, even as my heart plummets.

I cannot be part of his life anymore. Not if he's going to exist in my old world, the world in which I am a nurse but not a mother. He would find out. He would find out, and Stella would be taken from me.

His next words confirm my fears. "I asked the doctor if he remembered you! He definitely knew the name, and he said surely the nurses would be able to recall—"

I pull him suddenly tighter, desperate to feel his skin on mine for the last time. Desperate too to stop the words he spews with such passion.

I crush my lips against his and grasp his face between my hands; he is as hungry as I, the weight of his desire sending me stumbling backward. Pressed against the wall, I pull Charlie closer. Every inch of his body is touching mine, so why, why, *why* does it feel as if we are still not close enough? His right hand reaches into my hair, his left down toward my waist.

This is the last time he will ever touch me. My only chance. I feel his heartbeat as strong as my own and pull open his shirt to reach it. *My only chance.* I moan when my fingers land on his chest. I have seen the skin of many men in my work, but the physicality of the body fades in the harsh light of duty. The body in the hospital is the body in an anatomy textbook: mere muscle, skin, and bone. But Charlie's body against mine pulses, summoning from somewhere within mine the tears I've buried for decades. He wipes them oh so gently from my face as they flow and then returns his hands with sudden violence to my hips, his hands fighting fabric in their search for skin. I'm in an ankle-length skirt over my shirtwaist, and Charlie is able to slide his hands beneath the waistband so his thumbs layer over my hip bones. I am warm as if I have stepped naked into a creek under the hot summer sun. The water rises to my thighs, flows between them, and I draw my nails across Charlie's sweat-soaked skin. I want to go upstairs, and the clarity of the thought shocks me. I want to pull Charlie into bed with me and tumble into sin. But Stella is up there.

Stella.

Stella.

Stella. The reason I can never kiss this man again, the reason it is so wrong to give him this impression. The reason Charlie can never see my naked body and the reason that now I can never see him again at all. *Oh, Charlie,* I think with a jolt, *what have I done?* I stumble sideways to stand apart from him, though the need for his body still rages in my own.

"Oh, no." He shakes his head, his own breath ragged. "I'm so sorry, Althea, I—"

"No. Please don't." I don't want the last memory of the man I love to be an apology for the same. *Love.* Dear God, I love him.

"No, but—" He scrabbles through the pockets of his coat where it hangs near the door. "I wasn't trying to take advantage"— he shakes his head—"I . . ." He pulls out a glittering silver ring. It is small and delicate; it would not slide loosely on my fingers like the gold ones I bought myself at the pawnshop. It would fit.

This is everything I've wanted. Everything I want for myself. Everything I want for Stella.

Except that now, marrying Charlie would plunge us all into danger. I imagine my daughter with the Perkinses. The violence of a father, the rejection of a mother. And the disappearance of the woman who'd raised her. Welfare Island and its desperate souls materialize in my mind for the first time in months. I swallow as Charlie thrusts the sparkling ring toward me. "Althea, I want to marry you."

Shoulders down, back straight. Chin up, eyes down. A nurse is composed even in the face of agony and death. "Mrs. Wallace will be waking soon," I say evenly. "I ought to go attend to her. I trust you can see yourself out."

fall into bed and cry. It seems Charlie has unlocked my tears, and Stella peers confusedly between the slats of her crib. The blanket at Mrs. Wallace's house felt so luxurious when I first moved in—so much softer than the standard-issue one I'd had at the dormitory. Now, I can hardly bear to be underneath its stifling heat. I itch where the fabric rubs against bare skin.

I'm trapped enough in my life. My complicated, convoluted life. My life of lies. My life of denial.

I tuck my thumbs into my palms and wrap my fingers around them till the joints pop. *Charlie, Charlie, Charlie.* My toes twitch with each iteration of his name.

Charlie. I love him. I want him. I want to slide my stiff, exhausted body into bed beside his warm one each night. I want him to be there when I wake in the dark to feed Stella. I want him there when we wake up in the morning, and then I want to spend the day with him: coffee and conversation at the breakfast table, picnics at the park with Stella. I want to work beside him, laugh with him, even fight with him.

I love Charlie.

But I love Stella more.

For her, I am of course filled to the very brim with gratitude; joy, even. If Couney's incubators can be introduced into Bellevue, St. John's, hospitals across Brooklyn and Manhattan—well, millions of lives can be saved. I don't doubt that Couney himself has already saved thousands. How much more can be done in hospitals?

But must Charlie, my Charlie, be the one to do it?

He is not your *Charlie*, I remind myself sharply. And indeed, he is certainly not my Charlie now. He cannot be. Not if he is going to be part of the circles I must forever avoid: those at Bellevue, at Coney, those who know that I am a nurse rather than a mother.

A true mother is not so selfish, I think. I should be overwhelmed with joy that other babies like my own will be saved.

But I feel so alone.

No. I gaze at my daughter's round face in her crib. Giving up Charlie guarantees one thing: I will always have Stella.

I wake the next morning before my daughter does. I do not forget even for a moment the events of yesterday, instead peeling through them again. I am desperate enough to hope my reaction was overly dramatic; I pray that I overstated the effects of Charlie's decision. There must be an alternative to leaving him. But no. Perhaps if I'd confessed earlier, told him the truth—but I can no longer risk it. Not when he is working with the very nurses I deceived, the very hospital from which I was let go. Now, telling Charlie would mean more than losing our blissful days together. It might mean losing Stella, too. And even Charlie would be in danger. Asking him to keep my secret would mean asking him to lie to his colleagues and his bosses; if we were ever caught, he'd end up in jail just as I would.

I've done all of this for Stella. I've lost my home and my job, broken the law, lied to a grieving mother. By taking Stella as my own, I've made a commitment to give her a better, safer life than her parents would have. And I can't stop now. I don't get to make decisions for me anymore.

My decisions must be for Stella.

I wipe the tears from my eyes and swing my feet to the floor. I pull the sheets up and make the bed. The reality of the situation is painfully simple. I must never see Charlie again.

CHAPTER TWENTY-FOUR

Stella Wright, January 1951

Hattie has dismissed me. My mother's place is full of ghosts. A doctor I've never seen before recognized me and knew my mother's name. I can't call Jack at work again without risking getting him in serious trouble. I feel like a stranger in my own life.

I flee the hospital, and my feet unconsciously carry me to Rockefeller Center. Disappearing into the masses of early-evening holiday visitors and the anonymity of my hometown will be a welcome respite. If only I were a tourist, with no connections to this place beyond joy at its spectacle.

I'm in anything but the Christmas spirit, two weeks and a thousand revelations after the holiday. But still the tree that dominates Rockefeller Plaza takes my breath away. I remember the height from my childhood—the tree is something like sixty feet tall—but the decorations have transformed in the decade-plus since I last visited. Hundreds of sparkling orbs dangle from the branches, and garlands thicker than my arms drape in gentle curves like frosting on a cake.

Last time I was here was the year they opened the skating rink. They celebrated by erecting not one tree but two, and I remember gaping up at the enormous set. At ten years old, I was too short to even graze the lowest branches with my outstretched arms. But Mom didn't let me stay disappointed for long. She hoisted me up, though I couldn't have weighed much less than she did by then, and gritted her teeth until I was able to snatch a snow-dusted pine needle from one tree. Then we both collapsed to the ground giggling—until a disgruntled employee chased us away from the display, that is. I smile to myself. That was the naughtiest I ever saw my straitlaced mother.

My grin disappears. That silly moment may be the only misbehavior I remember from Althea, but I know now it was the least of her crimes.

I walk over to the ticket seller by the rink and purchase admission for seventy-five cents. Finding a bench to sit on and removing my pumps, I stuff my feet into the rented shoe-skates and then hobble to the rink to join the other skaters.

I haven't skated in years, so I should start slow. But I don't. I pump my legs until I'm gliding, the muscles in my thighs beginning to burn. I want to escape myself, escape the jumble of my thoughts. The skates chafe at my ankles. I keep going. The chilly air is freeing, refreshing. It stings my eyes and freezes the tears on my eyelashes.

Suddenly a child stops a few yards before me. His big, blinking eyes widen as I speed in his direction. His freckles look like my student Robby's. I try frantically to stop and finally throw myself to the side in a desperate attempt to avoid hitting him.

I fall hard on my shoulder, splinters of ice spraying my face. My groan is muffled under my scarf. My hat has flown off and landed who knows where.

I'm testing my ability to sit up when a pair of ice skates stop on a dime before me. I look up. A man holds my soft green hat in his left hand and reaches with his right to help me up. I stand but wobble, and he steadies me.

"Thank you." My words come out stiff with embarrassment.

"Happens to the best of us." The man pulls my hat over my head, his large hands on either side of my face. I recoil slightly, my eyebrows drawing together. His gold eyes suddenly look like a snake's.

"Well." I turn to skate away, but the man grabs my wrist. He yanks me back toward him.

"I don't think you're ready to get back out there yet."

"I am." I pull back, but his fingers tighten on my wrist.

"You took a pretty hard fall."

Speak up. I find my voice. "And you're about to as well, if you don't let go of me."

He raises his hands, releasing my wrist so aggressively that I lose my balance again. I brace the muscles in my legs to keep from falling.

My "rescuer" skates away with a huff, and I stare after him. Jack is protective, but he'd never be physical like that. My father—God, to think that Michael Perkins is my father—is violent, but my husband is not.

Jack. I see his golden hair, his bright eyes, his broad shoulders.

"Damn it," I whisper under my breath. Even here, under the sparkling Rockefeller trees, I can't escape my story. I can't forget my mother, the Perkinses, Jack. And when that child stopped in front of me, I could have sworn it was Robby, out of his wheelchair and not just walking but skating for the first time in his life. It's been a month since I've seen my children—and they aren't mine anymore—but I can't forget them, either.

I make my halting way off the rink and turn in my skates. Whether I want to or not, it's time to face my childhood home.

grimace as I pull open the door to our unit, dreading the cold. I'm hit instead with the thick, warm scent of tomato soup and the flicker of candles.

Has someone been in the apartment? Terror rising, I peer sideways into the next room. I grab the coat rack between two hands and prepare to lift it—and then I recognize the coat hanging from its spindly arms.

"Jack?"

"Stella!" Jack comes barreling out of the kitchen as if I've conjured him. He reaches his arms toward me, and I wrap my own around his back. I nestle my head against his chest.

"You came."

"Of course I came! I wanted to come to the hospital, but I didn't know which one. I stopped at the café instead and got you some soup."

There's no *of course* about it. Jack will do almost anything to avoid the city. The fact that he's here means more than I can express; it shows me that even if he can't share his past, he can push it aside when it matters.

"Thank you," I say as we move to the kitchen to eat. "Speaking of the hospital . . ." I tell him about my conversation with Hattie. "She didn't claim me, but—Jack, we're identical. It's obvious."

Jack squeezes my hand. "I can't imagine how hard this is for you, sweetheart. But if it counts for anything, I don't care if your mom was Eleanor Roosevelt herself."

I smile at him and squeeze back. "Wouldn't that be neat."

Jack scooches closer and puts his lips to my hair. "I just care that you're you."

I sigh. "It's just that I hardly even know who that is, now. Because of all this—and quitting. I don't really have any of *me* left."

Jack pulls back and looks into my eyes. "Stella Wright. You are fearless and curious and obstinate. You are smart and beautiful and persistent. Do you need me to go on?"

I shake my head. "Am I *too* persistent and obstinate? Am I . . ." I whisper my final words. ". . . like Michael?"

"No." Jack grips my shoulder. "You're the daughter of a brilliant, gentle mother. You're the daughter of her husband, protective and kind. And perhaps you're the daughter of Hattie Perkins, who atoned for her earlier sins by sending you away as an adult to save you from her husband. But you are not Michael Perkins's daughter, Stella. No matter whose blood runs through your veins."

I trace Jack's jaw with my fingers, take in his bright eyes. For him, what matters is the present. He cares who I am, not where I came from. It's no wonder he can't understand why I need to probe so deeply into his dark past; he wants to focus on the here and now.

"Jack." I lean into him. "Thank you for coming."

He takes my hand and laces his fingers with mine. "It was easy to make the 5:47 train after work." He feigns nonchalance.

Despite the lightness of his tone, he knows what I'm really saying. I'm not thanking him for the train ride or the time taken from his day. I'm thanking him for being here. I'm thanking him for showing me that, however much I've doubted it, I matter more to him than his demons.

An hour later, Jack and I lie tangled in my childhood twin. "More cramped than the back seat at a drive-in movie," Jack teases, and I scold him.

I reach out so that my fingers graze my mother's charm box on my nightstand. "Do you want to see?"

Jack nods and watches as I pull everything out. I show him the flower, the obituary, the photograph, the letter.

"What's that?" he asks when I'm done.

"What's what?"

He points to the faded newspaper clippings pressed into the bottom of the box.

"Oh, those. Just scraps. Mom used them as lining for the box. She said the wood could degrade the paper, or something."

"Anything interesting on them?"

"I doubt it." The side facing up is part of an advertisement for soap. I peel the brittle pages from the wood anyway, flipping them over to find cutouts from the classified pages.

I scan through the ads.

Neat-appearing widow, past 40, refined, good house-keeper and cook. Wishes to meet gentleman who can give good home, object matrimony; best references.

Young widow, 24, and mother of infant girl. Seeking kind man; object, matrimony. Direct letters to A., c/o M. Wallace, Times Square.

Young man wishes the acquaintance of beautiful girl, age about 25 years: I like hiking and theaters, do not dance: anyone interested please answer; object matri-mony. Box 3251.

"They're ads for matrimony!" I exclaim. "What would mine say? 'Stubborn, obstinate girl seeking easygoing husband'?"

Jack chuckles. "Better than mine: 'War vet, twenty-six, seeking passionate young woman who will put up with his epi-sodes.'"

I squeeze Jack. "I don't put up with you. I'm lucky to have you. In fact, yours should read: 'Dashing young man, seeking woman to make laugh.'"

Jack kisses my forehead. "Is that woman coming home with me tonight?"

I suck in my cheeks. "I'm sorry, Jack. It's just—I've been thinking. I want to talk to the doctor. The one who does the in-cubators at Bellevue. He recognized me and I have no idea how. He knew my mom's name."

Jack nods. "Okay. That I understand. But you aren't going to go see Hattie again, are you? I don't want either of you getting hurt."

I look up sharply. Jack knows me too well. I had been considering it; she's my birth mother, for God's sake. And I know nothing about her.

But maybe Jack is right. Dismissing me earlier today may have been the only way she knew to save me. And regardless, I don't want to put her in danger yet again. I look Jack in the eye and promise. "Just the doctor."

"I'd like to come with you. It sounded like he frightened you today."

I shake my head. "I was just overwhelmed, and shocked that he knew me. I can't imagine he's dangerous."

Jack sighs. "Okay. But you'll call me after? And you'll come home tomorrow night?"

"Absolutely."

Jack kisses me. "I'll stay the night too, then."

"But you have work in the morning," I protest weakly, hoping he'll say it doesn't matter.

"I can leave early tomorrow."

I reach over and hug him. "I love you."

"I love you, too," he says. "But I'm starving."

"I'm sure we can rummage something up in the kitchen," I say. We have leftover soup, and I bought a loaf of bread and cheese the first day.

"You don't want to go out?"

I look at Jack, who was too frightened three days ago to even come to the city. "No." I grin at him and wink. "Let's stay in."

The next morning, I wake up early alongside Jack so I can walk him downstairs and kiss him as he steps into the taxicab. "I love you," I tell him, and I've never meant it more.

Once he's gone, I climb into my own taxi and head for Bellevue. It's too early for visiting hours, which is a blessing. I'm afraid that I won't be able to resist the temptation of stopping in on Hattie otherwise.

I knock on the doctor's door again. This time, I'm prepared for his recognition.

"Stella! You're back."

"Good morning, Doctor. I'm so sorry about the way I left yesterday. I was overwhelmed. But I do have a few questions for you, if you have time to chat with me?"

"I have a few minutes now," the doctor says, staring at me. "But if you want to come back around noon, we can take an hour and go get lunch."

I remember Jack's fears and decline. "Now is fine." Nothing can happen to me in the hospital.

The doctor ushers me into his office, and I sit.

"We didn't officially meet," the doctor smiles wryly as he offers me a hand. "Dr. Morrison."

"Stella Wright." I shake it. "But you already knew that. And you knew my mother, Althea?"

Dr. Morrison nods. "I did. Isn't that why you're here?"

I shake my head. "It is now. Yesterday, I was just dropping in to ask you about the incubators for premature babies. I think I was premature, but back before the incubators were at Bellevue. When they were only out on Coney Island."

"You *think*? Stella—"

I cough. "Mrs. Wright."

"Mrs. Wright." He runs a hand through his graying hair. The color matches his eyes. "I'm sorry. I knew you when you were a baby. I almost—I almost felt as if I were your father."

"How is that possible? I had my own father." I narrow my eyes. "Horace Johnson."

Dr. Morrison opens his mouth to speak, but I raise an eyebrow. "Let me explain why I'm here," I say first. "Then you can tell me what you know."

I explain about the pink ribbon and what I learned from Hildegarde and Louise, and Dr. Morrison's face slowly drains of color. He shakes his head slightly, and his lips move. No sound comes out.

"Doctor? Are you all right?"

He closes his eyes. "All of these questions you have . . . why are you asking me, instead of her?" His voice falters like he already knows the answer. "And you're sorting through her things . . ."

"Oh," I say softly. "Oh, I'm so sorry. My mother . . ."

Dr. Morrison puts up a hand, and I stop. I don't want to say it any more than he wants to hear it.

"When did it happen?" His voice is choked, and I feel my own tears threaten.

"September fifteenth," I whisper. "Cancer."

Dr. Morrison's eyes close again, and his chest rises and falls. I sit awkwardly across from him, used to being on the receiving end of sympathy for my mother's passing and not knowing what to say now that the roles have reversed. "I'm sorry," I repeat. "You didn't know?"

"It's been years since I saw her." He shakes his head. "Last time I saw you, you were an infant."

I need to keep us talking so we don't fall apart. "I don't understand," I say. "How did you know my mom? Did you meet here when she was a nurse?"

He shakes his head. "I've only been here the last seven years. I used to be a private physician, and I treated Mrs. Wallace."

"Mrs. Wallace . . ." The name sounds familiar, but I can't place it. "I don't know her."

He explains that my mother worked for her as a caretaker when I was an infant. "Althea was so proud of you and Couney's incubators. I can't believe she never told you about the island."

"There was a reason for that," I say slowly. I hesitate to share my mother's secrets with this man, but then I have nothing more to lose. "I don't think I was truly hers."

Dr. Morrison looks at me quickly with an emotion I can't pinpoint, and then sits with his head bowed as I tell him the rest of the story. I explain Hattie's note, Margaret's birth and death certificates, my missing birth certificate. When I tell Dr. Morrison I was born September 5, 1926, he looks up at me and shakes his head. "I met you in September. You were already two months old, born July 5."

"Just like Margaret," I say.

Dr. Morrison cradles his head in his hands. "Yet you're so like Althea."

"What?" My whole life, people have commented on our differences: my rounder face, lighter hair, softer body.

"Your mannerisms. You pull your ear the same way she did."

I can envision it so vividly, the way she would tug on her ear when she was eager or impatient. I feel a rush of affection for my mother so strong I nearly collapse.

"You also see things as clearly as she did, as black and white."

"Except that I don't see anything clearly right now."

Dr. Morrison collapses into the chair behind his desk, head in his hands. He deliberates for a moment, my foot tapping impatiently, and then looks up. "Your mother never did anything without great intention, Ste—Mrs. Wright."

"It's okay," I interrupt gently. Something in his voice—and his grief—tells me he may have been more than a colleague to my mother. "Stella is fine."

"Stella. Althea was the most devoted mother I've known. She took you everywhere, stayed up with you all night when you were sick, put you first in every decision she ever made. Sometimes I worried about her own well-being, she was so concerned with you. Your mom hardly had any money for your baptism, but she went without buying her own food—ate your leftover purées for a week—to save up for your gown. She was so proud of you, Stella." He shakes his head. "I'm sorry. I have so many memories . . . but what I'm trying to say is that, if your mother did lie to you about who your father was—or even who *she* was—she had good reason to do so."

The Althea the doctor describes sounds like the mother I knew. Selfless almost to the point of weakness.

Or so I thought. Maybe she was selfish to the point of strength.

"But she lied to me."

"Oh, Stella." Dr. Morrison circles the desk to crouch before me. "Stella. She lied to me, too. But it doesn't change how I feel about her."

"And how *do* you feel about her?"

"I loved her." He doesn't play coy. "I still do, even if she's gone." His voice breaks. "Even if I didn't know her story. Even if . . ." His mouth twists in pain. "Even if she walked out of my life the day I asked her to marry me."

"To marry you!" I gasp, nearly forgetting my own saga in the midst of his.

"I thought she loved me too."

It isn't impossible to believe my mom loved this man. His eyes have a magnetism to them, an intensity quite unlike my father's. I can see how my focused mother would have been attracted to Dr. Morrison's passion. And his love is genuine. His grief is no act; his body slumped when he realized Mom was dead, and he has yet to straighten.

"Why did she marry my father?" I murmur. "Or—Horace Johnson. I suppose he wasn't my father."

"He *was* your father," Dr. Morrison says gently. "If you saw him as such."

There's a question in his eyes I don't know how to answer. Did Althea see Horace Johnson as a husband the way I saw him as a father? Did she love him?

I don't know. They weren't passionate or even romantic. But they lived in peace together for decades.

"I don't know anything anymore," I admit. "I don't know who my parents are or if they loved each other or who I belong to."

"There's a lot I don't know, too," Dr. Morrison says. "But I knew Althea. She was smart and brave and always certain of what was right. She was careful and caring and protective. And no number of lies can change that, Stella. No secrets can." He's crying, and it occurs to me for the first time that I never saw my father cry. But Dr. Morrison's tears don't seem a sign of weakness. They're signs of love. He's one of the few people still alive, I realize, who still loves and grieves my mother like I do. He understands.

And he's right. My mother was kind and selfless to a fault. I never once doubted her devotion over the years, even when I was a bratty teenager out for a fight. Biological mother or not, lying or not, she was my mother.

But I'm still desperate to know with certainty who I am. "She never told you the truth about me?" I plead. "You never saw her again?"

"I don't know anything else." He shakes his head, as mournful as I. "And—" He falters. "I never saw her again."

CHAPTER TWENTY-FIVE

Althea Anderson, April 1927

I craft an ad for employment as Stella sleeps. Twenty-six words take two hours to write, but I deliberate over each one. I reread the results: *Widow with young daughter. Experience as nurse. Seeking live-in work with invalid, family, or single woman. Full-time. Apply to Althea Anderson, c/o Mrs. Wallace, Times Square.*

Nothing astounding, but I suppose it will do. I pick up a paper I'd discarded earlier in the week and flip through its chalky pages. Running my eyes down the personals, I check to ensure I didn't skip anything important. Age, experience, position wanted, and contact. Satisfied, I move to put down the paper and pause. There, mixed in with the employment advertisements is a word that could have been mine: *matrimony.*

Don't look, Althea. Any wedding-related advertisement will merely upset me, after what I've turned down. I don't want to read about the flowers I could have ordered or the beautiful gown I could have worn walking down the aisle toward Charlie.

But my eyes jump quickly to the advertisement despite my best effort. *WANTED—Female companion; single; about 35 years for single business man; object matrimony. J.J., Times Office.*

Not an advertisement for wedding-related services, then.

An advertisement looking for a bride.

The chemical smell of the newsprint ink nauseates me as I reach for another old paper. I run my finger down the line, not sure whether I do or do not want to find more advertisements in the same vein. For a while I don't, but then here is one: *Young man wishes the acquaintance of beautiful girl, age about 25 years: I like hiking and theaters, do not dance: anyone interested please answer; object matrimony. Box 3251.*

Shaking my head, I turn the pages. The ads go both ways; here is one for a woman seeking a man. *Neat-appearing widow, past 40, refined, good housekeeper and cook. Wishes to meet gentleman who can give good home, object matrimony; best references.* I cringe— *good housekeeper and cook?* The ad befits a prospective employee more than a prospective wife.

My stomach turns the way it did that long-ago day at Coney Island as I watched the kids on the roller coaster scream. If a woman can put this sort of advertisement in the paper, couldn't I?

I turn the pages quickly. They seem to be everywhere. Here is another.

Another.

Another.

I set the papers down, the tips of my thumbs and pointer fingers black like soot. Turning my palm away, I knead the bone of my wrist against my forehead and look to Stella. She sleeps on her tummy, her bum in the air like a baby bear.

A baby bear without a father.

I stagger to the bathroom as my thoughts crystallize. Stella needs a father. She needs a father and—the thought is sour—she needs someone who can support her. Without a nursing position, and now that I must give notice to Mrs. Wallace, I won't be able to do it. Being a woman alone in this world is a dangerous gamble. Alone, Stella and I would barely stay afloat in the best of times, and if one of us gets sick—if she has complications from being born premature or I end up with the same cancer that killed my father—we'll sink.

And if I have one job, it's to keep my baby girl afloat.

CHAPTER TWENTY-SIX

Stella Wright, January 1951

I do one final sweep of the apartment before leaving. I've packed my valise and filled a box with things to take home—china plates, a few pieces of jewelry, a blanket. The charm box I place in my purse. I want it safe and close to me. It started all of this, after all.

The train ride home is long, and I pick through Mom's box with new eyes. This time, I look at the flower and wonder if it could have been from Dr. Morrison. I look at the note and marvel at the thought that that fingerprint—its tiny whorls and smudge of impatience—is my own.

When I tuck the note away and see the print from the newspaper clipping, it hits me. I know now where I'd heard Mrs. Wallace's name before.

> Young widow, 24, mother of infant girl. Seeking
> kind man; object, matrimony. Direct letters to A., c/o
> M. Wallace, Times Square.

I stare at it in shock. So that was where my mother met my father, twenty years her senior. But why? Why on earth would she leave Dr. Morrison, a doctor her own age who truly loved her, when she was willing to settle for a stranger?

I close my eyes. Marriage is complicated; I know that well enough. I may never understand why my mother married my father, but he was that. He was my father, like Dr. Morrison said.

I left Dr. Morrison my Poughkeepsie address before leaving this morning. "If you can pass a copy to Hattie, too," I whispered, "safely? I'd appreciate that."

I hope the doctor reaches out. I'm hungry for the pieces of my mother he can return to me: What did she wear to my baptism? What was her relationship with Mrs. Wallace? Did she read poetry even then? What was her favorite flower? Did she still talk about nursing when the doctor knew her? Did she feel about it the way I feel about teaching?

I'm also hungry for someone who can understand my grief. Hungry to connect with someone who loved my mother as much as I do.

Jack is not yet home when I get back; he'll work until five p.m. I leave my box of things behind the desk at the train station, promising to come back for it with my husband and the car later, and then walk home with my purse and my valise.

I let myself in, change into a fresh skirt and blouse, and head to the town library. I've spent so much time untangling my mother's life; it's time now to untangle mine.

It's time to protect my students the way my mother protected me.

"Good morning." I greet the older woman behind the circulation desk. "Do you have any volumes on the education of handicapped children?"

Her eyelids twitch. "Handicapped children?"

"Yes."

"I don't think so." She rifles through a card catalog. "Does such a thing even exist?"

"Education"—I glare—"or the handicapped child?" I'm quick to take offense where my students are concerned; I blame Gardner's abuse.

"L-literature about them," the woman stammers like a scolded child.

I'm too embarrassed to admit that after a year and a half of teaching special education I don't know. Embarrassed I never thought to educate myself on this before, to do more for my students than just love them. "They must."

"I'm not seeing anything in our catalog. Perhaps you ought to check the Vassar library," the woman suggests.

It's a good idea, and I thank her with a smile.

I pass several of Jack's and my favorite college spots as I make my way to Thompson Library. There's the vast Vassar Farm, which I tilled endlessly during the war but which I remember more for Jack getting kicked by a cow during a milking. I dissolved into laughter at his indignation, until the cow turned its stony gaze toward me. Then Jack was the one laughing through the pain in his side.

Beyond the farm, I see the tree under which Jack kissed me

the first time. The bench on which we shared our first Vassar Devil. The building in which we attended our only shared class, whispering and snickering in the back of the room.

And now Thompson Memorial Library rises ahead, its white spires out of a European fairy tale. I pull open the heavy wooden doors and step inside, my shoes clomping on the gleaming trapezoid tiles below. I turn left to the circulation desk as the grandfather clock across the room chimes twelve times for the hour. The girl behind the desk cannot be too much younger than I am, but her bare left hand and easy smile widen the gap. "Good afternoon." I incline my head slightly. "Do you know where the books on teaching students with handicaps are kept?"

"Of course." The girl searches the card catalog and reads a number, then points me in the correct direction. I'm headed away from the famed Cornaro Window, and I make a note to return and pay it my respects as I leave. I can't help but notice as I turn away that the circulation girl's lips are a perfect Cupid's bow. Just like Hattie's. Just like mine.

I force myself back into the present moment. Only two books sit shelved under the classification given me: last year's *Journal of Exceptional Children* and a recently published *Education of Handicapped Children.*

"Exceptional." I taste the word and decide I like it.

Settling into a seat, I open the first book. It consists of various articles, some of which are relevant and some of which are not. I skim over the various options on visual impairment or private school or infancy, skipping instead to articles that may be of use to the kids I teach. *Taught*, I correct myself.

By the time I'm done with both books, I have a long list of

notes. Some of them are functional, such as separating desks so students are less distracted by those beside them. Some are academic, like R. N. Walker's "realistic arithmetic" tips or the suggestion that even nonreaders be taught to recognize common street signs. And some, best of all, are fun. Entire articles sing the praises of teaching children music, puppetry, and crafting to foster expression, communication, and even cooperation. I've even sketched a silly little drawing on my notes sheet. Mary Ellen stands in the center, a cheerful Snow White. Judy holds an apple, a defiant grin slashed across her face. Seven kids surround Mary Ellen as the dwarves, and James stands apart to read the narration. Sweet, gentle Robby is the prince waiting in the wings.

I tuck the clumsy drawing into my purse, clasping it shut with the golden latch, and rise. Before leaving, I pad to the south side of the library where the Cornaro Window filters in rays of colored light. Lady Elena Lucrezia Cornaro-Piscopia commands the center of the stained glass awaiting her crown of leaves; men in shades of yellow and green and blue and purple and red bow down before her. I give the lady a mock salute as my friends and I were wont to do in our college days. As the first woman in the world to receive a doctorate degree in 1678, Lady Elena serves as an inspiration for the women at Vassar riddled with doubt.

"You didn't give up either, did you?" I trace the outline of the woman's long white robes. "You didn't, and Dr. Morrison didn't, and Dr. Couney and Hildegarde and Nurse Recht didn't." And my mom, more than anyone, never gave up on me. Like the doctors and the nurses, she fought for me when I was too young and weak to fight for myself. She sacrificed for me, poured love into me, gave me all the chances to pursue the romance and career she never had.

I can never thank her for what she did, and the pain of that realization is visceral and sharp.

I breathe deeply. I can't thank my mother, but I know what she'd want me to do instead. She'd want me to give the gift of love to someone else. To intervene for someone else the way she intervened for me.

I take a deep breath. The nurses, the doctors, and my mom fought for me. But who is fighting for my kids?

J ack runs to meet me when I open the door to our house that night, and I embrace him. "Something smells good. Did you cook?"

"No." He looks sheepish. "I picked up those Italian sandwiches you like as a welcome home."

I laugh and kiss him. "Sounds more like you. And yummier, too." Over our meal, I tell him what I learned from Dr. Morrison. "He loved her, Jack. And I never knew he existed."

I expect him to crack a joke—maybe, *Our daughter better know I exist.* But instead, he reaches out and touches my hand. "He's loved her for twenty years?"

"More."

"I can't imagine," Jack whispers, "not being with you for all that time."

I squeeze his hand and wipe my eyes before they can well up with tears. "Me neither. I don't understand. Why do you think she married my dad, some stranger she met through a newspaper ad?"

"I have no idea. But with everything else we've learned, we can probably assume she did it for you."

We sit in silence for a moment, both of us thinking. "Your mom did the same thing for you, in a way. Raised you on her own to keep you safe from your father."

He shrugs. "A mother's love."

It's a testament to how hard he's trying that he doesn't mention my becoming a mother, too.

"How do you feel?" he asks me instead.

"Overwhelmed, mostly." I shake my head. "I felt betrayed at first, but after everything I've learned I'm grateful to her. She gave me a good life."

Jack nods along. "Even when it wasn't easy for her."

"Exactly." I lean forward. "Jack, I've been thinking. She didn't let all the opposition get in her way, and I know she wouldn't want me to, either." I tell him about what I learned at the library. "I know that the school won't hire me again this year, what with the new teacher being there, but—"

"Actually, Stella, I have something to tell you." Jack puts down his sandwich. "I was afraid to mention it before."

"What? What happened?" My head shoots up, hands sending my plate spiraling toward the center of the table.

"The woman they hired to replace you—Miss Dickerson, I think—she quit."

"What?" I jump to my feet. My skin prickles with fury. "After a *week*? She just left the kids? What are they doing now? Jack—" I grab his shoulders. "What if this is *it* for them? What if their parents send them off to Willowbrook or Rome State?" I can feel heat starting to gather behind my eyes. The emotions of the last few days are catching up with me, casting my fears for my former students in high relief. "You know what they call that place? Rome State Custodial Asylum for Unteachable Idiots. Unteachable idiots!" I'm sobbing openly now. "Imagine Mary Ellen there. They claim the places are nice, but, God, Jack, I've heard things . . ."

I've heard things that would horrify even Michael Perkins. Medical experiments—radiation, vaccination—conducted on nonverbal children unable to say no. Eight-year-olds stranded in cribs like cages. Hundreds of cots crammed into single rooms. Children used for free labor. Infants entirely isolated from their families. Straitjackets, restraints, beatings. Nakedness and cold.

I picture Judy at Willowbrook or Rome. I don't doubt she would be the first to go, her behavior "troubled" enough to justify it. *No*, I want to cry, *the more chains you wrap around that girl, the harder she'll try to break free.* And what about Carol and Robby, confined to wheelchairs and incapable of moving on their own? In an overcrowded, understaffed institution, they'd be all but ignored. Would anyone notice Carol's quiet determination or Robby's sudden laugh?

I pull the Snow White image from my clutch. "Jack." I hold the sheet as if its scribbles carry the wisdom of the Bible. "Those kids can learn to sing, and dance, and read, and do math. Not that they should be abandoned otherwise—they deserve an education. But Jack, they need this opportunity." I go on and on, blubbering until I can hardly understand my own words. I am like a child myself, flailing my limbs and gushing snot and tears. Only my final statement comes out clearly.

"Jack." My eyes implore him to understand. "If Hildegarde or Nurse Recht or my mom had quit, I would be dead."

Nighttime, and Jack and I both lie restless and awake.

"Jack?" I speak into the darkness.

"Stella?"

"I'm sorry if my going to the city scared you. You must have been worried sick, and I wasn't exactly gentle about it. And then you showed up anyway."

A slight rustle; his head turning on his pillow. I wish I could see his hair spread across it: curly and golden like the perfectly crisped edges of a cake.

My own hair, and Hattie's too, is similar. Any child of Jack's and mine will grow hair like a crown, thick and bright and dripping with ringlets. *Our child*, I think, *will be adorable*.

"Our child?" The bed shifts as Jack sits abruptly.

"My damned mouth," I laugh weakly. My throat is still sore from crying. "I didn't realize I'd said that aloud."

Jack eases back onto his pillow. "I won't press it, then."

The smile of his voice pushes through even in the darkness. *Our child.*

"But I will press on this," he continues. "Don't feel guilty, Stell. You needed to be there."

"I'm not sorry I went," I amend. "I just wish I'd talked to you about it more. Not left the way I did."

"You're here now." His fingertips brush my face, and I turn to meet his eyes. He kisses me softly and then pulls back. "Do you need me to tell you, Stella? About France?"

I've burned for a year and a half with the frantic desire to know exactly what Jack saw and heard and did overseas. But now that he offers, I'm not sure I need to hear it. His words about me reassert themselves now—what does it change, really? Whoever birthed me, I am still Stella. Whatever he experienced, he is still Jack. I know he saw things that changed him. I suspect he did things that scarred him. But whether he's reliving his own actions or others', I know he would never become anyone but himself. I know he would overcome any scars he needed to for my sake. He came to the city when I needed him, after all, the same city he's feared since his discharge in '44.

Yes, I know he's Jack. My goofy, good, beautiful Jack.

I kiss him again.

"Stella." He pulls back. "I mean it."

"Shh." I bite his lower lip. "I don't care."

And truly? I don't.

CHAPTER TWENTY-SEVEN

Stella Wright, January 1951

Jack and I spend Saturday morning at Vassar's library collecting newspaper articles and publications about special education laws. I wanted to march into Principal Gardner's office kicking and screaming on Friday, but Jack convinced me otherwise. I'll go on Monday with a plan—and with well-written letters to the county seat and the governor, citing several laws and research studies. I'm determined that Gardner's going to let me start back up with my students, and he's going to give us a full day and real supplies. If he doesn't, I already have the envelopes addressed.

Now, Jack is distracting me in the cocktail lounge at Arlington Lanes Bowling Alley. We've both been scoring too high to make the game exciting, so we're hoping to become tipsy enough to throw off our aim. It's a ridiculous plan and an utterly frivolous date. Jack's not been subtle about its goal: to cheer me up. To give me a treat, a night of pure fun, after all the emotional turmoil of the last days. With Jack's characteristic zeal, he's been successful, and the date has been simple and fun.

Until now. Jack must have had one too many cocktails, because he turns to me with a look more serious than I'm used to seeing on his face.

"What's wrong?"

"It's foolish."

"Tell me."

"I was afraid when you were gone. Afraid you'd decide not to come back. I'm just so afraid that—one day—I'll run you off with all my problems. The phobias, the nightmares."

Jack's eyes glisten, and I take his drink from his hand.

"Jack." I cup his face in my hands. "You are so much more than the war, just like I'm so much more than an incubator baby. I am the spunky girl raised by a mom who loved me so much she broke the law for it. You're the sweet boy raised by a woman who loved *you* so much she ventured out alone because of it. That's who we are. That's who *you* are." I lay my head on his shoulder. "And Jack . . . when you're a father, you'll see that that's what really matters. That you know how to love." We are both silent for a moment before I speak again. "And maybe . . ." *Oh, Stella.* I'd meant to bring this up tactfully . . . and in private. The topic I'm about to broach is anything but casual. But, even with all I've learned, some things never change. I can't stop the words from bursting out of me as they come. "Maybe," I repeat, "you'd like to start thinking about becoming one soon?"

Jack looks up sharply. "Becoming one what?"

"A father."

"Stella, really?" Jack leaps from his spot beside me and wraps his strong arms around my chest. "You think we're ready? You think *I'm* ready?"

I roll my eyes. "I think you've always been ready. I suppose I wasn't."

Jack lifts me so my toes are just brushing the floor and spins me around. "But wait." He thumps me inelegantly back to the ground. "You're just getting back into teaching again. Surely you aren't ready to be done?"

"Ah . . ." Complications like this one are part of the reason I should have saved this conversation for later. "Well. I was hoping I wouldn't *have* to be done."

"But—" Jack hesitates. "Is that . . . possible?"

"Well, I can't work once I'm visibly with child. Obviously. I'd be fired on the spot. But I thought that maybe . . . once the baby was born . . ." I say the rest of it in a rush. "I thought I could go back. Your mom could probably watch the baby a couple of days a week. And I've gotten to be friendly with some of my kids' moms—I think that if we babysit some weekends, they'd be happy to look after an infant during the day. Carol's mom, maybe—she asked me to let her know if I ever needed anything, and she could watch a baby for us while I had Carol at school. And"—I take in a great breath of air—"speaking of school, I'd like to go to school this summer. College. There are special education credits I can take, Jack. It will be so much better for me and for the kids, too, if I really know what I'm doing. I'll meet people. People who know what it's like. People who will appreciate the work I do."

"*I* appreciate the work you do."

Not a no. He's just piecing it all together.

"Of course. But it's different. I am so grateful for you; it means so much to have you on my side. I need people who aren't just understanding but who *understand*. Who know exactly what I'm up against in the administration and the district and the state. What if—imagine if they even had ideas for reform? New schools, different eligibility requirements, trained teachers?"

"Ah."

I nod eagerly. I know my husband takes time to make decisions, but I need to hear his response. Is this fanciful life I describe a possible one? Could I be a woman with a job *and* a child? Could I continue to work in the school and learn from my babies?

I'm waiting for his answer when a sharp cry pierces the thin walls of the cocktail lounge. "Strike!"

I laugh slightly, but Jack rolls from the sofa to the floor and covers his head, his movements crisp and rapid.

Shit. I squat next to him as I have in the past to mitigate the damage. "Jack." I place my hand on his back.

His face is twisted in panic, and I think of my own turmoil on Coney Island when I found out my mother wasn't who I'd thought she was. It wasn't the betrayal that hurt me as much as the fear that I didn't know myself anymore. Could Jack feel the same way?

Rather than accost Jack with my usual questions—*what are you remembering, how can I help?*—I say his name. "Jack." I rub my hand in firm circles along his spine. "You're Jack Wright. You're safe, in Poughkeepsie, with your wife. Stella. I'm Stella. You're kind to me. You make me laugh. You're patient." I repeat it again and again. "You're Jack. You're kind. You're patient. You're Jack. You're kind. You're patient. You're safe here."

His face floods with color as his body finally relaxes. I pull him up to standing, and he grits his teeth. "Let's get out of here." The other men and women look away quickly, but Jack isn't stupid. He knows they've been watching.

"Let's get out of here," I repeat. "Of course." I grab his arm and lead him outside to the car. We climb in, and he rests his forehead on the steering wheel.

He breathes deeply for a few minutes, and I give him time. I turn my head to look out the window and watch the couples coming from the bowling alley, expecting the pang of envy as girls cling to their boyfriends and laugh. It doesn't come, though. I love my husband. Episodes and all. I wouldn't trade him for anyone.

"Do you still think I'm ready to have kids?" Jack finally lifts his head, bitterness in his voice.

"Oh, Jack. You know what a big hug Mary Ellen would have given you after that? Jack, kids are *kids*. They won't judge you. At least"—I chuckle slightly—"not if you don't judge them."

"But what if I . . . hurt them?" He recoils from his own question.

Hattie's face looms large: her purple-clouded eye, her twisted arm, the chain of thumbprints at the base of her neck.

"Jack, you would never. I've slept next to you every night for more than a year, and you've never so much as shoved me away from you. Not when you have nightmares, not when you wake up. You've never hurt me when we fight. You've never hurt me when I've provoked you." I try to laugh. "You've never come close or even threatened it. And Jack . . . I wouldn't let you." Hattie's bloody lips, Hattie's fine knotted hair. "If you touched our child once, we'd be gone."

"Where would you go?"

"Your mother would take us in. Even Dr. Morrison probably

would. And I have a degree, Jack, I could find work. I would find a way." *Like my mother did.*

"You promise you'd leave?"

My heart breaks for my husband, who one minute ago feared my leaving him and now is begging for me to promise I'd do just that. "Yes, Jack. I promise."

Thank you again for being here." I smile sideways at my husband. He's taken the Monday off from work to stay with me, and he's making a great show of being "sick," staggering around dramatically and speaking in a low rasp. Uncharacteristically nervous, I'm grateful for the excuse to laugh. On cue, Jack swoops in to kiss me, and I push him away playfully. "No, sir, not when you might be contagious!"

"I was miraculously healed." He shrugs. "Amazing."

I roll my eyes. We're approaching the school building: red brick and wide windows. Different from out here than from within the basement, that's for sure.

"Good luck." Jack grasps my hand and brushes my cheek. "I'll be right here."

And in I go.

"Ah." Principal Gardner looks up from his desk as I enter. "Stella Wright."

I don't waste any time. "I hear Miss Dickerson quit?"

A short nod.

"Where are they now? My kids?"

"I do not have psychic powers, Mrs. Wright. I imagine most of them are at home with their mothers."

"But it's a Monday." *Foolish, Stella. That is his point.* I recover: "You could get fired."

"Alas, not if there are less than ten students in our region. The few we have can travel to other schools in the district if they must."

Hours away? It's impossible. Especially without buses. "There are eleven. Nancy, Stanley, James, Judy, Robby, Carol, Mary Ellen, Giovanna, Patricia, William, and John."

"Hmm."

God, how I loathe this man.

He continues. "I'm afraid not. There are just nine now. Giovanna has been tested, and her IQ does not fall below the seventy-five maximum for your class."

"Surely you don't mean to say she hadn't previously been tested."

"She'd failed."

"Was the test given in English?" His silence is all the answer I need. "For God's sake, the girl had just moved to America!"

"And as for Robert," Gardner continues as if I haven't spoken, "his IQ has been determined to be at the imbecile level. So, he does not qualify for class. A shame."

Robby: scruffy red hair, freckles, a permanent coating of milk dried atop his upper lip. "Robby . . ." I am speaking as if around stones. "Robby is nonverbal. And he can't write."

"Exactly."

"No. No, you aren't getting it. Those are physical disabilities. They have no bearing on his IQ. But they keep him from being able to answer the questions, even if he knows the right responses."

"That being said, he tested below a fifty."

"Yes." I gritted my teeth. "Because he couldn't give his answers."

Principal Gardner shrugs lightly. "Slow classes are for children with IQs between fifty and seventy-five. Robby does not qualify."

"Who tested him? I'll talk to the psychologist, I'll—"

"I'm afraid you won't change the psychologist's mind, as I tested Robby myself."

A principal testing a student's IQ is not procedure. I have a sneaking suspicion it might not be legal. He's just given me more leverage.

I slap the two addressed envelopes onto the principal's desk and pull out the letter. "I'll have to revise this now," I say. "It described all the laws you were breaking before: not providing bus service, only allowing my students half days, withholding public funds . . . I could go on, but now I suppose I need to add that you administer your own IQ tests, keep immigrant children out of regular education, and are currently denying services to ten deserving district children."

"You wouldn't," he scoffs. "Imagine the pushback. You know the other parents resent the resources your children take away from the others, and with my connection to the superintendent, I could turn every school in the district against you, too. I'm sorry, Mrs. Wright, but who's going to listen to a flighty, hysterical woman over a seasoned principal?" He shrugs, not at all sorry. "When it comes down to it, you'd never dare send those letters. Not unless you wanted to be out of a job for good."

Speak up, Mom always told me. I think of "The Gift of the Magi," the way Mom equated sacrifice and love.

If risking my own career is what it takes to show these students I love them, it's what I'll do.

"I'll send the letters on the first of next month," I tell Gardner. For the first time, I'm glad I quit. He knows I'll uphold my end of the bargain just as I did before. "I'll be back with my kids next week. And if you haven't fixed these problems by the end of the month . . ." I nod to the envelopes. "Well. You don't need me to remind you that I keep my promises."

Robby's mother swings open her door at my knock. "Mrs. Wright?"

Accusation and relief war in her face when she recognizes me. I am the woman who let her son down, but also—I am here.

"Mrs. Givens. Is Robby inside?"

Her face softens slightly. "Yes."

"Lunchtime?" I grin.

"Yes." The word is the same as before, but her voice turns sheepish. Glistening beige goop drips slowly down the front of her blouse, and her cheek is smudged with puréed peas.

"I know how that can be. Do you want a hand?"

"I—are you certain?"

I nod.

"Please, then, come in."

I can't blame her for being surprised. Likely, she's not often offered help with her son. We find him in the kitchen, secured to his seat with layers of zippers and straps. Puréed food dries in crusty lines across his face, and the room stinks of peas.

"Here." I take a washcloth, wet it, and gently scrub the boy's face while his mom feeds him. To my surprise, Robby lets me. When I have finished, he smiles widely. He dips his fingers in the green gook of his peas. And then he smears the liquid slowly and intentionally across the curve of my cheek onto my chin.

"Ack!" I choke on the smell. "I suppose I did deserve that." I crouch by his side. "I'm sorry, Robby." And to think Gardner denies this boy's intelligence. "I never should have left."

We're back in our musty basement by eight a.m. the next Monday. Ten kids sit in a circle before me—six on the carpet, two in wheelchairs, two sprawled separately on the hard tile. "We're going to be doing things a bit differently now," I tell them. I post my Snow White drawing on the chalkboard to remind myself.

Not that the change is an easy one. God, no. The kids are conflicted, uncertain whether to be excited I'm back or insulted I'd gone. Their routine has been interrupted, and if there's one thing they all agree on, it's a love for structure. We muddle through four hours and then stand aside as the choir class files in at twelve o'clock. Twenty-five little bodies press into the room, and I line my ten in a row in front of them. For those who can't sing, I pass out the instruments Jack bought according to the list I gave him last week: a tambourine for Carol, a drum for Robby, a triangle for Mary Ellen, and maracas for William.

"What's this?"

I smile at the choir teacher, Miss Edwards. Likely, she's paid more than my three thousand dollars a year despite teaching just one hour per day. "We are extending our day to two p.m. so the children can take the same buses as their peers."

"But why are they *here*?"

"For choir, of course!" I relish presenting the words as if they are obvious.

She blinks. "Principal Gardner must have forgotten to notify me of this change," she says stiffly.

Judy catches my eye and smirks. "He must have."

"Well!" Miss Edwards claps her hands. "Let's get started, then. Ah—" She leans over to me and whispers, "Can they read?"

"James and Stanley can." I point. "Judy and Patricia can read when they want to. Nancy will know the song as soon as you start; she's got quite the ear for music. Four of them won't be singing; that's what the instruments are for. Which just leaves John, who's not discouraged easily. He'll figure it out." I flash him a thumbs-up, and he responds in kind.

Miss Edwards hands James a copy of the music, dropping her own in the process. "Oh, dear." She bends to pick it up. "I don't know why I'm so flustered."

I do. Faced with the actual humanity of my students, looking into their eyes, she's suddenly unsure how to treat them. No longer can they be ignored or patted on the head like good little dogs. Not after she sees Judy smirk or James's face crack open in delight. Not now that she sees they are human.

get home just after three forty-five p.m., and supper is ready by the time Jack comes home with my name on his lips. "Stella. You have mail. Two letters, one from Dr. Morrison."

I forget dinner immediately, grabbing the letter and seeing the return address: *Charles Morrison, Bellevue Hospital, New York, New York.*

I tear the envelope open and four sheets spill out—more than just a friendly hello.

The first paper I pick up isn't part of the letter. It's a certificate printed on thick paper. I unfold it and read.

In the name of the Father, and of the Son,
and of the Holy Spirit.

We do Certify that, according to the ordinances of
Christ Himself, we did administer to

STELLA ANDERSON the Sacrament of Holy Baptism,
thereby initiating STELLA ANDERSON fully by water
and the Holy Spirit into Christ's Body the Church: on this
second day of December in the Year of our Lord 1926 in
the Church of the Transfiguration, in this Diocese of New
York. Signed: Reverend Paul Grover. Parents: ALTHEA
ANDERSON. Sponsors or Witnesses: Mrs. MOLLY
WALLACE and Dr. CHARLES MORRISON. Date of
Birth: July 5, 1926. Place of Birth: Manhattan, NY.

I am so fixated on the names—Molly Wallace, Charles Morrison—that I nearly miss the birthdate. July 5, 1926. Not my birthday, but Margaret's.

I think I know what Dr. Morrison's letter is going to say.

Dear Stella,

I trust you have made it home safely. Please give my regards to
your husband.

I write you today because I fear I was not entirely honest when we met. I held back some truths because I thought I was protecting Althea and you, whom I still see as an infant learning to crawl. But you are no longer a child, and you have dealt with enough lies.

After my failed proposal, I did see your mother one more time. I did not know how to tell you the nature of our visit, so I didn't try. I suppose even doctors can be cowards.

It was July 1946. You had just turned twenty years old and had finished your first year at Vassar. You were still in Poughkeepsie with a young man and his mother—Jack's, I suppose. Your mother showed me pictures of you, which is how I recognized you in my office, and told countless stories of the girl you had grown up to be. I must confess I laughed aloud, Stella, when she told me of the engineering class you had taken simply to spite the boy who told you you would not. I had last seen you at nine months old, but I could so easily reconcile the two versions of you. A fighter, feisty at nine months and at twenty years. And today, too. Your mother was so proud of you, and I know she would be still.

That day was the first time I had seen her in nineteen years. I told you I had not seen her since the day I proposed in 1927, and I hadn't. Not until that July night in 1946. It was a Tuesday, a strange day to appear out of the blue. But still your mother showed up at my door late at night, eyes raw from crying.

She wore a wedding ring, Stella. She did not try to deceive me. But I had loved this woman for twenty years, and though she talked endlessly about you, she did not mention a husband.

I thought perhaps he had passed away. I stopped just short of hoping it. Instead, I chose not to wonder.

Your mother was a loyal, moral woman. I would later learn that your father had indeed passed away before that night; I don't think Althea would have come had he not.

And so, Stella, I am not writing to further tarnish your view of the woman who raised you. If you truly love your husband, I hope you understand. Love makes us do things we would not otherwise consider.

I write you because I am a doctor. I am familiar with the human form, Stella; I have delivered babies and treated new mothers. And it was evident to me even twenty years after your birth that Althea Anderson had never had a child. Childbirth was a brutal surgery in hospitals in the 1920s, and women carried its scars for life. Your mother, who claimed to have delivered you at Bellevue itself, did not bear those telltale markings. Her husband was not a doctor and would never have noticed. But I am certain.

Your mother never bore a child.

I did not ask her about it. It was a night we had waited two decades for, and I dared not spoil it or drive her away. As I told you in New York, I knew your mother to be an ethical young woman and nurse. I knew that, whatever her secrets, she had good reason for them. But I also believe that you have the right to know. Your mother did not give birth to you; she was not your biological mother.

I never saw her again after that day. That is the honest truth. But I wondered constantly whether her secrets were part of the reason she had left me, somehow.

*Now that you have come to me with what you know, I be-
lieve I finally understand. I had just told your mother of Dr.
Hess and my plans when she left me. I had just told your mother
I would be at Dr. Couney's every day. If she did not want me
to learn your story, or what we can now surmise your story
was, she could not be there alongside me.*

*Your mother picked you above all else, Stella. Above her
work. Above me. Above her oath as a nurse. And even above
the law. I do not tell you this to make you feel guilty. I tell you
this because I have just told you your mother is not your mother.
But I want you to know she still is. She loved you enough to
give you everything, Stella, and that will never change.*

*With love,
Dr. Charlie Morrison*

I turn to Jack. The letter confirmed everything I've learned; I
was Hattie and Michael's natural-born daughter. I was Hattie's,
and though she gave me up once, she found a way to save me
twenty-four years after that original sin.

Hattie. "Who is the other letter from?"

"It's unmarked."

I take it from my husband and open it carefully.

Dear Stella, it reads.

*A doctor gave me your address. I hope you don't mind my writ-
ing. But I wanted to let you know I got a P.O. box. I think I
did it because I wanted you to be proud of me.*

I have so much to say, and no idea how to say any of it.
Please write me if you'd like me to try.

With love
Hattie Perkins

I trace the address of Hattie's P.O. box. Three simple numbers, but they're a brave step toward freedom.

"She did it for me," I whisper.

"They've all done so much for you."

The nurses and Dr. Couney. Dr. Morrison. Hattie.

And Althea, who saved me from the beginning. She raised me as her own, and she loved me. She loved me more than anything or anyone else.

I throw my arms around Jack. To think that my mother ran to the man she loved twenty years after she'd last seen him—to think of the love she had to give up to keep me safe. The love she gave up to give me a chance at finding that kind of love myself.

"I love you, Jack. I love you so much."

"Forever, Stella. I love you, forever."

CHAPTER TWENTY-EIGHT

Althea Anderson Johnson, July 1946

The door swings open and sends me back two decades. Charlie's hair is speckled with gray, and fine lines radiate from his eyes like dendrites. But those small changes disappear as I stare at him with the same breathless anticipation I felt at twenty-four.

His firm jaw and deep gray eyes center me, help dissolve the guilt that's plagued me since receiving Hattie's letter this afternoon. For the first time in twenty years, I am not just a mother. This man remembers me as more than that: as a nurse and as a woman.

I feel my spine straighten as I regain some of that old sense of competence.

"Althea?" Charlie's voice is low and hoarse, and a thrill runs through me like I'm still twenty-four.

I feel myself blushing as I say his name, surprised my body remembers what it is to react to a man. "Charlie."

He steps back wordlessly, inviting me inside. I step across the threshold into the apartment and immediately gasp to see a picture of Charlie and Dr. Couney sitting on the sideboard.

Charlie sees me looking. "He shut down the place at Luna Park three years ago. You probably heard."

I nod.

"It wasn't necessary anymore. Cornell opened their own dedicated incubator ward first, and other hospitals are following suit. Believe it or not"—he smiles—"I'm at Bellevue myself now."

I steady myself with a palm against the wall. My entire history is coalescing before me now: Hattie's letter, Dr. Couney's photograph, Charlie at Bellevue.

Charlie in front of me, in the flesh.

"You've done such good," I whisper. It's all I can think of to say. "Saving babies like Stella."

Charlie's face breaks into a sad smile. "Stella. I've thought of you both so often." He looks at me in question. "How is she?"

A rare note of pride is evident in my voice. "She's studying education at Vassar."

"She's healthy?"

"Completely."

He raises his eyebrows. "Happy?"

I let myself smile. "Yes. She loves school, and she's met a boy. She's at his family's place in Poughkeepsie now for the holiday weekend."

"And you?"

"Me?"

"Are you happy?"

I'd forgotten how penetrating Charlie's eyes can be, how deeply they swim with emotion.

I lift one shoulder slightly. "I'm a mother, Charlie. If Stella's happy, I'm happy."

"That's not what I mean," he says.

I exhale. "I know."

And then he's kissing me. His hands are on my shoulders, his lips are on mine, and I want to tell him that happiness is not so simple. That even though I chose this life without him and without nursing, even though I had countless moments of perfection with Stella, that I never stopped thinking about what—and who—I lost.

But in this moment, happiness is simple. I forget everything else as my back hits the wall. His hands are on me, fewer layers of fabric between his skin and mine in this decade than there used to be. I am bold and wrap my own arms around Charlie's upper back, run my fingers through his hair. It's still thick and soft despite its gray, and I pull Charlie closer.

"Wait." He pulls back, breathing ragged, and his gaze darts to my wedding ring and then back to my face. "Is this all right? Is this what you want?"

It's not why I came. I needed to run from the guilt that Hattie's letter opened in me like a sinkhole, and despite the years, my mind turned immediately to Charlie—a man who always understood me, made me feel safe. My thoughts have turned to him more and more since Stella left for college, and with Horace gone a year, with Stella away—happy and finding love—I did something I haven't done in twenty years. I acted on impulse.

My eyes meet his. This wasn't why I came, but I've been waiting for this for two decades. And it seems that he has, too.

"Yes," I say as I reach for him again. "This is what I want."

I open my eyes at five a.m. Mom hours are similar to nurse hours, and I can't break the early wake-up habit even with Stella away at school. I usually take the time to go on a walk, but not today. Today, I'm content exactly where I am.

I shift carefully to look at Charlie. His hair is tousled, and thin strands of silver glint in the early-morning light. I resist the urge to run my fingers through his hair and straighten it, not wanting to wake him.

I snuggle up against him, and his eyes open. Slate gray, same as they were the day I met him. Our bodies may have changed, but our eyes are still our own.

"Hi."

"Hi." I feel momentarily ridiculous peeping up through my eyelashes, like I'm playing at being twenty-four again. But then Charlie kisses me, taking his time, and I'm no one but myself.

"Are you hungry?" He pulls back.

I don't want him to go out of his way. "Only if you are."

Charlie throws the blanket off and stands. I watch as he gets dressed, the muscles in his back moving like waves. It's hard to believe that I didn't know about the freckle on his left shoulder until last night, or that he has a scar on his calf from a childhood fall out of a tree.

I sit up in bed. "Do you want me to help?"

Charlie shakes his head. "I'm okay. But no promises you'll enjoy my cooking."

I smile. "You could make Jell-O salad, and I'd still be thrilled to *not* be the one doing the cooking for once." I feel immediately guilty. It's not as if I've ever asked Stella to cook, and it never occurred to me that Horace might have. "Not that I mind cooking," I say. And it's true. I like taking care of people. If I can't bind their wounds and deliver their babies, at least I can fill their bellies.

I hear Charlie fiddling around in his tiny kitchen, and then he returns to sit on the edge of the bed. "Does Stella have a favorite food?"

I laugh. "She's usually too busy talking to taste much."

"I can imagine that." He chuckles as he puts a hand over mine. "What's she like? Now that she's all grown up."

"Oh, Charlie. She's wonderful." I'm so proud of my Stella: her confidence, her determination, her kindness. With bravery and strength, perhaps she'll have the fulfilling future I robbed myself of. I want her to have it all—the man she loves, the job that inspires her.

I look at Charlie. "You never had kids?"

His lips flatten. "No." His gray eyes are dark. "But I never stopped feeling like Stella was mine."

To keep from telling him she should have been, I kiss him. I press my lips to his and wonder at how clearly the touch evokes those kisses in Mrs. Wallace's kitchen so many years ago. I can almost feel the edge of the counter, as if an entire lifetime hasn't passed between those days and this one.

But an entire lifetime *has* passed. So many years have gone by without this man by my side.

I pull back and gaze at Charlie. In a perfect world, he'd have been mine. The longing for that reality is so strong it hurts, and I squeeze Charlie's hand without having realized I'd grabbed it in the first place.

"What's wrong, Althea?"

I shake my head, the pain intensifying as he says my name. It's not that this moment isn't perfect; I'm just mourning all that could have been, all that wasn't. All the years I missed with Charlie. All the moments I wanted to clap with him over Stella's accomplishments, all the times I pulled out his pressed flower and tried to find any remaining hint of its scent. The nights I woke up drenched in sweat after dreaming of Michael stealing Stella away, the nights Charlie could have held me and whispered into my hair. The days that stretch so long now that I am home alone, without purpose or companionship. My hours could be filled with discussions and debates: about the female biochemist who identified the active agent in tuberculin, the men who used a moldy cantaloupe to develop penicillin. So much has happened in the world since Charlie and I last met, and I wish we could have shared it all.

"Althea? What's wrong?"

"Nothing." I exhale, eternally adept at keeping my thoughts to myself. But because Charlie deserves the truth, I give him as much of it as I'm able. "I've just missed you."

"And I, you. Every day." He pauses, and his face suddenly looks like an older man's. "Can I ask you why you left?" He rubs his forehead with the palm of his hand. "I tried to find you, Althea. I didn't know if it was what you wanted, but I needed to know where you'd gone. *Why* you'd gone. But I never could figure it out." He dropped his hand to his lap, his gray eyes beseeching. *Why.*

All my visions come crashing down. There was a reason my life and Charlie's had diverged. There was a reason he couldn't be the one to give Stella piggyback rides or kiss me late at night.

Being with Charlie would have meant Stella would never be safe. Charlie's world was that of Dr. Couney, Louise, Hildegarde. He works now at Bellevue, where—somewhere—a certificate exists that labels Margaret Perkins as deceased. Where Ida Berry, now Head Nurse Berry, knows the truth of my dismissal.

If I had married this man—this beautiful, considerate, intelligent man who has always seen me as an equal—Stella could have lost everything.

I've missed Charlie every day of my life, but I don't regret the decision I made to leave him.

I give Charlie one final, lingering kiss, and he leans into it without question. He doesn't know that it will be our last. This time, forever.

"I can't tell you," I whisper. "But please. Know that I love you."

I just love Stella more.

Author's Note

When I stumbled upon an article about Dr. Martin Couney's in-cubator wards, I was struck by the utterly bizarre nature of it all—lifesaving technology on the Luna Park boardwalk, spectators paying to watch infants fight for their lives. I immediately bought and devoured Dawn Raffel's *The Strange Case of Dr. Couney: How a Mysterious European Showman Saved Thousands of American Babies*, and I knew without a doubt that the subject would be perfect for a novel. Althea's story, which itself is entirely fictional, came to me as I wrestled with a question posited by Raffel in her nonfiction text. After Dr. Couney's death, investigations into his past revealed he'd been lying about who he was, where he was educated, and with whom he trained. Those who discovered his lies grappled with what to make of a man who was by all accounts a liar and a con man—but who saved thousands of innocent lives.

I crafted Althea's story to reflect the same ethical question. If saving a child's life meant usurping the parents' role, lying, and ostensibly kidnapping—would it still be the right thing to do?

In regard to the necessity of the lie, or Cybil's and Margaret's parents' rejection of Coney Island's services, this really did happen. Dr. Couney operated several incubator wards, the one in Luna Park from 1903 to 1943, but he was not necessarily trusted by medical professionals or the general populace. Beth Allen, born prematurely in 1943, recalls that her mother initially refused to take her to Luna Park; Dr. Couney himself came to the hospital to convince her. While Cybil's parents and the Perkinses are not directly modeled after real people, they very well could have been.

Regarding the other characters, many of them are lifted directly from history. Dr. Martin Couney, Hildegarde Couney, Louise Recht, Ms. Caswell, and Director Rottman were all real people. Charlie is a figment of my imagination, but Dr. Julius Hess— the man with whom Charlie works to bring incubators to the hospitals—was real. The first incubator ward training program at a hospital in New York City was created in 1939 at the New York Hospital; the advent of premature baby wards in hospitals was part of the reason Dr. Couney closed his own ward in 1943. Until then, hospitals had deemed it too difficult or too expensive to care for low-weight babies.

Their attitude was also influenced by the eugenics movement, which originated not with Adolf Hitler but with the American scientific community. As with most of the ugly parts of our history, we like to ignore that. But as Stella points out, the remnants linger. Special education didn't take off until the Kennedy administration; it was just beginning in the 1950s, as Stella fights for her kids. Much of the support students with special needs did receive in that decade came not from the government or school districts but from parent advocacy groups such as the National Association of Parents and Friends of Retarded Children, now known simply as the Arc. However horrifying it may seem, straitjackets really were believed to be a useful educational tool, and most doctors recommended that students with severe diagnoses be institutionalized rather than raised at home and educated.

Stella, Jack, and Stella's students are all invented characters, as is the awful Principal Gardner. I've been lucky enough to work in inclusive schools with students with special needs, and I hope that the love I feel for my students comes through in the pages. Luckily, I've never worked with an administrator like Gardner!

In terms of the other historical pieces in the novel:

Most of the newspaper articles and headlines are real, as is Martin Couney's obituary. Yes, men and women really did place classified ads for marriage in the papers!

I tried to do Bellevue Hospital justice, as it was often on the forefront of treating people rejected by society. It was also pivotal in the training of female nurses, though requirements were strict (e.g., no married women). Many hospitals sent babies to Luna Park or Atlantic City for Dr. Couney's treatment, and Bellevue may well have been one of them; however, I took the liberty of creating a doctor who was opposed to Dr. Couney's practices, as many were.

All the details regarding World War II veterans at Vassar are true. Thirty-six men enrolled at Vassar in 1946, and many more had taken classes at the school by 1953. The sixteen who graduated held diplomas not from Vassar but from the State University of New York; Vassar did not become officially coed until 1969.

For more information on Coney Island's incubators, check out Raffel's book or Claire Prentice's *Miracle at Coney Island: How a Sideshow Doctor Saved Thousands of Babies and Transformed American Medicine*. The Internet also has several articles about the wards, many of which include photographs and interviews with survivors. Bellevue School of Nursing records, including year-books and bulletins, can be found online as well.

Finally, if you're interested and able to donate, the International Rescue Committee (rescue.org) provides premature baby incubators to countries in crisis.

Acknowledgments

I wrote eighty thousand semi-intelligible words on a Word document over the course of a semester at Vanderbilt; the following people helped me turn those words into this novel.

Eternal thanks to:

Early readers, including Ellen Armstrong, Ryan Armstrong, Mary Lee Bass (Mimi), Lori Martin, Karen Crow, Lindsay Galvin, Jorge Nuñez (my own Jack, minus the war bits), and Eric Armstrong.

The rest of my supportive family and friends, including but not limited to Stan Bass (PawPaw), Jay and Nancy Crow (Pops and Nan), Adam Crow and Jennifer Lloyd-Crow, Mike Crow, and my education cohort at Vanderbilt (Doing It for the Money and the Fame).

My agent, Melissa Danaczko of Stuart Krichevsky Literary Agency, who believed in this book before it was worthy of being called one, and who is as caring and supportive as Althea herself.

My editor, Tara Singh Carlson, and her assistant, Ashley Di Dio, the pair of whom continually astounded me with their incredible eye for sharpening both the most sweeping emotion and the tiniest details.

The rest of Putnam's publishing team.

The teachers at Water's Edge Elementary and Saint Andrew's School, for always encouraging me to write.

The Miami Writers Institute and The Porch Nashville.

Robin Oliveira, for her careful read and helpful suggestions.

My sister Ryan, again, for taking my author photo and being the most supportive and loyal person I know.

Dawn Raffel, author of *The Strange Case of Dr. Couney*, and Claire Prentice, author of *Miracle at Coney Island*.

Dr. Martin Couney himself, without whom thousands of babies would not have lived and this novel would not have been written.

THE

Light

of

Luna Park

ADDISON ARMSTRONG

A Conversation with Addison Armstrong

Discussion Guide

BOOK
ENDS

PUTNAM
— EST. 1838 —

A Conversation with Addison Armstrong

One might be surprised to hear that you wrote *The Light of Luna Park* at twenty-two years old. What inspired you to write this emotionally nuanced novel?

I wrote the type of book I've always read. The first novel I remember reading was *Little Women* by Louisa May Alcott in first grade, and I suppose I've read about women and the past ever since! I love stories about history, women, family secrets, complicated relationships, and moral gray areas. So I may not have as much life experience as some other authors, but I've lived it all vicariously!

The Light of Luna Park is rooted in the real history of medicine behind the "incubator babies" of Coney Island. How did you perform the research required for this story? Was there any information that surprised you?

My research started when I was reading a completely unrelated history piece. As I scrolled through the article, a clickbait-style heading popped up as my next suggested read . . . and even as I rolled my eyes at the unlikelihood of its being legitimate—baby incubators at an amusement park?—I found myself clicking the link. Obviously, I was immediately hooked. I scrambled to read everything I could on Dr. Couney's incubators, nonfiction books and primary sources like newspapers, photographs, and interview transcripts. I even got to visit Bellevue Hospital, which has a historical gallery that displays a hospital timeline, an old ambulance, and a centuries-old medical kit.

As to what I found surprising? Everything! I couldn't believe that people paid to see babies struggling to survive, for one thing, and so it blew my mind that the shows even existed at all.

But as surprising as the existence of Couney's incubator wards was the fact that some parents turned them down. Several interviews with living survivors of the incubator wards report that their mothers were offered spots only after mothers of babies born before them refused the offer. Notably, only the babies who did go to Coney Island (or Atlantic City) are still around to remember.

Finally, I was shocked by the juxtaposition between Couney's exhibits and the eugenics-related displays proliferating at the same time and place. In every way, the incubator wards were just so incongruous to the setting in which they found themselves. They were an oasis of calm in the frenzy of an amusement park, a bastion of hope and acceptance in a world that had the rest of the scientific field calling for selective breeding and sterilization.

How did you come to craft the two heroines—Althea and Stella? Are they based on real people, or were they inspired by anyone in particular?

Neither was inspired by anyone in particular, though of course I can't write about Althea as a mother without thinking of my own mom. Both characters have elements of myself in them—from

Althea's single-mindedness, which often translates as standoffish-ness or anti-socialness (oops) to Stella's career as a teacher. In some ways, Stella also has elements of my sister Ryan in her; they're both fiercely loyal and will fight with every last breath for those they love.

What is your favorite scene in the novel, and why?

This is a hard one, because I've rewritten and reread every scene so many times that I can no longer read a single sentence without remembering all the versions of it that have come and gone. So while there's no one scene that sticks out to me, I do love those depicting Stella and her students. One of my favorite moments is when Robby smears his pureed food all over Stella's face—it makes me laugh, because I've been on the receiving end of the same thing!

I also like the scenes with Althea and Charlie, because I think their intensity is so well-matched. The way Althea handles the doctors at the AMA meeting leaves me feeling smug, too.

This story examines the complicated ties of motherhood and the lengths a mother will go to protect her daughter. What drew you to portray this relationship and the choices Althea makes?

I'm lucky. My mom and dad are my foundation; I don't know who I'd be without them. They love me unconditionally, and I know that, like Althea, they would sacrifice everything for me. I also know that if I were to find out they weren't really "mine" bio-logically, none of that would change. What matters isn't the blood we share but the bond we share.

I've also spent years working with children myself—teaching, tutoring, nannying, you name it. I'm not yet a mother, but still I wouldn't hesitate to sacrifice for the kids I've known. Of course, let me put on the record that I would *not*, like Althea, kidnap them!

If Stella's timeline was set in present day, how do you think the school would have handled her professional situation? Do you think that would have changed the path her story takes?

Stella would definitely have the opportunity today to take legal action against the school if they tried to use undue physical restraint against the students. That being said, Stella's situation is not as distantly past as it may seem. The Individuals with Disabilities Education Act (originally the Education for All Handicapped Children Act) wasn't passed until 1975, and the Americans with Disabilities Act came fifteen years later. Even today there is more to be done.

Of course, I don't mean to be dire! Many of Stella's kids today would be in inclusive classrooms, use Augmentative and Alternative Communication (AAC) devices to communicate, self-propel their wheelchairs, and take advantage of a host of other resources. Unlike in 1950, schools are required to provide a free and appropriate education in the least restrictive environment to all students with (and without) special needs.

As for how this would affect Stella . . . I can imagine her suing the school over their abuses and getting fired as a result. I think she still would have ended up in New York City chasing down the ghost of her mother, because she would have needed Althea's strength and guidance just as much in this new scenario. Still, she would wonder whether she was doing the right thing for her kids; still, she would need to fill her grief and time away from work with meaning.

Why did you choose to include Jack's PTSD from World War II in the story? What do you think this adds to the novel?

A third of the adult male population of the United States in the 1940s served in World War II, plus hundreds of thousands of American women. But despite the fact that virtually no one came out of the war unscarred, there was very little understanding of PTSD (which wasn't used as a term until the 1970s or a diagnosis until 1980). While the trauma of war tormented veterans, and by extension their loved ones, there was little done to effectively combat the problem. The effects were so far-reaching that I felt I couldn't write a story that took place in 1950 without considering them.

Additionally, I saw a clear link between the eugenics movement in Althea's era and the war in Stella's. Just as Althea's actions led to Stella's circumstances, the eugenics movement in the 1920s laid the groundwork for Hitler's atrocities during World War II and their aftermath.

I think Jack's struggles are also necessary for Stella. She's a fighter, and I wanted her to go from fighting *against* her husband to fighting *alongside* her husband. For them to have the strong marriage I wanted, they had to be right for each other—but there had to be something in the way. For Stella, it was grief. For Jack, it was the trauma of war.

What do you hope readers will take away from *The Light of Luna Park*?

I hope readers come away with a sense of how powerful unconditional love is. More than that, I hope they see that every human being is deserving of it. There are people in the novel (and in our history and even our present) who try to claim that some people aren't strong enough, smart enough, able enough, healthy enough—but I want readers to see how, on every level and in any circumstance, a person has the capacity to love and be loved.

Without giving anything away, did you always know how the story would end?

I always knew how things would end for Althea, Stella, and the others, but I wrote the last chapter (Althea's) at the suggestion of my editor. My mom had actually proposed the same thing after reading the manuscript months earlier, but I'd (foolishly) ignored her! I knew what would happen in that chapter, as I'd already alluded to it in the doctor's letter to Stella, but I didn't know I was going to include the scene itself in the novel.

What's next for you?

I'm finishing my master's in Reading Education at Vanderbilt University and hope to stay in Nashville to teach elementary school when I graduate. In the meantime, I'm continuing my writing! I don't think I could stop if I tried. My upcoming projects, like *The Light of Luna Park*, take little-known historical eras or events and explore the choices (or lack thereof) women were given within them.

Discussion Guide

1. What did you think of how Stella's grief over her mother's passing was portrayed in the novel? If you've experienced grief, did you feel Stella's emotions mirrored yours, or were they different?

2. What were your feelings toward Stella's husband, Jack, in the beginning of the novel? What about at the end? Do you feel he is a good husband?

3. In chapter 7, when Althea views one of the circus acts at Coney Island featuring children and adults with deformities, she tells a woman, "The whole thing feels exploitative." The woman counters this by saying, "Way I see things, the circus is a haven for people like that." Discuss these differing opinions and your own in relation to this conversation.

4. Which character was your favorite, and why?

5. *The Light of Luna Park* calls into question how far someone would go to save another. Do you think Althea ultimately made the right decision for Stella? For herself? Why or why not?

6. How do you think Althea and Stella are similar? How are they different?

7. Much of the information regarding Luna Park and Dr. Couney—the "Incubator Doctor"—is rooted in fact. Which piece of information was the most surprising to learn?

8. Do you think Stella handled her professional dilemma well in the beginning of the novel? If you were in her place, how do you think you would have reacted?

9. How did you feel about Althea and Charlie's relationship? Were you satisfied with how it ended up?

10. Do you think Dr. Couney's lies or omissions were justified by his motivations?